ALSO BY MARGARET TRUMAN

First Ladies
Bess W. Truman
Souvenir
Women of Courage
Harry S Truman
Letters from Father:
The Truman Family's Personal Correspondences
Where the Buck Stops
White House Pets

IN THE CAPITAL CRIMES SERIES

Murder at the Watergate
Murder in the House
Murder at the National Gallery
Murder on the Potomac
Murder at the Pentagon
Murder in the Smithsonian
Murder at the National Cathedral
Murder at the Kennedy Center
Murder in the CIA
Murder in Georgetown
Murder at the FBI
Murder on Embassy Row
Murder in the Supreme Court
Murder on Capitol Hill
Murder in the White House

Murder

at the Library
of Congress

Murder
at the Library
of Congress

—

MARGARET
TRUMAN

DOUBLEDAY DIRECT
LARGE PRINT EDITION

RANDOM HOUSE

NEW YORK

Copyright © 1999 by Margaret Truman

All rights reserved under International and Pan-American Copyright Conventions. Published in the United States by Random House, Inc., New York, and simultaneously in Canada by Random House of Canada Limited, Toronto.

Random House and colophon are registered trademarks of Random House, Inc.

ISBN 0-7394-0642-6

Printed in the United States of America

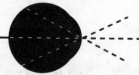

**This Large Print Book carries the
Seal of Approval of N.A.V.H.**

To Gates Bennett Daniel,
with love from Grammy

"They [the Declaration of Independence and the Constitution] are more than historical relics. . . . We may think we have them safely bottled up, but the ideas they express will go on forever. They will continue to give energy and hope to new generations of men, here and in other countries, in the long struggle to create a better society on earth."

—HARRY S TRUMAN, president of the United States, addressing the Library of Congress on its 150th anniversary honoring its founder, Thomas Jefferson, May 17, 1950

Murder

at the Library
of Congress

Esteban Reina looked down from the tall stepladder. Above him was the skylight he'd just repaired. He'd explained to his boss, the museum's manager, that the repair he'd started that morning was more complicated than he'd anticipated, and that he would have to remove the entire skylight to do the job right.

"Before it rains," the manager said. "Make sure it's fixed before it rains."

Reina had taken his time, but kept an eye on the sky. Rain wasn't forecast until the night, plenty of time.

It was now five o'clock. The skylight had

been removed, the weather stripping replaced, and the skylight again rested in its opening, allowing gray light to filter into the small, single gallery of Casa de Seville, a not-for-profit museum of sorts supported by a grant from two Hispanic-American businessmen and donations at the door. Devoted to bringing a taste of Seville, Spain, to Miami, it was located on Southwest Eighth Street—"Little Havana."

The collection wasn't especially important in a historical sense, nor was the worth of the displays, maps, dioramas of fifteenth-century Seville, and costumes replicating what was then fashionable very high. If worth was determined by size, a large painting by an obscure, modestly capable nineteenth-century artist, Fernando Reyes (influenced by the respected seventeenth-century religious painter, Murillo), was the most valuable offering in the small space. The scene was Columbus on his knees in Seville offering up his Book of Privileges to King Fernando and Queen Isabel. It was but one of myriad paintings done over the centuries depicting that event; Reyes's work was considered by collectors to be barely adequate; he was perhaps not influenced enough by Murillo.

Reina, Casa de Seville's part-time maintenance man, went to a rear door, opened it, and placed the ladder outside. He then went to the men's room, where he washed his hands, changed out of work clothes into slacks, a floral shirt, and sandals, and left the museum, pausing to say good night to the manager.

"Fixed good as new," Reina said. "And before the rain."

"Excellent. See you in the morning, Esteban."

"*Sí, mañana por la mañana.*"

Warren Munsch assiduously avoided Miami's fancier Chinese restaurants in favor of the one he sat in this night, a small storefront take-out place with four tables, in a strip mall near the airport. He wasn't particularly concerned with the quality of the food on his plate, as long as it wasn't foul. Warren Munsch ate to satisfy hunger, to fill the void three times a day. That's how he approached most aspects of his life.

The ribs and fried dumplings rested heavily in his digestive tract as he left the harsh fluorescent lighting of Go Go Hunan and stepped into the relative darkness of the parking lot. It was oppressively hot and humid; he felt as though he were wrapped in a rubber sheet. He looked up at the sound of a jet approaching Miami International, the aircraft slicing across the full moon like a thin bug. Munsch hummed the old song "Moon Over Miami" as he walked to where he'd parked his new black Cadillac at a far end of the lot, away from other cars. He got in, cracked open a window, turned on the AC, lit a cigarette, and checked his watch. Morrie would be leaving his house about now, he thought. Garraga, too, if he hadn't drunk his dinner and fallen asleep in a stupor. Two hours to go.

Another jet screeched overhead. Munsch opened the glove compartment and fingered an envelope containing airline tickets. He wasn't fond of flying, although he could brace himself when flight was unavoidable. He closed the glove compartment, leaned back against the vehicle's headrest, and closed his eyes. Maybe I'm getting a little too old for this, he thought. Lately, he'd found himself becoming forgetful, small lapses but annoying: Why-did-I-come-into-this-room? sort of things. It wouldn't have worried him if he were in some other line of work. But since coming out of Raiford a year ago, his second stint behind bars, he realized that forgetting something, even a seemingly insignificant something, could land him back there, which he was determined to avoid. Maybe this job should be his last. It promised a good pay-day, plenty of money to get out of Miami, maybe go to his daughter's house in Oregon. He grimaced at the thought. Not with all those kids running around. W. C. Fields was right about kids: "Anyone who hates children and dogs can't be all bad." The Bahamas, the British Virgins, maybe even South America or Cuba. He opened his eyes, lit another cigarette, and smiled. Cuba was appealing. Warren Munsch liked Cuban women, and if there were plenty of them in Miami, imagine what Havana must be like.

"Buenos días, señorita," he said to no one, drawing deeply, and coughing.

An hour later, after having dozed off, he left the parking lot and drove south on Red Road into Coral Gables, a ten-minute drive, where he slowly circumvented the European-style fountain at the intersection of Sevilla Avenue and DeSoto and Granada boulevards, one of fourteen such round-abouts written into the city plan back in the 1920s. He pulled to the curb, turned off the lights, and lit up, leaving the engine and air-conditioning running. The heavy heat and humidity, and now the rain, had cut down on the number of people on the street that night, although it wasn't deserted. It never was. Coral Gables, "the City Beautiful," seldom failed to draw tourists day or night, summer or winter. Nothing dumber than a tourist, Munsch thought; he'd relieved his share of them of their vacation money. No easier creature on earth to scam than a dumb tourist.

Garraga was the first to arrive. He walked slowly, stopping to stare at the fountain as though it held some special fascination, making too much of a point that he wasn't going anywhere in particular. Eventually, the tall, lanky Cuban, wearing jeans and a yellow tank top, sidled up to the Caddy, looked around, opened the front passenger door, and slid in.

"How are you, amigo?" Munsch asked, a fresh cigarette sending a cloud of blue smoke in Garraga's direction.

"Good," Garraga said, adding his pungent whiskey breath to the Caddy's interior atmosphere.

"You have the other car?"

"*Sí.* A Taurus. Silver."

"Not too new."

"Ninety-five. Where's Morrie?"

"Late, as usual."

"There he is."

Garraga pointed to a green four-door sedan that had entered the traffic circle and approached where Munsch and Garraga sat. It was driven by a blond woman wearing large round sunglasses. The man next to her sat resolutely, looking straight ahead, like a husband being driven by a wife to a hospital for life-threatening surgery. He was bald on top but had long silver hair slicked back at the sides and tied into a small ponytail. He was tieless; the collar of his white shirt protruded inches above the back of his blue suit jacket.

"I told him to leave the bitch home," Munsch muttered.

She pulled up behind the Caddy. Munsch saw in his rearview mirror that she was using her mirror to adjust her hair. Morrie turned to her and said something. It looked to Munsch that they'd started arguing. Morrie opened his door and started to get out, but turned and yelled something at her. She responded with a pointed gesture. He slammed the door, walked to the Caddy, and got in the back.

"Why the hell did you bring her?" Munsch asked.

"I needed a ride."

The blonde put her car in reverse, jerked back a dozen feet, then pulled out from the curb, almost sideswiping another vehicle.

"You should get rid of her," Munsch said.

"Forget her," Morrie said.

"You tell her what we're doing?" Munsch asked.

"No, of course not. Hello, Garraga."

"What 'a you say, Morrie?"

"I say let's go do it. My sinuses are killing me."

With Morrie noisily using an inhaler in the backseat, Munsch drove to Coconut Grove, following Garraga's directions, until reaching Alice Wainwright Park, a lush waterfront recreation area surrounded by mansions, including one owned by Sylvester Stallone and another by Madonna. The light rain started to come down harder, and Munsch turned on the wipers.

"Over there," Garraga said, indicating a silver car parked on Brickell Avenue.

Munsch parked the Caddy in a well-lighted

area and they walked to the Taurus. "Damn rain," Munsch said. "I hate rain."

He took the keys from Garraga and got behind the wheel of the Taurus. "Where did you get this?" he asked.

"Opa-Locka. The airport parking lot."

"You couldn't have gotten better?" Morrie asked from the backseat.

"What do you want, a Rolls?" Garraga said. "Munsch told me: nothing fancy."

They drove into the Little Havana area of Miami, also known as the Latin Quarter because a heavy influx of immigrants from Central and South America had made it less exclusively Cuban, and parked across the street from Casa de Seville. They sat there quietly, Munsch chain-smoking cigarettes, Morrie chain-inhaling loudly, Garraga slouched passively in the front passenger seat.

"This Esteban, you trust him?" Munsch asked Garraga.

"He needed the money. He's a snowbird."

"That cocaine is garbage," Morrie said. "Only animals use it. You have to smoke so many goddamn cigarettes, Munsch? I can't breathe in here. It kills my sinuses."

Garraga laughed. "You want me to smoke a cigar, Morrie?"

"Better not put a match near your mouth, Garraga. You smell like a brewery," Morrie said.

Munsch ground out his cigarette in the ashtray and turned off the engine. "Okay," he said.

They stepped from the car into the rain and quickly crossed the street. Casa de Seville was a one-story white stucco building with a blue tile roof. The public entered through carved double oak doors set in the middle of the building. Two windows covered with black wrought-iron grillwork flanked the doors.

Attached to one side of the building was another one-story structure housing a bodega in which an old Cuban, illuminated by overhead fluorescent lights, stood behind a counter talking to a man seated on a stool. They were the only people in the small grocery.

A narrow alley separated the other side of the museum from a two-story apartment building with four units. A woman stared at the rain through a glass door on the ground floor. Aware she was watching them,

Munsch led Morrie and Garraga into the bodega. Munsch now saw that the customer talking to the owner wore a tan uniform. A security guard? He didn't look to Munsch as though he could provide much security for anything or anyone. He was fat, probably in his paunchy fifties, with strands of shiny black hair pulled over the top of his bald head.

The old man behind the counter eyed them as Morrie browsed a magazine rack and Munsch looked at a platter of *coquitos* on the counter, the coconut candies brought in daily from the Caribbean. Garraga stayed by the door. He'd become edgy, moving from foot to foot.

"Cuánto es?" Munsch asked, pointing to the candies.

"Seventy-five cents," the bodega owner said.

Munsch threw a dollar on the counter and accepted his change. He took a candy and joined Garraga at the door. "Morrie," he said sharply. Morrie replaced the men's magazine and followed the others out to the sidewalk.

"What about the cop drinkin' coffee in there?" Morrie asked.

"What cop?" Munsch said. "That fat slob

with his belly hanging out of his shirt? Forget him. He doesn't even have a gun."

They walked along the front of Casa de Seville to avoid the rain, and stopped at the far end of the building, by the alley. Garraga nonchalantly crossed it to where he could see the glass door leading into the apartment building. The woman was gone. He looked up and down the street, then motioned with his head. The others followed him into the alley to the rear of the museum.

Behind Casa de Seville was a small grassy area bordered by a high chain-link fence and containing two Dumpsters. A red metal door provided rear access to the museum. Above it was a slatted red-and-white metal awning; the pinging sound of raindrops was magnified as the three men huddled beneath it.

"There's the ladder," Garraga said, pointing to where one rested against a Dumpster.

"And there's no guard?" Morrie asked.

"No," Garraga said. "No guards."

"Don't light a goddamn cigarette," Morrie said to Munsch, who was about to.

Munsch ignored him and lit up.

"There's just the alarm system," Garraga said. "No guards, no night watchmen. Reina says there's no money. They pay him peanuts."

"All right," Munsch said, coughing and extinguishing the cigarette with his shoe. "Go on. Let's get it done."

Garraga leaned the unfolded stepladder against the wall and started up. He paused once he'd climbed onto the roof's overhang, looked down and said to Morrie, "Come on."

Morrie said to Munsch, "Why don't you go up with him?"

"I have to get the car," Munsch said. "You don't drive."

"I don't have to."

"You don't have to *what*?"

"Drive."

Another cigarette went to Munsch's lips. "It doesn't matter why you don't drive, Morrie. Get up there and help Garraga, like we planned."

Garraga scrambled higher onto the roof and waited for Morrie to reach the top of the ladder. Morrie took Garraga's extended hand and clumsily joined him. They crouched low as they made their way to the skylight, Morrie muttering under his breath about pain in his knees. Garraga pulled a penlight from his jeans pocket and directed its beam on the skylight. "There it is," he said, "the alarm wires, just like Reina said." Two small sheathed wires protruded from where one edge of the skylight made contact with the roof.

Garraga withdrew a pocketknife and a small roll of black electrician's tape from his jeans and handed the flashlight to Morrie. "Hold it steady," the Cuban said. "I have to splice these to kill the alarm lead to the skylight."

"Why didn't your guy just cut it?" Morrie asked.

"Because, Morrie, that would have shown up on the alarm panel, a break in the system. Just shut up, huh, and hold the goddamn light."

"You'll get electrocuted in this rain," Morrie grumbled, keeping the penlight's beam squarely on Garraga's hands.

"Okay," Garraga said, slipping the knife back in his pocket. "Grab that edge of the skylight and lift. It's not attached."

Morrie slid his fingers beneath the skylight's metal lip and tried to lift it. "It's stuck," he said.

"Just gunk Reina put on it for a seal. Come on, lift, it'll come free."

It did, with a sucking sound, and they slid the skylight away from the opening.

"The rain'll mess up the floor down there," Morrie said.

"So what?" Garraga said.

Morrie handed the penlight back to Garraga, who directed its beam down into the gallery. Morrie peered over the edge. "That's a hell of a drop," he said.

"Yeah, well, *you* don't have to worry about that, Morrie."

Garraga dangled his legs through the opening, lowered himself until his elbows on the roof supported him, then continued his descent until he hung by both hands. He let go, the sound of his contact with the floor joined by a Spanish obscenity.

Morrie trained the light on Garraga as he got to his feet, looked around the gallery, and limped to the wall on which the Fernando Reyes painting of Columbus offering up his Book of Privileges hung. Morrie shifted the light to the painting. That's what we're supposed to steal? he thought. Must be worth plenty for what Munsch said they'd be paid once the painting was delivered.

Garraga expected the painting to be firmly anchored to the wall, but it was attached only by two brackets at the top. Some gentle back-and-forth movement caused them to eventually pull free of the wall, leaving the large framed canvas in Garraga's hands. He leaned it against the wall and went to a supply room in which Reina said there would be another stepladder. Garraga positioned it beneath the opening in the roof, brought the painting to it, climbed the ladder until he was close to the ceiling, and pulled the painting up behind him. Morrie positioned himself to receive it.

"It's too big," Garraga said as he tried to wedge the painting through the opening.

"Try it on an angle," Morrie suggested.

"I did. It's too big. Can't you see that?"

"Take the frame off. Munsch said to get the painting, not the frame."

Garraga returned to the floor, opened his jackknife, and began to cut the canvas away from the simple wood frame, staying as close to the perimeter as possible. That task finished, he rolled the canvas, went up the ladder, and pushed it through to Morrie. He hoisted himself up to the roof: "We got to put the skylight back."

They did, the painting was dropped to Munsch, and Garraga and Morrie joined him on the ground. Garraga tossed the ladder in a Dumpster and they turned to leave the area,

Munsch in the lead. As he turned to start down the alley, he stopped abruptly. Morrie and Garraga came to his side. Coming toward them was the fat man in the tan uniform they'd seen in the bodega.

"Hey, what are you doing back there?" he asked, continuing to waddle in their direction.

"Who the hell are you?" Munsch asked.

"What'a you got there?" he asked, still narrowing the gap.

"Come on," Munsch said, starting to lead his colleagues up the alley again.

The guard placed himself squarely in their path.

Munsch and the others now saw that the guard was carrying something in his right hand.

"He's got a piece," Garraga said, his voice rising.

"Stop!" the guard ordered.

Garraga answered by pulling a small Saturday night special from the waistband of his jeans, pointing it at the guard, and pulling the trigger. The shot struck him in the stomach.

"What the hell did you do that for?" Morrie asked.

"Stupid," Munsch said. "Let's get out of here."

They ran past the guard, moaning and writhing on the ground, his stubby fingers pressed to the wound. The "piece" he'd held in his right hand was lying next to him. It was a cell phone. Morrie started to bend over the guard but Munsch grabbed his collar and pulled him upright.

"Leave him," Munsch said.

"I think he's dead," Morrie said.

"He ain't dead," Garraga said. "All that fat stopped the bullet."

The three men reached the street and continued running to where they'd parked the silver Taurus. They jumped in, and Munsch drove too fast to his Cadillac.

"I thought there wasn't supposed to be no guard," Morrie muttered.

"Why the hell did you shoot him?" Munsch asked, running a light. "There were three of us. The guy didn't even have a gun."

"I thought I saw one," Garraga said. "Just shut up and drive. Forget about it. Just get the money, Munsch, and we split."

"The buyer's not going to be happy there's no frame," Munsch said.

"The hell with that," Morrie said. "It's the

best we could do. It was too big. Dumb bastard, shooting the guy."

"He won't be happy," Munsch repeated.

"Who?"

"The buyer. Maybe he wanted the frame, too."

"What do we do with the Taurus?" Morrie asked.

"Just leave it. Do I have to think of everything?"

Munsch dropped Garraga and Morrie where they'd met up with him at the DeSoto Plaza and the fountain.

"How about a lift home?" Morrie said to Munsch.

"Call your cheerful blond chauffeur. I don't have time."

Munsch handed Garraga and Morrie envelopes, each containing two thousand dollars in cash.

"When do we get the rest?" Morrie asked. "I got bills to pay."

"When I get back from L.A. Cool it till then. And keep your mouth shut, huh, especially with your bimbo."

"I'm outta here," Garraga said, leaning through the open driver's side window, his long, thin face inches from Munsch's face.

"You bring the money back, Munsch. I'll keep in touch with Morrie. You bring it back, understand?" Munsch thought Garraga was about to draw the gun again but the Cuban left it in his waistband.

Garraga and Morrie watched Munsch drive off.

"I never liked Munsch," Morrie said. "What'd you shoot the guy for? You're nuts. You're one crazy Cubano."

"Forget it. It never happened. He better come back from L.A. with the loot. You want a drink?"

"No. My sinuses are still killin' me. It's all this humidity, and the rain don't help. I ought to move to Arizona or some other desert."

"Yeah, why don't you do that, Morrie?" Garraga said. "Stay in touch."

"Yeah, do that, Garraga. Enough art appreciation for one night. *Hasta luego.*" He disappeared into the rain.

"Mac, it's Annabel."

2   The five o'clock rush hour within New York's La Guardia Airport was as busy as the roads surrounding it, thousands of people moving methodically and with purpose, many running, jackets flapping, glasses sliding down noses, narrowly avoiding knocking each other over, leather briefcases in hand or slung over shoulders, the constant stream of flight announcements over the PA fueling the mad scramble to leave New York.

"Mac, I'm at the airport running for the shuttle. I—I'm losing you. This cell phone is . . . Oh, there you are. What? . . . The meeting went very well—I'll fill you in tonight. . . . What about the doctor?—Excuse me—No, not you, Mac, I bumped into someone. . . . Surgery? Really? Are you okay? . . . No, I— I'm losing you again. . . . You'll pick me up? Great. See you in an hour—love you."

Annabel Reed-Smith dropped the tiny phone into her oversized bag and picked up her pace in the direction of the Delta Shuttle gate. Senator Menendez, with whom Annabel had spent the day at the offices of *Civilization,* the magazine published in concert with the Library of Congress, had already checked in.

"Reach Mac?" he asked.

"Yes. He'll pick me up."

"Good."

Richard Menendez was in his third term as United States senator from Florida. His position of political power, coupled with a reputation, before running for the Senate, as a champion of Hispanic-American causes, thrust him into the role of leading spokesman of that large, and growing, constituency. He was rakishly good-looking, sword thin and erect, on the tall side of six feet, with senatorial gray at his temples, the rest of his hair coal black and precisely cut. His expensive suits draped nicely on him; this day he wore a gray one with the unmistakable look of English bespoke tailoring, the whitest of shirts, and a muted gold tie splashed with dozens of tiny replicas of the Spanish flag. But what people usually remembered about Richard Menendez's physical presence was his smile, a warm, wide, genuine one that said all was well, or would be.

They settled in adjacent seats on the 727.

"What did you think of the meeting?" he asked.

"I thought it was useful," she replied. "You?"

He ran his tongue over his lips. "I was pleased to see the level of enthusiasm for the theme. From what I'd been told by the library's public affairs people, there was some resistance to devoting an entire issue to Columbus."

Annabel smiled. "There's been a lot of consternation at the library since this new publisher started publishing *Civilization* for them. The conflict is evidently over whether the magazine is publishing enough articles that reflect the Library of Congress."

"Yes, I've heard that," Menendez said. "Of course, there's always a debate when a magazine is published on behalf of an institution or organization, balancing the need for a 'real' magazine with it being used as a public relations vehicle for the sponsor."

"I got the feeling from the new editor in chief that he's capable of handling that balancing act."

"An impressive young man."

"How do you feel about being *Civilization*'s guest editor for the Columbus issue?" Annabel asked.

His laugh was low and gentle. "I should be flattered, being in the company of such notable guest editors—Martin Scorsese, Spike Lee, Julia Child, Jules Feiffer—a heady experience for a humble U.S. senator."

A laugh from Annabel. "You show me a humble senator and I'll make you guest emperor."

"And you, Annabel? Writing the lead article for the issue should be quite a challenge."

"I love it. I've always been fascinated by the idea that Las Casas might have written his own diaries about Columbus's first three voyages."

"If he did," said Menendez, "and if those diaries are ever found, history will be enhanced—and someone will become very, very rich."

"Or famous," Annabel said, "or even infamous. Hopefully, whoever does uncover the diaries—and let's not forget they say there's the possibility Las Casas included a map where Columbus might have buried gold—ideally, that person will be altruistic enough to see that the materials end up in a place of public learning."

"Like the Library of Congress."

"Yes, like our library."

The plane had been taxiing during their conversation. Now, the captain's amplified voice said: "We've been cleared for take-off, ladies and gentlemen. Flight attendants, prepare."

Seconds later, thrust from the 727's three powerful jet engines pressed Annabel and Menendez back in their seats. The aircraft lifted off La Guardia's main runway, made a gentle left turn, and headed south, for Washington, D.C., for home.

It was raining in Washington when Annabel walked from the terminal to where her husband, Mackensie Smith, stood next to their car. Rather than providing a cooling respite, the rain simply added to the August humidity, which, when combined with a ninety-degree day, gave credence to the old D.C. joke that the first-prize winner in a contest receives one free summer week in the nation's capital, the runner-up two weeks. Like all such gags, it applied to Philadelphia, Baltimore, and Miami, too.

They embraced fully despite the heat and

the rain, got in the car, and Mac pulled away from the curb.

"So, tell me all about it," he said.

"After you tell me about your knee."

Mac smiled. "Sounds like the title of an art movie. 'My Knee.' Dr. Scuderi says I need arthroscopic surgery to solve the problem. It's the meniscus, he says. It's ragged and torn."

"Sounds like you're getting off easy. At least Giles didn't suggest a knee replacement."

Mac accelerated. He said without taking his eyes from the road, "It's called planned obsolescence."

"It is?"

"Yeah. Like car manufacturers. Make sure the product will wear out so consumers have to keep buying new ones. God has the same plan. Make sure *we* wear out—."

"So that I have to buy a new Mac?"

He looked at her. "I'm getting old, Annie."

"Nonsense. You're young, or at least youthful, and vigorous. Your problem is you've never been sick a day in your life, never had an operation. Have the surgery. You'll stop limping and be the terror of the tennis courts again."

He grunted, turned onto the Theodore Roosevelt Bridge, crossed the Potomac, and took local streets until driving down into the underground parking garage of the Watergate's South Building. They'd purchased a three-bedroom apartment there a little over a year ago and loved it.

They were greeted upstairs by Rufus, their Great Blue Dane.

"I've only been away a day," Annabel told the welcoming dog, almost as tall as she, rubbing behind his ears to keep from being devoured. "Both you guys know how to welcome a girl."

Mac called from the kitchen, "Drink?"

"Maybe one and a half."

The rain ruled out having their drinks on the terrace, so they settled in the living room, where they clinked glasses and took a first taste of Mac's perfect Perfect Manhattans.

"Speaking of same, how was Manhattan—perfect?"

"On its best behavior. They say the crime rate's down . . . but that hasn't slowed them down."

"The meeting," Mac said. "It went smoothly?"

"Very. The issue is going to be devoted to Columbus, and not just the usual recounting of his voyages and discoveries, but to his personal side, too. You know, he came out of obscurity, Mac, the son of a shopkeeper and weaver. He and one of his brothers went to sea at an early age."

"But that's not the specific thrust of your article."

"Right, the article I've been commissioned to write will focus on Bartolomé de Las Casas, the real controversial figure in the story. He's always been considered nothing more than Columbus's friend and confidant who worked on Columbus's daily logs and helped him write his Book of Privileges."

"Which was? Refresh me."

"It was the book Columbus presented to judges and notaries in Spain back in 1502. He wanted to convince Queen Isabel and King Fernando to grant titles, money, and other privileges to him and his descendants in return for having risked his life to discover new lands for the Crown."

"The explorer was a pragmatist as well as an adventurer."

"Can't blame him. But Las Casas might have been more than just a pal and editor. If certain scholars are correct, Las Casas kept his own diaries. And never told Columbus he was doing it."

"And your friend's alleged diaries might be in conflict with Columbus's version of things?"

"My *friend*?"

"Las Casas will be your friend when you're done researching him. What's your deadline?"

"Two months."

"When do you start your research?"

"First thing in the morning. Consuela is setting me up with a cubbyhole in the Hispanic and Portuguese reading room. I'm scheduled to interview Michele Paul."

"Who's she?"

"He. Paul is probably the leading scholar in the world where Las Casas is concerned. There are plenty of others, but he seems to be the most respected. He's been researching the Las Casas diaries at LC for much of his career."

"That sort of single-minded focus always amazes me," Mac said. "Snack?"

"Thank you, no. Too close to dinner. Are we eating here?"

He nodded and stood. "I picked things up

this afternoon at the French Market. Simple fare." As Mac headed for the kitchen, he stopped for a moment and winced.

"Your knee?"

"Yeah. Comes and goes."

"It woke you up last night."

He smiled. "You were awake?"

"Uh huh. Sit. I'll get dinner." She got to her feet.

"Oh, no. I'm the chef in this house, torn meniscus or not. Enjoy your drink. Glad you're home. So's he."

Rufus, who answered to many things, including *he,* wagged his tail. Annabel watched her husband enter the kitchen, followed by the dog. Mac wasn't limping, but it was clear he was favoring his right leg.

As minor a procedure as arthroscopic surgery to repair a knee might be, that anything was wrong with her husband was anathema to Annabel. Since marrying seven years ago—he'd been a widower since losing his first wife and only son in a Beltway head-on car crash; it was Annabel's first marriage—they'd been almost adolescent in their view of their mortality. They would live happily forever now that they'd found each other, no problems, no threats to their love, never aging, doctors to be seen only for routine checkups that showed them to be, of course, in the pink of health, remarkable physical specimens, the perfect couple in every way and destined to remain that way.

Need help? she almost asked, but didn't. Instead, she picked up that day's *Washington Post* and read of the latest scandals in the nation's capital. She often told herself, sometimes aloud when no one was looking, that she was fortunate that neither she nor Mac were involved in politics. It had become a nasty business, the courtly debates and back-room maneuverings with the nation's best interests in mind replaced by vituperative, blatantly partisan attacks, too many of them personal as far as she was concerned. Owning an art gallery and being married to a law professor were exactly her cup of tea, smooth Darjeeling with just enough lemon to make things interesting.

She was about to drop the paper and join Mac in the kitchen when an article about the Library of Congress caught her eye. A wealthy woman in Massachusetts had died and left her late husband's collection of legal documents from eighteenth-century Cape Cod to the library. Upon opening the boxes and examining the contents, librarians discovered an urn with the husband's ashes. She grinned. Happens. A year earlier, the article pointed out, another donation of rare books included two plastic bags of cocaine.

Annabel smiled. She'd loved libraries since childhood, their once dusty shelves filled with the thoughts and talents of the ages, the quietude of their reading rooms, and the intensity of persons using them to learn about something they hadn't known before.

Two months at the Library of Congress, she thought, her smile broadening. She couldn't wait to get started.

4 The Library of Congress is America's oldest national cultural institution; the year 2000 will mark its two-hundredth anniversary. It is, quite simply, the largest repository of recorded knowledge in the world, as well as an active symbol of the symbiotic relationship between knowledge and democracy.

While continuing to serve as the primary reference source for Congress, the Library of Congress, known as LC by Washingtonians, houses more than 115 million "items" on 532 miles of bookshelves in three large buildings: more than 17 million books.

And it is not all books. There are 2 million recordings, 12 million photographs, 4 million maps, and 47 million manuscripts. Some national libraries in other countries confine themselves to their own languages. The LC has holdings in 460 languages. It has four thousand employees, some of whom serve in overseas offices in Rio de Janeiro, Cairo, New Delhi, Islamabad, Jakarta, and Nairobi, and in acquisitions offices in Moscow and Tokyo.

Each year, almost a million visitors pass through the metal detectors of the Jefferson, Adams, and Madison buildings for a weapons search and subject their handbags and briefcases to personal examination. Annabel Reed-Smith was among them, entering the newest of LC's buildings, the Madison, the morning after her return from New York.

She passed inspection, having nothing suspicious in her bag except the usual womanly too-much-of-everything, and went directly to where she'd been told to report, the Office of Public Affairs, on the ground floor.

"Good morning," she said to the first person she met. "I'm Annabel Reed-Smith. I'm working on an article for *Civilization* and was told to check in here. I'll be working in the Hispanic-Portuguese section."

"Of course," the attractive, middle-aged woman said, smiling, extending her hand, and introducing herself. "I'm Joanne Graves. I've been expecting you. *Civilization* is my baby, so to speak. I'm the library's liaison. Coffee?"

"Thanks, no, I've had enough." Annabel didn't add that having married Mackensie Smith, an avowed coffee snob, had turned her into a caffeine parvenu in her own right. Office coffee? Either bring it from home or skip it.

The public affairs specialist fetched a fresh cup of coffee for herself from a small kitchen, sat behind her desk, and asked pleasantly, "Ready to settle in to the life of scholarly research?"

"More than ready," Annabel said. "It was a bit of a scramble to cover the gallery. I have an art gallery in Georgetown. But it worked out."

Annabel had once been a matrimonial attorney in Washington, one of the more respected ones, according to *Washingtonian* magazine's annual issue on the city's best lawyers. Having never married had nothing to do with a lack of suitors. Annabel simply was constitutionally not content with second best. She'd spend a year and a half shopping for just the right rug, never succumbing to those that were almost what she wanted. It was the same with men. Better to remain single than to make a mistake.

Then she met Mackensie Smith, former top criminal attorney whose clients had included a number of inside-the-Beltway notables. With his wife and son gone so suddenly, Smith lost interest in his practice, eventually giving it up and becoming a law professor at George Washington University.

"I'm thinking of leaving the law," Annabel told him one night after their relationship had been firmly established. "I've had this life-long love of pre-Columbian art and history, and I've always wanted to open a specialized gallery. What do you think?"

"Do it!" he said without hesitation. "Change your life before life changes you."

She found an attractive space in Georgetown and filled it with baked-clay Tlatilco statues, stucco death masks, beaded belts, and silver jewelry from that vastly rich and artistic era before Columbus and other Europeans set foot on the shores of Central and North America and transformed those places forever, not always for the better. Simultaneously, Annabel immersed herself in pre-Columbian history, eventually finding the study of Christopher Columbus and his four voyages to the New World to be of great interest. And she started writing articles on the subject, first for esoteric journals, then moved on to publications with wider circulation and enhanced influence. These activities helped to make the name she'd forged for herself in pre-Columbian art circles—the gallery was now twice its original size—and led to the offer to write the lead article for *Civilization* on the Las Casas connection to Columbus.

"I know your gallery, Mrs. Reed-Smith. I've been there but never bought anything. A little—no, a lot beyond my means."

"Buying things for the gallery is often a lot beyond my means, too," Annabel said modestly.

"Let's head over to Hispanic," Annabel's host said, taking a final sip of coffee.

"Do you know whether I've been set up to speak with Michele Paul?" Annabel asked as they left the public affairs office and went to the main entrance, where Annabel's briefcase and handbag were again searched—

this time for books belonging to the LC—before exiting to Independence Avenue.

"Too nice a day to use the underground tunnel," the pert, enthusiastic public affairs specialist said, striding briskly in the direction of the researcher's entrance to the Jefferson Building on Second Street, SE. The main entrance was on the other side of the building, on First Street.

"Michele Paul," Annabel repeated.

"Oh, him."

Annabel laughed. "Should I read something into your tone?"

"Please don't. Telling tales out of school—in this case, a library—is a popular sport, especially where Michele Paul is concerned. He's a brilliant scholar."

Annabel waited a beat: "And?"

"He can be . . ."

"Difficult?"

"A rare bit of understatement in a town that thrives on overstatement."

"Don't feel you're betraying any confidences," said Annabel. "I've heard harsh comments about him, too, although I can't speak from much personal experience. The last time I was in the Hispanic reading room, Consuela introduced us. He was terribly rude."

"I'm not surprised. You and Consuela go back a long way, I hear."

"Yes. She's a dear friend."

"And popular around here. If she has a dark side, I've yet to see it."

"How does Consuela deal with the temperamental Mr. Paul?" Annabel asked.

"Pretty well, I guess. When you deal with someone with his credentials—he's the sole reason some donors to the Hispanic collection look to us first—Consuela might not have been able to find a way to—well, there I go again."

"Find a way to get rid of him?" Annabel felt like she was on a game show where one person starts a thought and the next contestant finishes it.

"Talk with Consuela about it. We'll go in that door over there."

"I get the feeling I *won't* be interviewing him," Annabel said.

"Oh, I suspect you will—eventually. Ever since he started his research on Las Casas six or seven years ago, he's defined secrecy, not just rudeness. Every note, every scrap of paper goes home with him at night."

"But he does give interviews," Annabel said as they approached the Jefferson, the oldest of LC's three buildings. "And he occasionally writes for the scholarly journals."

"Under threat of decapitation from the Librarian's office. But you've probably noticed that he never writes about what his research has uncovered. All he does is add fuel to the rumors about Las Casas."

"He claimed in one article that he would prove the existence of the diaries and map within two years. That was a year ago."

"Typical of Paul—predict something but don't back it up. He's very good at provocation."

They paused before entering the Jefferson.

"Mrs. Reed-Smith," Joanne Graves said, placing a hand on her arm, "don't listen to me when it comes to Michele Paul. Okay? I don't want to color your perception of him. He's not popular with colleagues, but that doesn't mean he won't be utterly charming and helpful with you."

"Fair enough, although I have to admit certain preconceived notions about Mr. Paul."

"And I'm delighted having you write for *Civilization*. It can use some new creative energy. Come on, Consuela's expecting us."

* * *

The Hispanic room occupies what is known as the Southeast Gallery on the second floor of the Jefferson Building. Until 1938, its space had been devoted to "Invention." The conversion of the space into the Hispanic room had obliterated a stained-glass ceiling with the names of twenty-nine famed inventors—Bell, Edison, Westinghouse, et al.—to the chagrin of those more interested in inventions than Hispanic-Portuguese history.

They entered the north vestibule and an entrance to the 130-foot-long vaulted reading room. Annabel stopped in the center of the vestibule and said of four dramatic murals: "Every time I'm here, these Portinari murals grab me. It's as though they're pulling me into the scenes."

"I have the same reaction," Joanne Graves said. "The Brazilian's powerful."

They turned in the direction of the reading room to see Dr. Consuela Martinez approaching. "Hello, you two," she said.

"Good morning, Consuela," Annabel said.

The chief of the Hispanic and Portuguese division was an attractive, vivacious woman of uncertain middle age, with a body language that spelled energetic. She was fond of vivid makeup—bloodred lipstick and dark blue eye-liner—and large gold jewelry.

"Coffee?" Consuela asked. "Let's go into my office."

"I left one behind, but thanks," Joanne said. "Have to be running now that I've delivered your latest scholar. Stop in and say hello now and then, Annabel."

"Shall do. Thanks."

"Annabel? Coffee?"

"Couldn't handle another," Annabel said, comfortable with small lies.

They settled in the cramped, overfilled office. Piles of books, maps, and file folders created small mountains on every surface.

"Ready to dig into the life of Bartolomé de Las Casas?" Consuela asked.

"Can't wait to get started."

"Good. I've reserved a cubicle for you on the upper gallery. Not terribly large but sufficient, I'm sure. As long as you don't sneeze."

"I'll feel important," Annabel said, "having my own space here."

"They considered giving you a carrel in the Office of Scholarly Programs," Consuela said, "but since you're focusing on a single Hispanic subject, it's better you settle in here.

Some of the material you'll want to see will be in Rare Books and Special Collections, or the manuscript division. Looking at maps, too?"

"Maybe. I'd like to start with Columbus's Book of Privileges. I had a brief look a year ago, but never really delved into it."

"LC's most prized piece of early Americana. It's a vellum copy, one of only three known to exist. The other two are in Paris and Genoa. But ours has the Papal Bull *Dudum siquidem.* Makes it that much more valuable. You'll need a translator."

"Probably, although I've been studying Spanish for the past three years. Took it in high school and college and promptly forgot most of what I learned. But I'm closing in on fluency now. *Más importante.*"

"Splendid," Consuela said. "Let's get you settled upstairs. I'll set it up with Manuscripts for after lunch."

"Before we go . . . ," Annabel said, "I was wondering about the interview with Michele Paul. Is that still on?"

Consuela's sigh spoke volumes. Next came a laugh. "Charm school didn't take with Michele," Consuela said, becoming conspiratorial. "The charm gene was missing at birth.

I couldn't pin him down, Annabel. He returned a day or so ago from a trip to Peru so I know he's in town. Michele single-handedly consumes our travel budget. I'd raise it with him but . . ."

"But it keeps him away from here," Annabel offered, not sure she should.

"From your mouth. Michele should be here by noon. I'll bring up the interview again."

"I don't want to make waves," Annabel said, following Consuela from the office and to a door leading to the Hispanic and Portuguese division's stacks. Consuela swiped one of several magnetic badges hanging from her neck through a slot on the door, unlocking it. "Make all the waves you like," she said over her shoulder as they ascended to the balcony overlooking the reading room.

Maybe he'll drown in them, Annabel silently translated.

The space that would be Annabel's for the next two months was one of four such areas, each approximately ten feet square, with a desk, lamp, empty bookcases, and a photocopy machine. A phone rested on a small table. "You can make all the local calls you want," Consuela said. "I see you've brought the requisite laptop. Here's an outlet for it, and there's a phone jack if you want to tap into the Internet from here."

"It's better equipped than my home office," said Annabel, placing the laptop computer and a compact, portable ink-jet printer she'd purchased especially for the project on the desk. She looked about: "Who uses these other spaces?"

"The cubicle at the end is occupied these days by a master's candidate from the University of Missouri."

"Oh? What's he researching?"

"It's a she—Mary Alice Warren. Nice gal. You'll like her. She's studying ancient Spanish burial rituals."

"Why?"

Consuela laughed. "Why not? It's the age of specialization. She's been hard at it for over a month, seems to love the subject. That next cubicle belongs to Richard Kelman. You'll get along fine with him. He's on a Fulbright to study how Spanish law impacted the way the indigenous populations of Mexico were treated under the Inquisition. He spends most of his time in Manuscripts poring over items in the Kraus Collection, and in the law library."

"And who's on this side?"

"Dr. Michele Paul."

"Oh," Annabel said. "I'm surprised he doesn't have bigger space considering his credentials."

"He does. His cubicle is eleven by eleven. Space is at a premium around here. Push come to shove, the books get more space, not people. Actually, we've kept this space you'll be using vacant as sort of a buffer zone between Michele and Dick Kelman. Michele read a paper Kelman had written and berated him in front of a group of people, told him he was a pathetic excuse for a scholar or something like that. No, worse than that. They aren't fond of each other."

"So I'll be a human buffer zone."

"Sorry, but it's the only space available, at least in Hispanic. If you're uncomfortable, I can call Wayne Brennan in Scholarly Programs and see if he still has space."

"No, thanks, Consuela. I'd rather be right here in Hispanic. We'll all get along just fine."

"Good. By the way, that desk in the hall belongs to one of our interns from Maryland U. Delightful gal. She splits her time between here and the main reading room. I've got her cataloging Cuban newspapers. We collect fourteen of them."

"Fourteen newspapers published in Communist Cuba?"

"Fidel, the benevolent dictator and champion of free speech. Sure I can't get you coffee to kick-start your project?"

"Thanks, no. I'll start bringing a thermos tomorrow."

"That locker with the padlock is yours. Lock your laptop, purse, notes, anything else in there. It's secure. Ever since they instituted the new security system, we haven't had any problems."

"That's good to hear. I'll unpack my briefcase and get set up. You say we'll go to Manuscripts after lunch?"

"Right. And maybe you'll have better luck than I've had with Michele about the interview. He might be partial to tall, shapely redheads."

Annabel settled at the desk and spread out the supplies and papers she'd brought with her. Her excitement level had risen. Although she'd done research at LC over the past few years, those had been short bursts lasting only a few days. Mostly, she'd used the main reading room, where the volumes she sought were housed, including thousands of books on Hispanic-Portuguese subjects that were circulated to the general public.

But this was different. She was settling in for two months, a chance to really get to know more of Las Casas's relationship to Columbus, and she hoped to add something useful to the debate over whether the Spaniard had, in fact, written his own diaries about Columbus's first three voyages. If she could accomplish that through her research, and the article she would write for *Civilization,* she would have made a worthwhile contribution. She wasn't seeking to actually find the diaries, if they even existed in the first place. Others had spent their entire professional lives attempting to do that, without success. But if she could pull together all the snippets of information, and all the rumors over the centuries, into a coherent case that the diaries did, in fact, exist, she'd be more than fulfilled. Make a case that continuing to search for the diaries wasn't a wasted exercise. The lawyer in her speaking.

Her contemplation was interrupted by thoughts of her husband, speaking of lawyers and things worthwhile. Mac had been totally supportive of her plan to leave the day-to-day operations of the gallery to others, and to devote months to writing the article. His support wasn't surprising, of course. He'd backed every move she'd made since they met, offering advice when asked but leaving the decisions very much up to her. He was, she thought, the most decent and loving person she'd ever—

"Sometimes you get lucky," she said quietly as she picked up the phone and dialed their number at the Watergate.

"Mac?"

"Hello. Adjusting to your new life as an academician?"

"I think so. Consuela has given me a wonderful little cubbyhole on the balcony overlooking the reading room. I feel like I've been here forever. I'm going to the manuscript division after lunch to take a long, hard look at Columbus's Book of Privileges."

"Sounds great. Even privileged, you might say. Like me, marrying you."

"Mac?"

"Yeah?"

"Are you okay?"

"Am I okay? Of course I am. Why would you even ask?"

"You sound down."

"That's because I'm gearing up for another semester teaching tomorrow's keepers of our system of jurisprudence."

"I'm sure you'll have a splendid class, including a few future Supreme Court justices. How's your knee?"

"Fine."

"No pain?"

"Not even a twinge."

"Do you have any tennis dates planned?"

"No. Too busy."

"Uh huh. Have you talked to Giles about scheduling the surgery?"

"No. I thought I'd try magnets."

"Magnets?"

"All the rage in alternative medical circles."

Annabel suppressed a giggle. "If you end up with a positive magnet, I'll strap on a negative one. No one can pry us apart then."

"Good idea, Annie. Dinner? What's your pleasure? In? Out?"

"Out. Chinese."

"All right. What time will you be home?"

"Five-thirty."

"See you then."

Annabel hung up and thought about the conversation. She knew he hadn't made any tennis dates because his knee hurt too much when playing. Yes, he was the most decent and loving person she'd ever known. And, on occasion, the most stubborn.

"Hi."

Annabel swiveled in her chair. "Hello."

"I'm Sue Gomara." A young woman with short blond hair, wearing tight jeans and an even tighter pink sweater, smiled and extended a hand. In her other hand was an intimidating box cutter with a long, curved blade sharp enough to cut down small trees, or cut off large heads.

"I'm Annabel Reed-Smith. So, you're the intern? And would you mind putting that lethal weapon down?"

"What? Oh, this. Sorry." She backed up and placed the cutter on her small desk. "They always have me opening boxes," she said, returning to Annabel, "so I bought this myself at a hardware store." She chuckled. "Yup, that's me, *the* intern."

"I just arrived," said Annabel. "I'll be here for a couple of months."

"That's great. Consuela told me all about you. That's exciting, writing about Columbus for *Civilization*."

"Yes, I am excited about it. I understand you're cataloging Cuban newspapers."

"That's *not* so exciting, but it's part of learning, I guess. I spend a lot of time in the main reading room. I really like it there. I'm studying to be a librarian."

"A noble profession. I read somewhere that the first Librarian of Congress only made two dollars a day."

"That's okay. I don't want to become a librarian for money. It's because . . . it's because I love books. I really, really love them. I mean, there's something special about bringing people and books together, serving others, like the living and the dead. Some day I want to be the Librarian of Congress."

"Run the whole show."

"Run the whole show. When I do, you'll always be welcome. I won't keep you from your work, and I have to get back to those Cuban newspapers. Great meeting you."

"Same here."

The intern's high spirits lifted Annabel's momentary concerns about Mac's knee, about the dour Dr. Michele Paul, about her own ability to research and write about Las Casas. She was suddenly restless, and decided to take a walk through the Jefferson Building, which had reopened in May of 1997 after more than a decade of modernization and restoration. When it originally opened in 1897 to house the overflowing collection of books and manuscripts that had been stored haphazardly in the Capitol Building, it was called the most beautiful public building in America. As far as Annabel was concerned, the building itself was yet another of LC's treasures.

She returned a little before noon, enjoyed lunch in the cafeteria with Consuela Martinez, and spent the entire afternoon in the Manuscript reading room in the Madison Building. Before being granted access, she had to fill out a registration form and secure all personal belongings, including outerwear, pens, pencils, and newspapers, in a locker. The only item she was allowed to bring into the room was a laptop computer without its case. Annabel was provided the division's own paper and pencils and a pair of white gloves and assigned a desk, where she waited for one of the Library of Congress's most precious pieces of early Americana to be brought to her, secured in a special clear plastic sheath.

The Book of Privileges arrived. It was a privilege in itself.

Viewing the document had a visceral impact upon Annabel, creating a sustaining physical tension. The rarity and fragility of the document played a role in this reaction, of course. But more pervasive was being transported into Columbus's world through the thoughts and words he committed to the vellum. She went word by word, soon realizing that even her intensive Spanish lessons of the past three years would not provide her with the ability to fully comprehend what the discoverer of the New World was saying.

Still, she plugged away, making extensive notes on the paper provided by the reading room's personnel.

At four-thirty, the Book was returned to its climate-controlled vault, and Annabel collected her belongings and returned to her space in Hispanic. She was alone on the upper gallery. Below, men and women doing research at reader desks packed up in preparation for leaving. The room's quiet was omnipresent, even unsettling.

She placed some items in her locker, secured it with the padlock, and came downstairs. Consuela Martinez was in her office.

"Productive afternoon?" the division chief asked.

"Yes, but just a start. I'll be back there day after tomorrow looking at it again. I see that Michele Paul never showed up."

"No, he didn't," Consuela said, leaning back in her chair and chewing on a pencil's eraser. "He pretty much comes and goes as he pleases, although he knows I expect him to keep me informed where he is."

"I'm sure we'll meet up one of these days," Annabel said. "Thanks for everything. As they say, I think I've hit the ground running."

The road from the hotel to the airport on Virgin Gorda, in the British Virgin Islands, was steep, narrow, twisting, and treacherous. It hugged the side of a mountain, with a drop-off to the rock-studded shore five hundred feet below.

Lucianne Huston sat in the passenger seat of the Range Rover and fought to stay awake. It had been an exhausting and frustrating three days, beginning with flight delays made more exasperating by a lack of information from the airline. It had taken her fourteen hours to get there from Miami, with a plane change in Puerto Rico. Then came clandes-

tine midnight meetings that failed to material-
ize, promises of cooperation that were bro-
ken, and a couple of veiled threats from a
midlevel official whom Lucianne had wanted
to punch. She didn't of course; it would not
have been the sort of behavior expected of a
TV journalist representing NCN, the world's
leading all-news cable network.

Worse than the fatigue had been the lack
of results. Her assignment had been to follow up on information she'd received
through good sources that certain government officials in the idyllic British Virgins
were on the payroll of South American drug
runners. She'd come up empty, with plenty
of promising leads but not enough to go with
the story. She knew such payoffs existed
because not only did she trust her sources,
she trusted her own instincts. But you needed facts to make such accusations on the
air, and Lucianne didn't have them—yet.

The Range Rover's driver had been her
guide for the three days on the islands of
Virgin Gorda and Tortola. He was a young
man carrying too much weight, with tousled
black hair, heavy acne, and a pleasant disposition. The network had hired him through
an intermediary, and he'd been at Lucianne's

beck and call since picking her up at the airport three days ago. If there was any reason for her to be sorry to leave, it was him. His name was Robert, and he spoke with a lilt, scattering English Creole terms throughout conversations with her, many of which she had to ask him to translate.

They were halfway down the mountain when a battered blue pickup truck appeared coming up the road, which was barely wide enough for two vehicles to pass. Robert slowed to a crawl as he waited for the other vehicle to come abreast. Lucianne looked down to her right. They were on the outside, the Range Rover's wheels on the extreme edge of the road.

When the pickup truck was twenty feet away, Lucianne saw the two men in the cab. The driver laughed as he pointed the truck directly at the Range Rover and gunned the engine. Robert stiffened and applied the brakes, causing the wheels on the right side to slip in the direction of the drop-off. "Stinkin' bastard," he said. There was no way to turn away from the truck, no room to maneuver. The pickup's left front fender hit the Range Rover's left front fender, causing the vehicle to move farther off the road. The front wheels went over the edge; the under-carriage rested on the drop-off's crest.

The driver of the pickup shifted into reverse, then roared forward, his right wheels literally climbing the lower edge of the mountain and tipping the truck in the direction of the Range Rover. It passed and roared up the road, kicking dirt and dust into the air.

Robert and Lucianne scrambled from the vehicle through the driver's door, careful not to step off the edge of the road. Robert shook his fist at the wake of the pickup while Lucianne let loose a string of longshoreman invective and threw a rock. The verbal warnings had turned physical.

Lucianne Huston was used to being in dangerous situations—civil wars in Third World countries, tribal uprisings, in Saddam Hussein's shadow during Desert Storm, Bosnia, Northern Ireland, interviews with serial killers in maximum-security prisons, the Middle East. But no one had ever tried to kill her because of her investigations and reporting. At least she hadn't considered all the mishaps she'd experienced to have been deliberate acts.

"You'd better call for help," she told Robert,

who carefully retrieved his cell phone from the vehicle. A half hour later, a tow truck arrived and pulled the Range Rover back onto the road. It was drivable, and Robert and Lucianne followed the truck the rest of the way down to the airport. Her flight to Puerto Rico had left—The one time it's on time, she thought, and it has to be today. She remained at the tiny airport for six hours until the next flight took her to San Juan. There were more delays. She arrived home in Miami at three in the morning.

She had intended to sleep late in her oceanfront Fort Lauderdale apartment and take the day off. But that plan to enjoy a day of leisure was dashed by the one message on her answering machine.

"Lucianne, this is Baumann. Sorry the BVI story didn't pan out, but I've got another one for you. Different. Top priority. Ten o'clock in my office. Welcome back."

She managed four hours of sleep, showered, put on jeans, white T-shirt, and tan safari jacket—at least she could dress as though it was a day off—grabbed a dough-nut and tea at a nearby outdoor cafe, and drove in her red Fiat Spider convertible to her TV network's broadcast center. Located on the Dixie Highway, it was a year-old, ten-story building whose glass curtain-walls reflected its surroundings, distorting shapes, and, when the sun shifted, wiped them off the huge, multipanel screen. As far as Lucianne was concerned, the building represented a rigid, unimaginative, and distinctly ugly blot on the landscape, not that the landscape was any great shakes, either. That she spent most of her working days on the road covering stories was fine with her.

She swore at the car parked in the slot with her name on it, pulled into another marked space, slung her large, heavy leather bag over her shoulder, and entered through an employee door, flashing her badge at the guard, who greeted her by name.

Robert Baumann's office was in the rear of the building, on the top floor. Lucianne fielded a succession of greetings as she passed desks in the spacious newsroom and breezed through the open door into the news director's corner office.

"Hello," he said from behind a boomerang-shaped black desk. He was in his shirtsleeves, a tie pulled loose from his neck. Baumann was a burly forty-five-year-old man with hair like a bear, a black thatch of it curling out from his neck through the shirt's opening. He'd come to TV news after a good career in print journalism. His news judgment was considered solid; management liked and backed him at almost every turn. Lucianne liked him, too, although she wasn't always in agreement with his judgment calls where her assignments were concerned.

She dropped her bag on the carpeted floor and pulled a director's chair closer to the desk.

"So," he said, "tell me about the BVI. They must be pretty good at covering up if they kept you at bay."

"I'll break through," she said. "I've got a few sources working on it."

Baumann looked up from something he was reading and laughed. "You have more sources, Lucianne, than Miami has Cuban restaurants."

"Lots more."

"How close do you get to them?"

Now, a laugh from her. "You mean do I sleep with them? A few. That they're still my sources must mean I'm pretty good at that, too."

Baumann dropped his reading material on his lap, leaned back in his high-backed black leather chair, and fixed her in a bemused stare.

Lucianne Huston was a star at the network. Her willingness—no, make that enthusiasm—to be where the action was, no matter what danger it posed for her, had made her compelling to millions of TV news junkies: hurricane winds threatening to blow her over, rockets whistling past her ear, fierce mountain freedom fighters glaring at her as she asked how they felt about killing their fellow countrymen. Baumann had occasionally considered moving her into an anchor chair to take advantage of her popularity and good looks, but reversed himself whenever the notion struck him. The one time he'd suggested it to her, she'd laughed it off, saying, "I'm not a talking head, Bob. I'm a *real* journalist. Keep your anchor job; just pay me what your pretty-boy readers get."

Baumann appreciated Lucianne's reporting skills. Her looks weren't lost on him either. It wasn't that she was beautiful in a magazine cover or Hollywood way. Her features were less than perfect, nose a little too broad, mouth a little too small. It was the overall impression that counted. She was five feet, seven inches tall, slim and fit, and carried herself with confidence. Her auburn hair was worn short but not too short, an easy style to maintain in the jungles of Central America or the winter winds of Bosnia. Her complexion was dusky, brown eyes large and round; many assumed she was of mixed parentage. She wasn't.

"So, what's this story you want me on?"

"Columbus."

"Columbus? You mean Columbo? Peter Falk?"

"Christopher. He discovered us."

"Oh, *that* Columbus. He's surfaced?"

Baumann grinned. "You might say that. See this?" He slid papers across the desk. "Just got these this morning."

Lucianne read quickly, dropped the papers on the desk. "So?" she said.

"Interesting, huh?"

She shook her head.

"Happened night before last."

"Bob, this was my day off. You said you had a story for me—'top priority,' you said."

"Right. This is it."

"A local murder? What's the big deal?"

"I'm not sure it is a big deal, Lucianne, but it could be. You do know that the Columbus celebration is coming up in six months."

"Uh huh."

"And that there's been this controversy for years over whether one of Columbus's sailing companions, Bartolomé de Las Casas, might have written his own account of the voyages."

"I read something about it."

"The security guard who was shot worked for a small museum called Casa de Seville. In Little Havana."

"Latin Quarter. You're behind the times."

"Whatever. The guard was on his first night at this museum. They never had a security guard before."

"Timing is everything. My condolences to his family."

"Whoever killed him stole a painting from the museum that same night."

"Uh huh."

"It was a painting that depicted Columbus on his knees in front of the king and queen of Spain. See the picture there?"

Lucianne took a second look at what Baumann had given her. The clip from *The Miami Herald* included a picture of the ribbon-cutting ceremony when Casa de Seville was dedicated two years ago. Posing in front of the painting by Fernando Reyes were the museum's curator, the two businessmen who'd provided the initial funding, and U.S. senator from Florida Richard Menendez.

"Okay, I see it," Lucianne said, "but so what? Some overly dedicated art connoisseurs break into this museum, steal a painting, and shoot the security guard. I see it wasn't considered a great work of art. They could have done better."

"The question, Lucianne: Why did they bother stealing this particular painting if it wasn't worth much, and murder someone in the process?"

"A bad eye for art and a ruthless disregard for human life."

"Maybe." Baumann got up, stretched against an ache in his back, went to the window, and looked down at a man-made lake. He turned, leaned against the sill housing the vital air-conditioning, and said, "I got a call last night from Joe Betz in Los Angeles." Betz was the network's L.A. bureau chief. "He thinks there's a story in this Las Casas diary business. My nose tells me there is. According to him, some people out there, identity unknown at this point, are offering big bucks for the Las Casas diaries and map."

"Map?"

"Yeah. Those who believe those diaries exist also believe that Las Casas drew a map showing where Columbus buried gold. A lot of gold. *Sixty Minutes* did a piece on it six months ago."

"Yeah, I saw it. Where's the news? If I find the gold, do I get a cut?"

"No, but you'll get a letter of commendation in your file, and have the satisfaction of having contributed to mankind's understanding of his origins."

"Cute. Forget it. Give me a nice little war. When do I leave for Africa?"

"You're not going to Africa."

"Why? I was supposed to cover the unrest in Mozambique."

"It's cooled off there, Lucianne. I want you to follow up on this art theft, the murder, and Las Casas. See if they're joined at the hip. Everybody loves missing treasure. Like who'll win the lottery."

"But we don't even know whether a map and diaries exist."

"Right, but I'd like us to be in the hunt along

with the eggheads. Speaking of them, there's a guy at the Library of Congress who's supposed to be the most knowledgeable scholar in this area. Name's Michele Paul. I pulled up some material from the Web on Las Casas. Dr. Paul predicted in a piece he wrote a year ago that he'd prove within two years that the diaries and the map are real. Go to Washington and get an interview with him. In the meantime, I'll keep tabs on the art theft and murder. The police say, off the record, that it looks like the museum's maintenance man might have set things up from inside, left a skylight unsecured for the thieves to get in. He's disappeared, never showed up for work after the theft. The cops say he had a record of drug use. If they find him, they'll probably know who pulled the heist. A couple of days off the stuff and every hophead spills."

"Washington? I'd rather go to Africa. Or some other war zone like L.A." Lucianne stood.

"Maybe when this is over. Might I add that our fearless leader has a special interest in this?"

"He does?"

"Yeah. Among his many charitable activities is raising money for the Library of Congress. He and Cale Broadhurst break bread together."

"Who's Cale Broadhurst?"

"The Librarian of Congress. By the way, it was him who killed your Africa assignment."

"The Librarian of Congress?"

"No, our fearless leader. Look, even if you don't come up with anything startling, we'll use what you get for the documentary on the Columbus celebration."

They locked eyes.

Baumann said, "Our crack research desk has info on Michele Paul and the stuff from the Web. Any of your sources happen to be in the Library of Congress?"

"Oh, sure, lots. But I'll have to go back through my files, search under 'egghead.' "

"I knew I could depend on you, Lucianne. Look at it this way. Instead of being where you might get your pretty head shot off by some rebel gunman, you can operate for a little while in the genteel safety of the Library of Congress."

"I'm thrilled. Yawn."

"Every library is more exciting than it looks. Ask any real reader. You're a hard-digging reporter. That's what people do in libraries—

they dig for information. Or entertainment or distraction, whatever. By the way, you look tired. Why don't you get more sleep?"

"Because of your phone message. I'll get plenty of sleep sitting in a library. Thanks for nothing."

Munsch waved off the flight attendant who came down the aisle passing out magazines.

Warren Munsch didn't read much. The last book he'd gotten through was during his second stint inside, two and a half years for possession of stolen property. The book was *Know Your Rights: A Layman's Guide to Criminal Law.*

Armed with knowledge from the book, Munsch decided he knew more than any lawyer on earth, and believed he had become expert at analyzing his future activities. He'd given it plenty of thought before agreeing to lift the painting from Casa de Seville and had written down his expert analysis:

1. Nobody cares about paintings unless they're worth millions, so stealing a piece of junk isn't a big deal.
2. Morrie and Garraga do the break-in. If we get caught, they do the hard time. I don't know when I drive them why they want to go there. They hand me this lousy painting and tell me to take it to L.A. and turn it over to some guy.
3. I know nothing. Any clown in Legal Aid gets me off on that rap, like they did with the last two busts.
4. Home free.

The problem, he knew as he pondered this on the plane to Los Angeles, was Number Five. He'd never figured on the shooting of a security guard. The book he'd read in prison stopped short at advising how to beat a murder rap. He added a fifth item to his list: "I'm shocked when this Cuban named Garraga shot that poor security cop. I would have gone to the police but he threatened to kill me."

Not bad. Prove otherwise.

Munsch was glad the buyer of the Reyes

painting had sent a first-class ticket. The drinks were free and plentiful. He'd fortified his nerves at the Miami airport bar before boarding and kept the liquid tranquilizers flowing throughout the flight.

He got in the back of a taxi at L.A. International carrying a small overnight bag and the rolled-up Reyes painting covered by brown wrapping paper.

"Santa Monica," he told the driver.

"Where in Santa Monica?"

Munsch fished for a slip of paper in his jacket pocket and read an address off it. "It's a restaurant," he said.

"I know it," said the driver.

Now, on the Santa Monica Freeway, Munsch wished he hadn't had so much to drink on the plane. There was bound to be some sort of confrontation once the buyer saw that the painting had been cut from the frame. Maybe I should offer to cut the price so he can get a new frame, he considered, popping two Tums in his mouth, followed by a squirt of breath freshener he'd bought at the airport. He squeezed his eyes shut tight against a fuzziness in his brain and shook his head. Don't offer to cut the price, he silently told himself. Never show weakness.

Cutting away the frame demonstrated they'd been resourceful. If they hadn't done that, he wouldn't have the painting. How much can a new frame cost? A few bucks?

The cab dropped Munsch in front of Ivy at the Shore, on Ocean Avenue, where throngs of well-dressed people clogged the street in front of the restaurant. Munsch paid the driver, watched him pull away, then threaded his way through the crowd and went inside, where he was stopped by a man at a podium wearing a colorful Hawaiian shirt.

"I'm going to the bar," Munsch said. "I'm meeting somebody."

The host pointed in the direction of an outdoor terrace overlooking the ocean.

The bar was four-deep, and every rattan chair was occupied. The noise level was high, exacerbating the pounding headache Munsch had developed during the slow trip on the freeway. A couple left one end of the bar, and Munsch quickly slipped into the space. A bartender appeared.

"You got any coffee?" Munsch asked.

"Coffee? Ah . . ."

"Gimme a beer."

"We have—"

"Anything."

Munsch placed his overnight bag on the floor between his feet and laid the rolled-up painting against the wall. He took in faces at the bar. He'd been told that the person to whom he was to deliver the painting would be wearing a white jacket and a large-brimmed straw hat. No such creature at the bar.

His beer was served and he sipped. You'd better show up, Munsch thought. I didn't go through this for nothing.

He became increasingly despondent as he waited, nursing the beer, massaging his temples, and grumbling to himself, mostly about that fool Garraga, until he felt a poke in his back. He turned to look into the face of a man with a neatly cropped red beard and wearing a white jacket and straw hat.

"You took your time," Munsch said.

The man smiled. "The traffic. I was delayed."

"Yeah, sure." Munsch grabbed the painting. "This what you're after?"

"Not here."

The red beard led them to a section of the terrace obscured from the bar by potted ferns. A table had just become vacant; they took rattan chairs across from each other.

"A drink?" the beard asked.

"No. I had a beer. I left it at the bar. I don't want any more."

The beard shrugged. "I see you have what my client has been waiting for."

"Your client? I thought it was for you."

"I'm acting as an agent for the buyer."

"Yeah, well, I don't care who it ends up with." He leaned forward. "Whoever you are, I—"

"Smith. John Smith."

"Right. John Smith. I'm Joe Brown. Look, we had to slice the frame off because it wouldn't fit through the skylight with the frame on it."

John Smith frowned.

"I'll cut my fee so you can get another frame, but not by a lot. A frame don't cost much."

"The frame's not important. You did what you had to do. We read the Miami papers, too."

"That's right. We used our heads."

"Want to give it to me?"

"Sure." Munsch handed him the painting. "You want to open it here, see what it is? Believe me, it's what you . . . what your client wanted."

"I'm sure it is, Mr. Brown." He withdrew a

fat envelope from the inside pocket of his jacket and handed it to Munsch. "What was agreed upon."

Munsch shoved the envelope into his pocket.

"Don't want to count it?"

"No. You trust me, I trust you."

"The way it should be. Sure you don't want a drink?"

Munsch shook his head. "I better get going. John Smith, huh? Probably your real name."

Smith smiled. "It was a pleasure, Mr. Brown."

Munsch, who had been eager to go, hesitated.

"I know it's none of my business . . . but how come your client wants this? It's worth a lot, huh?"

"Staying in L.A. for a while?"

"A day or two."

"Enjoy your stay."

Munsch exited to the street and looked for a cab. There were three lined up at the next corner. He got into the first in line and told the driver to take him to the Beverly Hills Hotel. He knew that was where movie stars stayed; his cellmate in prison had told him he'd stayed there once. "They got a bar called the Polo Lounge, Warren," he'd said. "You should see the broads hang out there, starlets wall to wall. Like calendar girls."

The clerk at the hotel's registration desk eyed Munsch suspiciously, with his cheap overnight bag, ill-fitting brown corduroy jacket, and no reservation.

"I'm just in from Miami. Last-minute trip. Had to meet with some producers."

The clerk said nothing.

"You got one of those cottages out back?" Munsch asked.

"No, sir, but we do have an available room."

"I'll take it."

He took a nap and felt somewhat better when he woke up. The headache was gone. He called Miami. The voice and tone told him that Morrie's blond girlfriend was answering.

"Morrie there?"

"Who's this?"

"Warren. Munsch. Put Morrie on."

"Call the jail. They arrested him and Garraga."

"Oh, man," Munsch muttered.

"They arrested Morrie at the dock. We were going to Nassau to gamble. I was there. I've never been so embarrassed. Where are you?"

"I'm—What about Garraga?"

"Him, too. They got him, too. I told Morrie you were a loser, not to get involved."

Munsch hung up, thought for a minute, then called his daughter in Oregon.

"It's Papa."

"Hello."

"How's things?"

"Things are just fine." She always sounded cold when she spoke with him.

"Good. That's good to hear. How are the kids?"

"Fine. Are you in trouble again?"

"Me? Nah. No trouble. Just thought I'd check in. I'm on the Coast. On business."

"What coast?"

"The West Coast. Got to run. Good talking to you. Say hello to the kids for me."

"I will."

He looked up airline numbers in a listing he found in a welcome package and called three of them. The third had a flight for Mexico City leaving in two hours. He opened his passport as though to make sure it was legitimate. It wasn't, but it looked good, good enough to get into Mexico. He'd picked it up in Miami six months ago at a bargain price.

Munsch didn't bother telling the hotel he was checking out. No need. He'd paid cash up front. He poked his head into the Polo Lounge before heading for the hotel's main entrance. A nubile redhead in a tight dress smiled at him from where she sat at the bar. Munsch considered having a drink, nodded at her, had one of the parking valets hail a cab, and headed for the airport.

No need to send Morrie and Garraga their share of the money now, he decided. Where they were going, they couldn't spend it anyway. Where he was going . . .

Where *was* he going?

The first thing was to get out of the country. You could fly to Cuba from Mexico City. That was it, he decided, Havana, drinking *mojitos* like Hemingway with a bunch of wild Cuban women hanging over him. As long as the U.S. and Fidel didn't decide to bury the hatchet, he was home free.

"A drink?" the flight attendant asked after they were airborne.

"Yeah, sure. Got any *mojitos*?"

"What's that?"

"Forget it. A vodka on the rocks, and make it a double."

7 Michele Paul, arguably the nation's foremost living scholar on the role Bartolomé de Las Casas played in the life of Christopher Columbus, as he would be the first to agree, was up early in his condominium on the top floor of an apartment building in Bethesda, in Montgomery County. This was north of the District, as Washington, D.C., is often referred to. The few close friends who'd been invited to the apartment over the years were impressed with its opulence, considering what Paul did for a living. Pursuing scholarly research was not destined to make one rich; the psychic benefits were expected to compensate.

There were, of course, the small advances paid by publishers for esoteric books he'd written, and the magazine fees for articles. But the three-bedroom apartment and its furnishings better reflected the lifestyle of a successful businessman or highly placed government employee. What was as striking to those few visitors as the apartment's handsomeness was its total lack of anything living—not a plant or flower, not even a goldfish—aside from Paul, of course. He was fond of telling friends, "I don't want anything in my life that requires my taking care of them. Taking care of me is challenging enough." He'd never married.

He'd exercised for the past forty-five minutes, an intense workout starting with stretching, then the treadmill set at a fast pace, followed by weight lifting. Michele was proud of his body to what some would consider a narcissistic point. Naked, perspiration highlighting the definition of his arms and shoulders, he posed before the bathroom mirror for a long time, smiling approval at what he saw. Not only did he consider himself the world's foremost Columbus and

Las Casas scholar, he was certain he was the best conditioned.

Now, showered and dressed in a robe and slippers, he enjoyed coffee and a large bowl of fresh fruit on a broad terrace overlooking a park, the National Institutes of Health its scrim on the far side. He flipped through the morning paper, then pulled a lined yellow legal pad from a briefcase at his feet and began reading his handwritten notes, the result of a meeting with a friend in New York the previous day.

He picked up a cordless phone from the table in response to its feeble ring.

"Hello?"

"Michele? It's Consuela."

"Good morning."

"Good morning." Her iciness was not lost on him. "We missed you yesterday."

"It's always nice to be missed."

There was silence, followed by, "I've asked you to keep me informed when you won't be here. I don't think that's asking too much."

"Didn't I tell you I'd be out of town?" he said playfully. "I was sure I did."

Another silence: "I assume you'll be here today."

"Of course I will. You know I'm incapable of

staying away from you or the library for more than a day at a time." He smiled and waited for her response.

"There are people I want you to meet with today," the chief of the Hispanic division said flatly.

"Oh? Who?"

"Annabel Reed-Smith. You were scheduled to see her yesterday. She's writing a piece for *Civilization*."

"Poor thing. It must have slipped my mind."

"Yes, it must have. And Lucianne Huston."

"Who's she? Oh, wait, that fearless television reporter who's always reporting from some bloody murder scene or in the middle of a global calamity. Am I her next . . . calamity?"

Preferably her next victim, Consuela thought. She said, "She's doing a story for the Columbus celebration and wants to interview you."

"Should I wear a suit? Will there be make-up?"

"What time will you be here?"

"On time. I'd punch in if we had a time clock."

She hung up with conviction.

Paul laughed as he pushed Off on the

phone. After dressing—a pinched-waist double-breasted blue pinstripe suit that hugged his trim physique, a chalk-white shirt, wide lemon tie, and a new pair of black loafers purchased recently at London's Poulsen & Skone—he checked himself again in the mirror. M. Paul looked every bit like a man who had found his grail. His honey-colored, oval face had a matte finish, smooth and dry and unwrinkled, except for tiny lines slashing upward from the corners of surprisingly blue eyes, creating the effect of pulling them up into perpetual bemusement.

He made a final call before leaving, this to the manager of the boathouse on the Potomac where Paul kept a thirty-foot sailing sloop. He was angry at minor damage that had been done to the boat during a recent storm and berated the manager for his lack of preparedness. Satisfied with the manager's apologies and promise to repair the damage, Paul drove his red Jeep Grand Cherokee from the underground parking garage and headed into the District, eventually pulling into the parking space reserved for him at the Library of Congress, a perquisite granted when Texas University tried to recruit him, and he'd used the offer to better his lot at LC.

The hard heels on his new shoes reverberated off marble as he walked smartly to the second floor of the Jefferson Building, entered the Hispanic reading room, returned "Good morning" with a nod or grunt, passed the open door to Consuela Martinez's office without looking in, then climbed the stairs and entered his own personal space on the upper gallery. Richard Kelman, whose space was on the other side of Annabel's, looked over and said, "Good morning."

Paul didn't reply. He carefully hung his suit jacket on a hook in the wall, sat, and went through a pile of mail on his desk, methodically tossing the envelopes in a waste basket. He checked the monthly calendar on the desk, picked up a phone, and dialed Consuela's extension.

"My day's getting jammed up, Consuela. What about these women you want me to meet with?"

"Annabel Reed-Smith should be here shortly. I've assigned her the space next to you. Lucianne Huston is due at two."

"I have a meeting at two."

"You can't change it?"

"Not without difficulty. I should be back by four."

"I'll see if she can interview you then."

"I assume you're still looking for larger, more private space for me."

"I'm working on it."

"But not very hard, I take it. Have you called Wayne Brennan in Scholarly Programs? Half those offices over there are always empty."

"And you know they're reserved for out-side researchers. I can't be—Oh, here's Mrs. Smith now."

"Send her up to my cell."

Kelman gathered up his papers and left the area without another attempt at civility, passing Annabel on his way.

"You must be Mrs. Smith," Paul said at her arrival, extending his hand to Annabel and displaying a strong set of white teeth, made more so against his tan face.

"Yes. And you are Michele Paul." She took his hand, aware that he held it a little longer than necessary. She didn't bother mentioning that they'd been introduced before.

"Welcome to the garret," he said, indicating the area with a sweep of his hand.

"An apt description," she said. "I'm thrilled to have space here."

"A badge of honor. I understand you're writing for *Civilization*."

"That's right. On Bartolomé de Las Casas."

"Please, sit." He pulled the chair from her area into his. "I should be concerned," he said after they were seated. "You're invading my area of expertise."

"I wouldn't view it that way," she said pleasantly, "but I do want to pick your brain about that expertise."

"Pick at any part of me you wish, Mrs. Smith. It's Annabel, isn't it?"

"Yes."

"I insist upon being on a first-name basis with anyone who's picking my brain."

"Of course."

"And you may call me Michele. My mother was slightly confused when she named me."

Annabel laughed, in spite of herself.

"Well, Annabel, I'm yours for the next hour. A meeting at ten, lunch with a collector who has the audacity to consider turning over his materials to another institution, and an equally boring afternoon. My hour with you will be the highlight of an otherwise drab day."

"I'm flattered."

"Exactly as I intended. What do you wish to know?"

"Everything you know about Las Casas, I suppose."

"Are you planning on spending a few years here?"

"I'm planning on spending a few months here. Are you convinced the Las Casas diaries exist, based upon your research?"

"Yes."

"Based upon what?"

"You want me to do your work for you?"

Remaining civil, Annabel knew, would test her.

"Mr. Paul—Michele—I'm doing research in order to write an article for *Civilization* on the Las Casas connection to Columbus. The entire issue will be devoted to Columbus. Because you're acknowledged as a Las Casas expert, I was hoping you'd be gracious enough to give me a few good quotes, perhaps tell me why you predicted you would prove in two years—that was a year ago—that the diaries do, indeed, exist. Will you?"

"Give you a quote?"

"Yes."

"The diaries written by Bartolomé de Las Casas exist."

"That's it?"

"Next year's federal budget will be squandered on military hardware and not on the arts. It will be a warmer winter in Washington this year than last year. And I will be out of this hovel and in a larger, private office this time next month, even if I have to kill someone to accomplish that. You can quote me on all three subjects."

"I'm sorry to have kept you so long," Annabel said.

"No, actually you saved me, but I should run. I'd enjoy continuing this conversation. If I come off as slightly prickly, it's because I am prickly by nature, especially when amateurs intrude on a subject to which I've devoted a considerable portion of my adult life."

"Thanks for your time."

"Dinner tonight? Been to Taberna del Alabardero?"

Annabel stared at him.

"The tapas and paella are good, don't you agree?"

"I'm having dinner with my husband tonight."

He raised his eyebrows. "Only tonight? Is it an event?"

"Every time we meet."

She watched him slip on his suit jacket, check himself in a small mirror he'd hung on the wall next to the coat hook, and leave.

"Bastard," she murmured as she moved to her desk and went over notes she'd made the day before in the rare manuscripts room. Before she knew it, it was noon, and she was hungry. She went down to Consuela's office. "Feel like lunch?" she asked.

"Can't. A division chiefs' meeting. How did it go with our Dr. Paul?"

"Hardly the picture of helpful cooperation. He's so arrogant it's almost charming. He hit on me, as the saying goes."

"I knew he'd like being interviewed by a tall, attractive redhead. Were you flattered?"

"No."

"Mac would be unhappy at the news."

"Mac would only be unhappy if I invited it, or fell for it. Paul reminds me of a bullfighter, dangling that red cape, and confident that no matter how strong the bull is, it can be killed at the end."

"An image I'm sure he'd enjoy. Rain check on lunch?"

"Sure."

Annabel turned to leave but her way was blocked by a woman standing in the doorway.

"Hello," Annabel said.

"Hello."

"Dolores, this is Annabel Reed-Smith," Consuela said. "I've told you about her."

"Of course." They shook hands.

"Dolores is one of our top specialists in Hispanic," Consuela said. "Her field is Mexican culture."

"More specifically the impact of the pre-Columbian era on later Mexican culture," Dolores added.

"Why don't you two grab lunch together?" Consuela suggested. "Annabel will be here for a few months researching a piece for *Civilization*."

"So I understand. I was just heading out. Join me?"

"Love to."

Dolores suggested they skip the cafeteria on the sixth floor of the Madison Building and "eat on the economy." They walked to a strip of small restaurants a block away on Pennsylvania Avenue, decided on a place called Hill Street Brews, and were seated by the hostess in a booth.

Dolores, whose last name Annabel learned was Marwede—"People tend to pronounce it Mar-*weed*, but it's really Mar-*wee-dee*,"

Dolores said—was one of those individuals to whom Annabel took an instant liking. They were approximately the same height, tall, and might have been mistaken for sisters if their coloring was ignored. The redheaded Annabel was fair-skinned; Dolores was dusky, her hair, which like Annabel she wore long, was inky black. It had crossed Annabel's mind while walking to the restaurant that the anachronistic stereotype of librarians as granny-goose types, hair in a bun, round glasses, spending their days quieting children and protecting copies of *Ulysses* beneath the counter, had long ago been dashed. Most librarians she knew didn't fit that description, and the woman sitting across from her was no exception.

". . . and so I got my doctorate at Columbia in Spanish history," Dolores said over coffee, "and looked for teaching positions. The Library of Congress had an opening and I grabbed it."

"How long have you been there?" Annabel asked.

"Nine years."

"Enjoy working in the LC?"

"Love it. I split my time between doing my own research and as a reference librarian for people using the Hispanic division. Consuela tells me you have a wonderful husband."

Annabel smiled. "Yes, I do. Mac—his name's Mackensie—is a terrific guy. He teaches law at GW." She'd noted that Dolores did not wear a wedding ring.

"And you have that great gallery in Georgetown."

"My pride and joy."

"I've stopped in a few times but never saw you there."

"I've been fortunate with help. College students. I've pretty much turned the place over to them while working on this article. I interviewed Michele Paul this morning."

Dolores winced.

Is there no one who has kind thoughts about him?

"He was—well, he was somewhat helpful." No sense adding fuel to the anti-Paul movement. "My article focuses on Las Casas and his reputed diaries and map."

Dolores's tone and mood changed before Annabel's eyes. A darkness seemed to come over her, causing what had been a face with an almost perpetual smile to pull down at the corners of the mouth.

"I was warned not to expect much from him but . . ." Annabel forced a laugh. "Maybe I caught him on an off day."

Dolores's smile didn't seem genuine either. She looked down at her watch. "Dr. Paul and I don't see eye to eye. I have to get back," she said.

Who would? Annabel thought.

They split the check and walked back, promising to have lunch again soon. Annabel had wanted to spend the day in Manuscripts poring over Columbus's Book of Privileges again, but another researcher had reserved it. She took the underground tunnel to the Madison Building and stopped in at Public Affairs to see if they had any biographical material on Michele Paul and a list of his publishers for her article.

Annabel immediately recognized the woman in one of the offices. It was the TV journalist, Lucianne Huston. Two men sat in the waiting room, one cradling a video camera in his lap, the other perched atop a pile of black cases. Joanne, the woman who'd escorted Annabel the day before, waved her in.

"Lucianne, this is Annabel Reed-Smith."

"Hi," Lucianne said.

"You might want to talk to Annabel about Las Casas," Joanna offered. "She's researching an article for our magazine, *Civilization.*"

"Happy to," Annabel said brightly. "But there are genuine experts around here."

"Sure," Lucianne said. To Joanne: "You say Dr. Paul won't be available until four?"

"That's what I'm told."

Lucianne looked at Annabel.

"I'm free now," Annabel said.

"Now is good. How about just a talk first?" Lucianne suggested.

"You two can use this office. I have to escort a reporter to an interview with Dr. Broadhurst."

Dr. Cale Broadhurst, the fourteenth Librarian of Congress, had succeeded James H. Billington after being nominated by the current administration and confirmed unanimously by the Senate. Mac and Broadhurst had been frequent tennis partners when Broadhurst was dean of GW's ancient literature department. They still stayed in touch, only less frequently now.

"Before you go," said Annabel, "do you have a bio of Michele Paul for my article? I think I should know a little more about him."

"I don't have one handy, but I'll have one

sent up to you later today," answered Joanne with a mixture of surprise and disgust.

After telling her two-man crew they were free for an hour, Lucianne sat with Annabel. "So," she said, "tell me why you're so interested in this de Las Casas character."

"I've never heard him referred to that way," Annabel said, smiling. "I was wondering why *you're* interested in him. I thought you only covered wars and famine and sensational murder trials and crooked governments."

"I was surprised when they sent me on this story, too. Something to do with a rare books underground offering big money for the diaries and maybe a map—*if* they even exist."

"I thought you might be doing this for a special on Columbus for the celebration."

"That's the fallback position to justify sending me here. Do you know anything about this so-called underground interest?"

"No. I mean, I'm aware there are such things, certain people who'll pay a lot of money for something rare. No different from the surreptitious art scene. But tell me more."

Lucianne shrugged and drew from a half-full bottle of designer water. "I'm supposed to learn all about it from people like you. There was an art theft and murder in Miami that triggered sending me to D.C."

"An art theft? Murder? What does that have to do with Las Casas?"

Lucianne gave a handsome shrug. "That's what I asked my boss."

"What was stolen? Who was murdered?"

"From what I've been told, a second-rate painting by an artist named Reyes, Fernando Reyes, depicting Columbus giving something called a Book of Privileges to the king and queen of Spain. A security guard, his first night on the job, was shot."

"How dreadful," Annabel said. "There's a copy of the book here at LC."

"LC? Oh . . ."

"I spent part of yesterday looking at it. It's the most important piece of early Americana in the collection. But the painting was second-rate? The thieves must not have known much about art."

"I guess not. It was an inside job. Or inside and outside. A maintenance man allegedly left a skylight open for the thieves."

"Who was the painting's owner?"

"A small museum in the Latin Quarter. Casa de Seville. I've never been there."

Annabel spent the next fifteen minutes

telling Lucianne what she knew of the Las Casas legend. He was alleged to have been Columbus's sailing companion on the first three voyages, and had been not only the explorer's close friend, he'd helped him prepare his logs and diaries, according to those who'd spent their professional lives delving into the history. She sensed that the TV journalist was listening more out of courtesy than interest. It was obvious that Lucianne was not happy having been assigned this story. Annabel could understand. Lost diaries and maps, if there even were such things, paled when contrasted to being in the midst of shell fire, turmoil, and strife in exotic places.

"I'd like to get some of what you've said on tape," Lucianne said.

"If you wish."

"This guy, Michele Paul. You know him, I assume."

"Yes. He's your best source. No one knows more about Columbus and Las Casas than Michele."

"Does he have a gender problem?"

A small smile from Annabel. "No, I don't think so. He's suave, sure of himself."

"A Romeo?"

"I suspect so, only you can't prove it by me."

"Available after I interview him, Annabel?"

"Uh huh. My husband is attending a going-away party for a teaching colleague. I'm not meeting him for dinner until seven."

Annabel went to her assigned space in Hispanic and had just begun reading a book about Columbus that Consuela had recommended when young Susan Gomara appeared. She was crying.

"Sue, what's wrong?"

"Dr. Paul. He's so nasty. I was looking at some papers he left on a table by my desk. He came by, saw me, grabbed the papers, and started yelling at me."

"Yelling at you about what?"

"About spying on him or something. I don't know. I really don't like him. I wish he'd . . . break a leg or something."

Annabel got up and placed her hand on the young woman's shoulder. "Hey, Susan, don't let it throw you. He's a little high-strung, that's all." It sounded like the right thing to say.

"I guess so. Sorry to be such a baby."

"Don't worry about it. He seems to do a lot of traveling. With any luck, Mr. Paul won't be around very much."

"I hope not."

"You look lovely. A heavy date?"

The intern had changed from her sweater-and-jeans outfit into a pleated gray skirt, teal blouse, and white cardigan sweater.

"No. Whenever I work in the main reading room, I have to dress up. Rules. I'm heading there now, working until closing."

"Better than going through Cuban newspapers?"

"Much better. Well, see ya. Thanks for playing shrink."

Annabel watched the young woman leave. The change of outfit made her look more mature and professional. How exciting to begin one's career as an intern in the library of all libraries. With her determination and spirit, she might well end up one day as the Library of Congress's first woman Librarian, Annabel mused.

8 The Librarian of Congress slowly replaced the phone in its cradle and sat back in his blue leather chair. The wall to his right had bookcases up to the ceiling, as well as a bottom shelf on which rested a television set and framed photographs. Three blue leather chairs with wooden arms were on the opposite side of the desk. A large area to his left was devoted to comfortable furniture including a tan couch and stuffed chairs, another wall of bookcases, and an oversized rotating globe. Doors on both sides of the room gave access to terraces providing sweeping views of the Capitol.

While the stereotypical perception of workaday librarians was demonstrably inaccurate, the image of Dr. Cale Broadhurst as the leader of the world's largest institution of information might not have been. He looked distinctly academic; that is, were he an actor, he would have been cast as an academician, perhaps as the Librarian of Congress.

He was a small man, almost half size, and bald with the exception of a fringe of salt-and-pepper hair. His half-glasses were tethered to his neck by a colorful strap, and he was fond of tweed jackets, gray slacks, button-down blue shirts, bow ties, which he took pride in tying himself, and sensible brown leather shoes with thick crepe soles. Beneath it all was a brilliant mind, verbal fluidity, and an occasional flash of pixieish humor. But the phone call he'd just taken had not stimulated amusement. Excitement and shock were more like it.

He checked a clock on the wall. Four o'clock. The reception for Senators Menendez and Hale was at seven, giving him three hours to respond to the call in a meaningful, proactive way.

"I'll be with Ms. Mullin," Broadhurst told his

secretary, leaving the office and on his way to the office of Mary Beth Mullin, LC's general counsel. The lawyer was a big woman as women go, rendered more so when standing next to Broadhurst. Although her official role at the library was clearly delineated by her title, over the years she'd become Broadhurst's confidante of choice. He liked her law school way of thinking even for matters having nothing to do with law. As his confidence in her grew, and she became aware of it, she never hesitated to tell him exactly what she thought, about almost anything, including an occasional personal problem he confided in her. Mary Beth Mullin was no yes woman, an attribute the Librarian appreciated and needed.

She was on the phone when he arrived, which didn't deter him from entering and taking a seat across the desk from her. She finished her conversation, hung up, and leaned back in her chair.

"You look satisfied," he said.

"For good reason. My older daughter aced her government course at Catholic, and the repair estimate for my car isn't quite equal to the national debt. You?"

"National debt? I thought we had all kinds

of surplus. If I didn't have to play the role of beggar over on the Hill, I'd be considerably happier."

Along with his duties as the Librarian of Congress, Broadhurst found himself spending more and more time recently making the case to Congress for library funds. Since 1950, the size of LC's collections and staff had tripled, and its annual congressional appropriation had soared from $9 million to more than $360 million. Still, there was never enough money, it seemed, to handle more than a half-million research requests from members of Congress and their staffs each year; to keep up with mandatory cost-of-living increases for the four thousand employees; to move forward with the electronic cataloging of almost 114 million items in the collections, swelling each year through the copyright division; and to keep pace with the daily demands of the three glorious buildings and their four thousand inhabitants.

"Somehow, Cale, I can't see you begging for anything," she said, looking toward the window. "Looks like rain."

"I hope it holds off for the reception. Always nice to have cocktails on the terrace."

Mullin's laugh was gentle and knowing. "It wouldn't dare rain on the senators," she said. "What's up?"

"I just had a call from David Driscoll."

"What did he have to say?" She ran fingers through short, dark hair streaked with splendid slivers of gray; she looked like a woman who preferred sand and surf to the sterile atmosphere of a general counsel's office. She wore just enough lipstick to make the subtle point that her lips were nicely formed. Dark suits and tailored blouses were slimming.

"Driscoll was his usual taciturn self," Broadhurst said.

"With all that money he can afford to be taciturn."

"Yes, I suppose he can. And afford to be the supporter he's been of the library, and the avid collector he is. He called to tell me he's been in touch with someone who claims to have knowledge of where the Las Casas diaries might be."

Mullin wasn't nearly as familiar with LC's collections as Broadhurst, nor was she expected to be. She was the lawyer, more interested in keeping the Library out of legal trouble than in its more esoteric side. But she'd certainly heard enough about the legendary Columbus-era materials, and the search for them, to realize the importance of what her boss was saying.

"That would be remarkable information. Did he specify?"

"No. I tried to get more information from him but he deflected my questions. He's good at that. He basically had one question for me. He wanted to know to what lengths we'd go to obtain the diaries if he was able to broker a deal for us."

"You mean how much would we pay."

"You might say that."

"What are the diaries worth, Cale?"

"Depends on a number of factors. *If* they exist. Their condition. What they say. Whether the alleged map is included. And, of course, the source."

"The source?"

"Yes. If they surface through a reputable dealer with a sense of honor, that's one thing. If they're offered up by a shady middleman, that's another. Agree?"

"Yes, of course. How did you leave it with Driscoll?"

"I said I'd have to think about it." His grin

was impish. "I think you should think about it, too."

"It would have to be private money, wouldn't it, with Congress continuing to tighten its belt?"

"Ideally, private *and* public. Maybe not as tough a sell on the Hill as it appears at first blush. Sure, the military budget goes up every year, and the budgets for the so-called soft side of government go down. I'm considering slipping an aircraft carrier into our budget and hoping it goes unnoticed."

"Not a bad idea. You could call it the *Santa Maria*. What do you want me to do?"

"Nothing specific at this point, maybe some informal asking around on the Hill. That congressman from Appropriations who's always looking at you with adoring eyes at parties might be sympathetic if you brought it up with him. Is your husband still Senator Hale's favorite bridge partner?"

"Only when he bids correctly."

"Tell him to keep doing that. I intend to bring it up with Menendez tonight if the time is right, and he is ripe. I think the appeal should be to national pride, not that the LC will benefit. Shame if the diaries end up in another country. A possible shining moment for Congress and the nation. I'm going to feel out some donors as to what they might come up with to sweeten the pot."

Mullin frowned. "Not afraid of having it become public knowledge?"

"I considered that, but I don't think we have any choice. Driscoll wants a response within three days."

"I ask because Public Affairs called me this morning. Lucianne Huston is here to do interviews about Columbus, including the so-called Las Casas diaries."

"I know. And Annabel Reed-Smith is writing an article for *Civilization.* I'd say we should clamp a tight lid on this, but that's like asking a politician to keep a secret. This will be all over LC by morning, maybe sooner. Obviously, Consuela in Hispanic will have to be consulted. Michele Paul, too, importantly. Guess I mean self-importantly." He chuckled. "If the diaries did actually surface, there's first of all the authenticating process to go through."

Broadhurst went to the window and stood with his tiny hands shoved into the pockets of his tan tweed jacket. He said to the pane, "People have been searching for those diaries and maps for centuries. People have died in that search, even though no one knows for sure they even exist." He turned. "If they *do* exist, and we don't pull out every stop to obtain them, it will be a blot on this library. They belong here."

"Or in Spain," Mullin said. "But we should land them."

Broadhurst cocked his head and smiled in response to the expression on her face. "Yes, you're right, Mary Beth, a blot on my reputation, too, if we don't."

"You'll do what you can."

"Hopefully, it will be enough. See you at the reception. The diaries may be merely a chimera. I'll let you know if I get a chance to talk to Senator Menendez. I'll leave Senator Hale to you. Another chimera."

He walked to the door, paused, and turned. "By the way, anything new on the stalker?"

Mary Beth had followed him halfway across the room. "No, and I wish there were. This nut has the main reading room librarians spooked. They've taken to wearing their name badges upside down to make it more difficult for patrons to read their names."

"The police have anything new to offer?"

"No. They've got an undercover officer hanging around the room every day. Fortunately, the incidents have been limited to phone stalking."

"Let's hope it stays that way. See you tonight."

"That's a wrap!"

9   Lucianne Huston told her crew to pack up after having interviewed Annabel for twenty minutes.

"I'm not used to being interviewed," Annabel said, "especially on camera. I'm afraid I didn't have much to say."

"You spoke volumes compared to your friend Dr. Paul," Lucianne said, removing the lapel microphone from Annabel's jacket.

"Oh, that's right. I forgot. You were interviewing him at four. How did it go?"

"A waste of time. He sat down with a chip on his shoulder and gave me a series of one-word answers. Grunts don't make for great moments in television journalism."

"I'm sorry. And by the way, he's not my friend."

"My estimation of you has just risen. Know what he did when the interview, or grunt fest, was over?"

"What?"

"Invited me to dinner, a 'cozy little spot where we can get to know each other better.' Spare me."

"Hate to take the wind out of your sails, but he invited me to dinner, too."

"He must operate under that old male adage that if you ask enough women, you'll find one who says yes."

"Well," Annabel said, "I'm sorry the interview didn't work out. He is *the* expert on the subject. Staying in town for a few days?"

"Just tonight. I'm flying back to Miami in the morning. There's really no story here, Annabel. If I could smell even a small story, I could blow it up into a bigger one. But all the links are missing links. I mean, your interview will be helpful when we put together the special on Columbus to coincide with the celebration, but this Casas wild goose chase is just that. With any luck I'll be in

Africa in a few days hoping I don't come down with malaria."

"Malaria doesn't stand a chance against you. I wish you well."

Lucianne and her crew left the Madison Building, and Annabel went to her space above the Hispanic reading room in the Jefferson. She'd just immersed herself again in a book when Michele Paul arrived.

"Got your article written?" he asked brusquely.

She ignored the flippant question.

"Feel like a drink?"

"Thank you, no."

"I might share some inside Las Casas stories with you, but only over a cold, dry martini, straight up."

"A sobering notion."

"That gal digging into ancient burial rituals is joining us."

"Joining *you.* I'm packing up to leave."

"Suit yourself. How was your interview with the famous Ms. Huston?"

"Fine. Yours?"

"A waste of time. She knows nothing, asked a series of stupid questions that didn't deserve an answer."

Annabel said nothing.

As Paul started to leave, Consuela Martinez appeared. "A minute, Annabel?"

"Sure."

Consuela waited until he was gone before saying, "You can see why he's never been married. He's insufferable. Lucianne Huston told me he was totally uncooperative during the interview, barely answered her questions."

Annabel shrugged. "A brilliant foul ball."

"But that's not why I wanted to talk with you. Dr. Broadhurst is having a reception tonight for Senators Menendez and Hale. A small gathering, sort of a thank-you get-together for all Menendez and Hale have done for us over the years. Dr. Broadhurst called to see if you would be available to attend."

"I don't know. I—that's very flattering. I would have dressed differently."

"You look just fine. Can you stay for it?"

"I think so. I was supposed to meet Mac for dinner at seven. Let me try to reach him on his cell phone. He's at a going-away party for a colleague at GW."

"You'll only have to stay an hour," Consuela said. "The Librarian is hosting a small dinner party after cocktails for the senators and their wives."

She was successful in reaching her husband. "Sorry to bust in on your party, Mac, but Cale Broadhurst has invited me to a reception this evening for Senator Menendez. Starts at seven, over in an hour. Can we push dinner back to eight, eight-fifteen?"

"Sure."

"I'll call and change the reservation."

"Good."

"How's the party?"

"All right." Obviously, it wasn't wonderful.

"Knee okay?"

"Fine. Let's be safe and make it eight-thirty."

"Okay. Oh, I was interviewed this after-noon by Lucianne Huston."

"I'm the husband of a celebrity. Fill me in at dinner."

At a little before seven, Annabel wandered up to the Librarian's office in the Madison Building, where she was handed a laminat-ed badge to add to the one she already sported on a chain. "This gives you access after closing hours," she was told. "You'll need it."

Annabel went to the terrace overlooking the Jefferson Building, where two dozen people had gathered for cocktails, served by white-jacketed staff. Senator Menendez spotted her immediately and came to her side, drink in hand. "I didn't know you'd be here, Annabel," he said in a rich baritone.

"A last-minute invitation," she replied, plucking a moving glass of white wine from a waiter's tray.

"Well, I'm glad you're here. I understand Lucianne Huston is doing a story at the library."

"She was. I was interviewed this afternoon. She was supposed to do a piece on the Las Casas diaries, but I don't think she's pleased with what she's gotten so far. Her network's doing a show to coincide with the Columbus celebration. I think whatever she got may end up on that special."

Cale Broadhurst joined them.

"Glad you could make it," the Librarian said to Annabel. "Senator Menendez tells me he's working closely with you on the special issue of *Civilization*."

"That's right. He's my editor."

"In name only," Menendez said. "I leave the real editing to the magazine's professional staff. It is a great magazine."

"I wonder if I might buttonhole you for a few minutes?" Broadhurst asked the senator.

"Of course. Excuse us, Annabel."

She watched them enter Broadhurst's office, stopping along the way to say something to another guest.

"Where's your husband?"

Annabel turned to face Michele Paul.

"At his own party," Annabel said. "We're meeting later for dinner." She was annoyed at herself for even volunteering an answer to the question.

"You didn't say you'd be here."

"Because I didn't know I would be. Excuse me."

She walked off, not with any specific destination in mind but simply to move away from him. The word *smarmy* came to mind as she joined Consuela Martinez, Dolores Marwede, and Mary Beth Mullin, who were chatting with Senator Bruce Hale, the central-casting, silver-haired senior Democrat from Massachusetts who chaired the Senate Appropriations Committee. Annabel was introduced to Hale as an expert on pre-Columbian art.

"Dr. Martinez was just telling me about these missing diaries," Hale said.

"Missing . . . if they even exist in the first place," Dolores offered.

122 / *Margaret Truman*

"What do you think, Mrs. Smith?" Hale asked. "A wasted exercise trying to find something that isn't there?"

Annabel shook her head. "No," she said, "I don't think it's a wasted exercise at all. There's enough tantalizing evidence—well, maybe calling it evidence is wishful thinking—let's say enough tantalizing *hints* in the literature over the centuries suggesting that Las Casas did, in fact, write his own diaries about the first three voyages. He *did* write about Columbus later. And there is reason to think that a real writer would not have passed up the chance to at least make notes while the little ships were under way. Anyhow, as so often happens, when you're trying to run down one story, you get on to something else. Do the diaries exist? It can't be dismissed out of hand."

"And a *map*?" Hale said. "A treasure map? Sounds like the stuff of fiction to me."

"Far less credence is given the map than the diaries," Consuela said.

"And is anyone close to coming up with either?" asked Hale.

"No," Consuela said, "but lots of dedicated people are looking, trying to trace other written links to Las Casas and his relationship with Columbus."

Annabel looked past the others to where Broadhurst and Menendez were emerging from the office. A single drop of rain landed on her nose. She looked up at low, dark clouds scooting quickly by, then saw guests being ushered inside. Annabel followed the crowd.

The hour passed quickly. Dr. Broadhurst stood at the door and personally thanked each person for coming. Left behind with him were the two senators and their wives, General Counsel Mullin and her husband, and Broadhurst's chief of staff, Helen Kelly, whose husband had arrived just as the cocktail party was ending; Broadhurst's wife, Patricia, was out of town visiting one of their daughters who'd given birth to their third grandchild.

Annabel looked at her watch. Oops. Five after eight. She was meeting Mac at B. Smith's in Union Station, a ten-minute walk at best, two minutes by cab. She started for the building's main entrance, opening her briefcase as she went in anticipation of it being searched, stopped, fished in the bag for the notes she'd taken in the Manuscript reading room the previous day, couldn't find them, went down the stairs to the underground tunnel leading to the Jefferson Building, and walked at a brisk pace, almost a run, muttering to herself how careless she'd been to have left them in her cubbyhole. She was to revisit the Manuscripts room the next day and wanted to spend an hour or two at home after dinner planning how to make optimum use of the time.

They joke in the Library of Congress about how the three buildings turn into ghost towns the minute the doors close to visitors. Annabel certainly had that feeling as she traveled through the tunnel. No one passed her, and frequent glances over her shoulder confirmed she was alone. The clack of her heels was the only sound.

She reached the Jefferson. The elevators could be painfully slow, so she took the stairs two at a time to the second floor and entered the Hispanic room. She peeked into Consuela's office, which was empty, then heard a noise, far off. She looked, saw no one.

She was about to swipe her magnetic card in the door leading to the stacks and the private research spaces but hesitated.

Somehow, she felt intimidated entering that off-limits area without an escort. She knew how important security was at LC, the new system initiated eight years ago in response to a rash of thefts and defacing of materials. Back then, almost anyone could wander into the stacks; more than one person had been found sleeping in them by security guards during routine morning rounds. Not anymore. The enhanced system prohibited everyone from the stacks except those staff members with an absolute need to enter. Even the library's hundred-person uni-formed police force wasn't allowed access to them, unless, of course, an emergency demanded it.

Silly, she thought as she swiped the card, opened the door, and started up the narrow stairs. I have every right to be here. That's why they issued the two passes, one for the Hispanic stacks, the other authorizing her to be there after closing hours.

She paused at Sue Gomara's small desk in the hallway dominated by tall piles of Cuban newspapers. She couldn't help smiling. A nice kid, she thought, continuing the short distance to her own desk. But she stopped short of reaching it and came to a halt before crossing

Michele Paul's space. It was dark on the upper gallery; the only light came from a gooseneck halogen lamp on Paul's desk. But that was all the light necessary to see him seated, sleeping, at his desk. Paul was hunched over, his arms on the desk, his head resting on them.

Well, Annabel thought, it happens to the most diligent of scholars.

"Michele?" Annabel said quietly.

He didn't move.

Louder this time: "Michele?"

She took a few tentative steps toward him, coming close enough to be able to reach out and touch his shoulder with her fingertips.

She recoiled, brought those same fingertips to her mouth.

"Are you—?"

But she knew the answer. He wasn't sleeping.

She returned to the reading room and picked up the first phone she came to. But she didn't know what extension to call. She hung up and went to the European reading room, where two uniformed officers stood talking.

"Excuse me," Annabel said. "There's been an accident."

"Accident?"

"Someone is—Mr. Paul is dead."

"Paul?"

"In Hispanic. Please, I'll show you."

Fifteen minutes later, Annabel took her cell phone from her purse and dialed Mac's cell number.

"Hi," he said. "I'm at the restaurant. Running late?"

"Mac, there's been a tragedy here at LC."

"Tragedy? Are you all right?"

"Yes, I'm fine. But Michele Paul is dead."

"Good Lord. How? What happened?"

"I'm not sure. I discovered his body at his desk and—"

"*You* discovered the body?"

"Yes. The Hispanic division is overrun with police—library cops, Capitol police, MPD. I can't leave."

"I'll be right over."

"They won't let you in. Why don't you head home. I'll call you there and you can pick me up once I'm free."

"Nonsense. I'm coming now. Right now. Does it look like the police will want to take you downtown?"

"I can't imagine why they would."

"I'll be parked outside the main entrance, cell phone on. Keep in touch."

"Mrs. Smith?" a Washington MPD detective said.

"What? Yes, I'm Mrs. Reed-Smith."

"Would you give me a few minutes, please? Just a few questions."

"Mac, I have to go. I'll call you in the car."

"Right."

The two uniformed members of the library's police force had taken immediate charge once Annabel had led them to the body. While one stood guard over the scene, the other placed three calls.

The first was to the library's twenty-four-hour security communications room. The second was taken by the officer on duty at the Capitol police's communications room beneath the Russell Senate Office Building. He immediately passed it on to the CERT commander—Contingency Emergency Response Team—who dispatched officers wearing bulletproof vests and carrying M-249 automatic weapons. The third call went to MPD headquarters on Indiana Avenue.

Within minutes, the elegant Hispanic reading room, with its specially commissioned painted steel mural of the Columbus coat of arms looking down, was swarming with police from the three agencies. An explosives expert from the Capitol police was called in to determine whether such a threat existed—just in case. The Capitol itself was sealed off, including the underground tunnel leading to the Cannon House Office Building from LC's Madison Building.

After assuring that the crime scene was properly secured, the first uniformed MPD officers to arrive sought out anyone who'd been in the immediate area, including Annabel. After giving her name and her reason for being there, she was asked to wait at one of the reading desks until homicide detectives arrived.

"I'm Detective Shorter," he said. He consulted a notebook. "You're Mrs. Reed-Smith?"

"That's right."

"You were the one who discovered the body?"

"Yes. I'd forgotten something on my desk and . . . my desk is next to the one used by Mr. Paul."

"You knew him?"

"Not well. I've really only had one conversation with him." Annabel saw Dr. Broadhurst and Mary Beth Mullin being escorted into the room by LC's director of security.

"When was the last time you saw him alive?" the detective asked.

Annabel judged Shorter to be in his early thirties, a light-skinned black man with clear green eyes and close-cropped curly black hair. He wore a gray suit, white shirt, and plain maroon knit tie. His manner was calm and seemingly detached, as though taking a political poll rather than asking about murder.

"I saw him briefly at a party on the terrace outside the Librarian's office," Annabel said. "That was maybe forty-five minutes ago. Could have been an hour."

"Who was he with? You?"

"No. I don't think he was with anyone in particular. We exchanged a few words, that was all."

"Would you describe for me how you came to discover his body, Mrs. Reed-Smith?"

"Sure."

Annabel provided a step-by-step description of having left the party, starting to leave the building, then realizing she'd left her notes and coming to the Hispanic room to retrieve them. Shorter took notes while she spoke.

"That's about it for now," he said, closing the notebook and slipping it into his jacket's breast pocket.

"Is there any indication how he died?" Annabel asked.

Shorter ignored her question.

"Oh, when I arrived at the Hispanic room this evening, I heard someone over on that side of the room."

"Who was it?"

"I don't know. I didn't see anyone, just heard movement."

"I see. Well, I'm sure we'll want to speak with you again. I have your address and phone number."

"Am I free to leave?"

"I'll ask my case supervisor."

"Can I call my husband?" she asked, pulling her cell phone from her bag.

"Sure."

The Washington, D.C., medical examiner

arrived while Annabel called Mac in their car. The ME was accompanied by medical emergency personnel wearing white lab coats who guided a hospital stretcher on wheels through the reading room's tables to the door leading to the stairs to the upper gallery.

"I suspect they'll let me leave any minute," Annabel told her husband.

Five minutes later, Detective Shorter and another man, who introduced himself as Detective Nastasi, came to Annabel and told her she was free to leave. She again called Mac before leaving the building. She spotted the Buick parked on the opposite side of First Street, away from the knot of official vehicles blocking the front of the library.

"Hell of a night for you," he said, pulling away after she'd joined him.

"Certainly not what we'd planned."

"How was he killed?"

"I don't know. I didn't see any blood when I discovered him. I mean, I wasn't looking for it. All I wanted to do was get out of there and find help. Not much of a witness."

"Of course you wanted to get out of there."

They stopped at a Chinese take-out restaurant and brought the food to their apartment in the Watergate complex. After Mac walked Rufus, and they'd changed for bed, they settled in chairs in front of the television set. The death led the ten o'clock newscast.

"One of the nation's leading scholars on Christopher Columbus, Dr. Michele Paul, who worked at the Library of Congress, was found dead tonight in his office at the Jefferson Building. According to a spokesman for the Metropolitan Police Department, who requested anonymity, the cause of death appears to have been a blow to the head. We'll report more details as we receive them."

"Murder," Annabel said to the room. "Guess I've been resisting the idea."

"Unless he hit himself in the head. You said you heard someone when you walked into the Hispanic room?"

"Yes, but didn't see anyone."

"No hint of perfume trailing behind, no male smoker's cough?"

"No. I fail the test."

"Not with me. I'm off to bed."

Annabel stayed up, her eyes focusing

blankly on the images on the TV screen, her mind sorting through the evening's events. It was a futile exercise, and she decided to join Mac in the bedroom. But before she did, she changed channels to the all-news network on which Lucianne Huston had built her reputation. Yes, indeed, Lucianne stood in front of the Jefferson Building, the flashing lights of police cars tossing shards of red light over everything, amplified voices creating a background din as she reported:

"This is the front of the Jefferson Building, the oldest of three buildings comprising the Library of Congress, the world's largest and most important repository of information. Tonight, a man I had interviewed this afternoon, Michele Paul, was found murdered in the small area he occupied above the Hispanic and Portuguese reading room. He was killed by a blow to the head, according to sources who spoke with me on condition of anonymity. Michele Paul was a respected expert on the subjects of Christopher Columbus and more specifically Bartolomé de Las Casas, whose diaries—and possibly even a treasure map—have been the subject of searches by many scholars, some of whom have lost their lives in the effort. Whether Dr. Paul's murder tonight is yet another tragic example of this remains to be seen. I'm Lucianne Huston reporting from Washington."

Annabel clicked off the set. Ms. Huston was certainly on the case, as the saying goes. Would she change her plans and stay in Washington to continue covering Paul's murder? Interesting, Annabel thought, as she headed for the bedroom, how Lucianne instantly wove Paul's murder into the larger but vaguer Las Casas story.

What had started out to be an enjoyable two-month hiatus from running the gallery had, in two days, mushroomed into high-profile murder against the sedate, genteel background of the Library of Congress.

Who would have wanted to kill Michele Paul? she wondered as she slipped into bed beside her husband.

A cast of thousands, she decided as the warmth of his body helped lull her to sleep.

11 "Warren A. Munsch, a two-time loser. Armed robbery, possession of stolen goods. Four other arrests—a couple of gambling charges, kiting checks—no other convictions. A wise-guy wannabe."

"A jerk. So, what's he doing stealing a painting?"

The two Miami detectives sat in a room used for interrogation, surprisingly clean and modern considering its use. An empty Dunkin' Donuts bag, paper napkins, and coffee cups cluttered the Formica table. A file folder containing the report on the theft of the Reyes painting from Casa de Seville and the murder of the security guard was between them.

One of the detectives said, "His two amigos gave him up fast enough once the maintenance guy with a habit surfaced. Honor among thieves."

"You believe the Cuban was the shooter?"

"Yeah, why not? The weapon was in his apartment, and his partner said he pulled the trigger."

"But the Cuban—what's his name? Garraga—Mr. Garraga says the missing Mr. Munsch did the deed."

"Where the hell is Munsch? He flew to L.A. We know that. Used his own name to buy the ticket."

"And then he goes to Mexico City. With the painting? Hey, I don't get what's the big deal about this painting they stole. The manager of the museum said it wasn't worth much, was just sort of a backdrop, like wallpaper."

"There's mega-bucks in some stolen art. Don't you know that?"

"Yeah, I know that, but come on. A lowlife like Munsch isn't out stealing art. What does he know from paintings?"

"Like Jankowski says, he must have lifted

it for somebody else, on assignment. Maybe some big-shot art collector."

"I feel bad for the guard who got it. Christ, his first night on the job."

"Guarding a second-rate museum. Who'd figure getting shot in a second-rate museum?"

"Yeah, who'd figure. You'd think that gut of his would have stopped a bazooka, let alone a Saturday night special."

"Look who's talking. You're not exactly a male model."

"What do you expect, you keep bringing in doughnuts. Did you see that newscast last night about some expert on Christopher Columbus getting killed in D.C.?"

"No. What about it?"

His partner shrugged. "Columbus, that's all. That painting had something to do with Columbus, and the guy in D.C. was an expert."

"On Columbus?"

"Yeah. Lucianne Huston was there reporting."

"Where?"

"In D.C. She's everywhere these days, huh? Never sleeps, it looks like."

"Who *with,* that's what I'd like to know. She's a real fox."

"Not my type. We going back out to the museum again?"

"No. Jankowski wants us on that automotive parts break-in. The after-market in car hardware is big bucks. Bigger than *C*-plus paintings. Finish your coffee."

The man in the white jacket and straw hat who'd relieved Warren Munsch of the painting on the terrace of Ivy on the Shore in Santa Monica had, as instructed, taken the rolled-up canvas home with him that night to his Venice apartment and put it in a closet. The next morning, with the painting on the seat next to him in his BMW convertible, he drove into downtown Los Angeles and parked in a garage on Olvera Street, near the El Pueblo de Los Angeles monument, the historic core of the city. The cafes, shops, and stalls along the brick sidewalks were busy, the surrounding streets swimming in go-to-work traffic.

He walked a block until reaching the entrance to a three-story building with a plaque announcing its architectural significance, went up the stairs to the second floor, and opened a door at the end of a short hallway. A sign on the door read: ABRAHAM

WIDLITZ, ART RESTORATION AND CONSERVATION.

Entering, he stood alone in the room, surrounded by easels on which large canvases in various stages awaited the next step. A lengthy table lined a wall with windows that overlooked the bustling plaza.

The sound of a door from a second room opening caused the visitor to turn. Through it came a wizened old man barely five feet tall who walked with a pronounced limp. His white hair was thin and unruly, his glasses thick and in need of cleaning. He wore a dirty white shirt covered by an equally shapeless sleeveless black sweater. His pants were baggy. His shoes were of the molded variety and looked as if badly drawn.

"Ah hah, Mr. Conrad," he said, smiling. "I see you brought me something."

Conrad laid the rolled-up Reyes painting on the table. "He called ahead, right? You knew I was bringing this."

"Of course, of course. Sit down. Tea?"

"No, thanks."

"Let me see what we have here."

Widlitz carefully removed the brown wrapping paper from the painting, then unfurled the painting itself. Its being rolled had caused hundreds of cracks to appear.

"It should never be rolled like this," he said.

"That's the way it was given to me."

"What do people know? This will take time, Mr. Conrad. It won't be easy."

"Well, you tell him that. All I do is deliver it."

"Of course."

"I need to call him, tell him it's here."

"By all means," Widlitz said, pointing to a phone in the corner.

"It's Conrad," he said after being connected. "It's here at Widlitz's place."

"Good," the man said. "Were there any problems?"

"No. The guy was nervous, though. Real nervous. Where did you find him?"

"It doesn't matter. Did he indicate whether he was staying in California?"

"A day or two," Conrad replied, running fingers through his mane of greasy, sunbleached hair.

"I need you to pick someone up this evening at the airport."

"All right." He wrote down the information on the back of an envelope. Conrad Syms was often called upon by his employer to chauffeur people from the airport to the house.

"That's all for the moment, Conrad."

Conrad said, "Any chance of getting some money for meeting the guy last night? I'm a little short."

"I'll pay you tonight when you deliver my guest." He hung up.

Conrad waved at Widlitz and left. He hung around the plaza for a while before driving home, where he lounged at the pool that was part of his apartment complex. He met the plane at nine, took his passenger to the house in the tony Brentwood section, received his pay in cash from a Filipino houseboy, and drove to Sunset Boulevard, where he handed over the BMW to a parking lot attendant at Carlos 'n Charlie's. Maybe today he'd get lucky and meet a producer or director looking for his type. When he'd come to Hollywood from Minnesota after acting in some community theater productions, he was told he was a natural for motion pictures. So far, three years later, his only starring roles were in three pornographic movies and walk-ons in industrial films. Maybe it was time to change agents, he thought as he checked his appearance in the window, readjusted his straw hat to a more rakish angle, and made his entrance.

12 Usually, it was Mac who was up first, often before the sun. But this morning, he awoke to find his wife missing from their bed.

He found her in the kitchen.

"Couldn't sleep?" he asked.

"No," she said, looking up from where she sat at the table, a steaming cup of black coffee before her. "The impact of what happened last night has hit home."

He poured himself a cup and joined her.

"I've only been at LC for two days. I was given a desk next to his, and interviewed him for the article. I saw him at the cocktail party.

And now he's dead. Something inside me says it didn't happen, but I know it did because I was the one who found him. I touched him." She wrapped her arms about herself and shuddered.

Mac took one of her hands in his. "Only natural, Annie, that there would be this delayed reaction. We get caught up in the swirl of the event, being questioned by the police, hearing more about it on television. Then we go to bed and it hits us like a bad dream."

"And so real when you wake up."

"Yes, so real. What's this business about others having died while searching for the diaries?" Annabel had paraphrased Lucianne Huston's broadcast for him.

"Nothing contemporary, Mac. There was a team of researchers trying to find the diaries in the Canary Islands a hundred years ago. They were killed, presumably by a competing team. And the same thing happened to another group in the Dominican Republic. Natives were blamed, as I recall."

He frowned, cocked his head. "I was thinking of something more recent, Annie."

"Oh?"

"Yeah. Wasn't there a scandal involving the library eight or ten years back? Some researcher there—I think he, or maybe it was a she—disappeared or was killed."

"It rings a bell, but only vaguely."

"As I remember it, the individual worked in the Hispanic division."

Her shrug was a statement: "It just doesn't register with me."

"I'll pull it up from the *Post*'s Web site."

"What did we ever do before Web sites?"

"Haunted the newspaper's morgue and got ink on our fingers, or went blind looking at microfilm."

"I'd better get showered."

"Why don't you stay home?" he suggested. "No need to go there today. You probably won't get much done. The office space Consuela assigned you will be off limits while the police continue their investigation."

"I'm scheduled to spend another day in Manuscripts looking at the Book of Privileges. Las Casas helped Columbus write it. I'm trying to link similarities between language he used in that document and in his other writings that he's been given public credit for. Finding a needle in a haystack isn't easy, but it doesn't mean a needle isn't in that hay. I don't want to lose a minute of my time at LC, Mac. It's such precious time."

"Your call, of course. More coffee?"

"A little fresh, please."

She took her cup into the bathroom, leaving him at the kitchen table with his own thoughts. He eventually got up and went to the terrace overlooking the Potomac. The first rays of sun sent its ripples dancing. The city was waking up to another day of politics and pressure, its primary occupations. Like the river, it would surge ahead of its own weight and volition, influencing the nation and world and being influenced by them, preaching lofty goals but falling short of them too much of the time, the most wonderful form of government ever put into practice—and the most difficult to make work.

While this was happening, he, Mackensie Smith, would go through his planned day, meeting with faculty colleagues at the university, walking the dog, buying the ingredients for dinner that night, and worrying about the wife he loved spending her day at a murder scene.

Whoever killed Michele Paul, Mac thought, presumably was someone from within the Library of Congress, a colleague or at least a person who'd had enough contact with Paul to want him dead. Of course, there was the possibility that the murderer was an outsider, perhaps someone who'd gained access to the library for the express purpose of killing him. But that was less likely.

Annabel had said Paul was disliked by many, with an intensity bordering on hatred by some. If he had to bet, Mac would assume it was a murder fueled by passion, a killer with a personal motivation. Passion of one sort or the other, not reason or greed or ideology, was behind most murders. At least that had been his experience when practicing criminal law, and the statistics bore it out.

But that was simply intellectual speculation. What really bothered him was that if Michele Paul's killer was someone from within the library, that person could still be there. And Annabel would be there, too.

He dropped her at the Jefferson Building before heading for his meetings at GW.

"Sure I can't convince you to stay home for a few days?" he asked as she was about to get out of the car.

"I really want to be here, Mac. I have so much to do in researching the article. Please understand."

"Of course I understand," he said, not adding that no magazine article, nothing in the world, for that matter, was as important as her well-being.

They kissed, and he watched her enter the elegant Italian Renaissance–style building named for the third and rather elegant president of the United States.

Mac had refreshed his knowledge of the Library of Congress by basic reading materials Annabel brought home with her. Quite a man was Tom Jefferson. After LC's original collection of books, three thousand volumes purchased from England, was destroyed by British troops when they burned the Capitol building in 1814, Jefferson, by then retired to Monticello, offered his personal library of more than six thousand books, and Congress appropriated $23,950 for the purchase. Unfortunately, subsequent fires destroyed two thirds of the original Jefferson library; fewer than 2,500 remain in the library's present collection.

Great books and murder.

Somehow they didn't go together.

As she approached, Annabel was surprised at the lack of police presence in front of the building. Inside, people passed through the metal detectors, and their bags were searched as on any other day. That a murder had taken place wasn't evident until she reached the Hispanic and Portuguese reading room on the second floor. Yellow crime scene tape had been strung across every entrance to the area. A distraught Consuela Martinez stood behind one strand of tape. When she saw Annabel approaching, she went to a uniformed officer and informed him that Annabel was a researcher working in that section. Annabel lifted her badges for his inspection, and he allowed her to pass.

They went directly to Consuela's office, where the division chief closed the door behind them. She sat heavily in her chair, directed a stream of air at her bangs, and shook her head. "Can you believe it?" she said.

"I'm afraid so. I was telling Mac it seemed unreal until this morning. The harsh light of day and all that."

"Incredible. I mean, I detested the man, truly detested him—and respected his work, of course—but to think of him dying like that. Who could do such a thing?"

"I'm sure the police are working hard at coming up with that answer. What happens in a situation like this, Consuela? What law enforcement agency has jurisdiction?"

"The Washington MPD. The Capitol police get involved to make sure there's no threat to anyone on the Hill. I think they offer some forensic help, too. But MPD's in charge of the investigation. They've set up an interview room in the original Librarian of Congress's office."

"Where's that?"

"In this building, first floor. It's only used these days for ceremonial occasions and small gatherings. A beautiful room. Shame it has to be the setting for a murder investigation."

"Who are they interviewing?"

"Everybody who knew Michele, I suppose. That takes in almost the entire professional staff. The press are being corralled in the theater. There's lots of them."

"The TV report last night said he'd been killed by a blow to the head. Do they have the weapon?"

"This is only rumor, but I was told it was a weight of a kind used by our conservation and preservation people."

"A weight?"

"Yes, pieces of Linotype lead that are

melted into bricks and covered with cloth. They've used them for ages to hold down curled pages, maps, that sort of thing."

"I saw one of those on Paul's desk. He had a bunch of papers under it."

"Makes a great paperweight." She picked up such an object from her own desk and handed it to Annabel, who weighed it in her hand.

"But not a perfect weapon. You'd have to really be struck by this for it to kill you. An impetuous act," Annabel said.

"What?"

"If a lead brick like this *was* the murder weapon, the murderer picked it up from Michele's desk because it was handy. Not premeditated."

"An argument that got out of hand?"

"Possibly. Mac was telling me this morning about another scandal in this division. Someone . . . a researcher eight or ten years ago? A disappearance or a murder?"

"John Bitteman. He wasn't murdered, but he was a link, possibly, to what's been going on."

"No. How?"

"John was probably the first one here really to start digging into the Las Casas story. It was before my time; I've only been here six years. He was obsessed with Las Casas and the idea of his diaries."

"But you say he wasn't murdered. I thought—"

"They don't know what happened to him. He disappeared. The police labeled it suspicious, but he was never found. As I recall, there was some evidence of foul play. His apartment had been ransacked, and there was blood, I believe. But without a body, I suppose they couldn't officially label it murder."

"And he's never been found."

"As far as I know. Some of the old-timers joke that the Hispanic stacks are haunted by Bitteman." She laughed. "There isn't an official building in Washington that isn't haunted by one ghost or another, including this one. Bitteman isn't the only supposed ghost around here. You've heard about the miserly librarian who hid all his life's savings in various books in the collection when LC was housed in the Capitol?"

"I can't say that I have."

They were interrupted by Dolores Marwede.

"Hi," Annabel said as the librarian stepped into the office.

"Hello." Dolores closed the door and leaned against a bookcase. "This is unreal," she said. "You discovered the body, Annabel?"

"I'm afraid so. Have the police spoken with you yet?"

"No, but I was told to be available this morning. You?"

"Last night. Briefly. They'll want more. I'm on my way now to Manuscripts to look at the Book of Privileges again."

"The show must go on."

"I was telling Annabel about our ghosts, Dolores."

"Oh?"

"Our miserly poltergeist who hid his life savings in the stacks." To Annabel: "Dolores is our resident expert on library ghosts."

Dolores said without smiling, "He didn't trust banks and hid his cash in books. Poor fellow died of a stroke before he could tell anyone where he'd put the money. When they moved the collection into this building, workers found more than six thousand dollars in old, dusty volumes. People swear they hear fingers desperately flipping through books in the middle of the night."

"Sad."

"And, of course, there's Houdini," said Consuela.

"The magician?" Annabel said.

"None other. He bequeathed most of his collection of books on psychic phenomena, spiritualism, magic, and witchcraft to us, along with a lot of the mechanical devices he used in his magic shows. We have a reference librarian who says Houdini still uses some of those devices at odd hours."

"Maybe Houdini killed Paul by popular demand," Annabel said, quickly uncomfortable with her uncharacteristic flippancy.

There was a knock on the door.

"Come in," Consuela said.

The detective who'd allowed Annabel to leave the night before—his name was Nastasi, she remembered—opened it. "Sorry to interrupt," he said to Consuela, "but I wonder if you could spare me a half hour or so."

"Of course."

"Good morning," Nastasi said to Annabel.

"Good morning, Detective. How's the investigation progressing?"

"Progressing. I'd like to speak with you a little later."

Annabel glanced knowingly at the two

women. "That would be fine. Am I free to go to my work area on the balcony level?"

"Afraid not. It'll be off limits for the rest of the morning."

"I understand. I'm scheduled to be in the Manuscript reading room. That's where I'll be."

"I'll find you there. Dr. Martinez?"

Annabel stayed in Consuela's office for a few minutes digesting what she'd been told about John Bitteman. His name hadn't surfaced in the little research she'd done on Las Casas, and she made a note to look for what work he might have left behind on the subject.

She eventually left the office, crossed the police line, and walked slowly through the European reading room, which was open and already busy with researchers working at desks. She was almost to the end of the room when her Public Affairs contact, Joanne Graves, came around a corner, saw her, and increased her pace.

"I've been looking for you," she said. "More accurately, Lucianne Huston is looking for you."

"I thought she was going back to Miami."

"The murder changed her mind. She wants to interview you."

"She already did."

"About having discovered the body."

"I don't want to talk about that, especially on camera. I'm trying to forget it, not broadcast it."

"I know, but I told her I'd ask. She's with the rest of the press across the street in the Pickford Theater. She's kind of a celebrity among them."

"The power of TV. What have you heard this morning?" Annabel asked.

"Nothing. They're saying he was killed with the kind of lead weight we use in Conservation."

"I heard that, too, but it's just a rumor."

"I suppose all we'll get are rumors for a while. Going to Manuscripts?"

"Yes."

"I'll tell Lucianne you're not available."

"Thanks."

"Sorry to see your two months here get off to such a horrible start."

"Not a problem as long as I can hide from Ms. Huston's hot mike and red-eyed camera. Thanks for the warning."

Once homicide detectives Frank
13 Nastasi and Marcus Shorter had
settled in at a round conference
table in what once was the office of the
Librarian of Congress, Shorter commented
that he'd never interviewed murder suspects
in such a nice place.

The old Librarian's office, with its large
inlaid antique desk, rich Oriental carpet,
bookcases, paneled walls, and two flags on
stands behind the desk, one the American
flag, the other bearing the official seal of the
Library of Congress, had been the scene of
numerous official events. Presidents and for-

eign heads of state had been feted in the room, as had business leaders and literary lights. The original Librarian of Congress, John J. Beckley, appointed by President Jefferson, would have been appalled at the use to which the room was being put this day.

"Too nice," Nastasi countered. "You need a little grunge to keep 'em honest."

Their differing takes on their surroundings summed up how they would approach their interview subjects—Shorter the good cop, Nastasi the bad. They'd been playing that time-honored game as partners for four years.

Consuela Martinez was the third person to be interviewed there that morning. The first had been chief of the Personnel Directorate Office; the detectives had wanted to gain an initial understanding of how the institution was structured, especially in terms of those working at LC. The second subject was General Counsel Mary Beth Mullin, who was asked about the cocktail party the night of the murder. She provided a written guest list.

"What was Mr. Paul's relationship with others at the party?" she was asked.

"He was a senior specialist on the Hispanic and Portuguese division staff," she replied. "The party was in honor of Senators Menendez and Hale, both of whom play an important role for us in the Senate. Because Senator Menendez has championed the Hispanic division for many years, various top people from that division were invited. Dr. Paul was one of them."

Nastasi said, "He may have been a top guy, but not in the polls. We get the word that nobody around here liked him."

Mullin smiled demurely. "Michele Paul was difficult to get along with. He was egotistical and opinionated. He was also a brilliant scholar. Such people are often self-absorbed."

"Who really had it in for him, Mrs. Mullin?" asked Nastasi.

"I really don't think I should be the one to—"

Shorter interjected: "What he means is, Mrs. Mullin, was there anyone who'd displayed a blatant, open hostility toward him?"

"Not that I can think of."

Consuela was next to be questioned. That she was visibly nervous as she took a seat held out by Shorter was demonstrated by the small handkerchief she twisted with her fingers and a tic in her left eye.

"You were the deceased's boss?" Nastasi said.

"Yes. Michele was part of my staff."

"How long did he work for you?"

"Ever since I became chief of Hispanic. That was six years ago next month. Michele had been at the library considerably longer than that."

"We have his personnel file," Shorter said. "He came to work here in nineteen seventy-seven, twenty-two years ago."

"If that's what it says."

"What did he do for you?" Nastasi asked.

"Do for me? What do you mean?"

"You say he worked for you. What kind of work did he do?"

Consuela sighed and dabbed at a bead of perspiration on her cheek. "I suppose it's misleading to say he worked for me," she said. "Scholars on Michele's level really don't work for anyone. They do their own thing, as the saying goes, pursuing their research at their own pace and on their own schedule. But there has to be organization, someone in charge. That's been me for six years."

"You get along with him?" Nastasi asked.

Consuela clutched the handkerchief in both hands and focused her eyes on it.

"Dr. Martinez?" Nastasi said.

She looked up. "I'm sorry, my mind wandered. What was the question?"

"You and Mr. Paul. Did you get along?"

She paused: "Not exactly."

"What does that mean?" Nastasi asked, as annoyed with her response as he was when his kids answered that way.

"Michele was . . . well, he was difficult. He was—no, we did not get along especially well. He was abrasive."

"To you personally?" Shorter asked.

"Yes. I think—I know Michele resented me from the day I became chief of the division. I suspect he was jealous."

"He wanted the job?" Nastasi asked.

"I think so. He spread lies about me."

"Lies?"

"Yes. When he heard I was being hired to head the Hispanic division, he told people I was a whore who'd slept her way into the job."

"A sweetheart."

"He planted other vile, false stories about me, hoping Dr. Broadhurst and others at the top would deny me the job. Fortunately, they didn't."

"That must have upset you," Nastasi said.

"Of course it did."

"Why didn't you fire him?"

"I would have if I'd had the option. But his credentials are—were impressive. There have been a number of important donors to the collection who gave their historic materials to us rather than another institution because Michele was here."

"Tough position for a boss to be in."

"Very tough."

"I assume you and he had more than a few confrontations about it."

Consuela managed a smile. "Many. He denied, of course, having been the source of the lies about me. Besides being unpleasant, Michele was an accomplished liar. Smooth would be the kindest way to describe it."

"Yesterday?"

"What about yesterday?"

"You had a confrontation?"

"No."

Nastasi looked up from the pad on which he'd been making notes. "No?"

"No."

"Sure you don't want to think about that before you answer?"

"Why should I?" Consuela said, changing position in the chair.

"I heard you *did* have a confrontation with him yesterday."

Consuela's brow furrowed. "I can't imagine who would say that. Do you mean a telephone conversation we had?"

"Yeah, that's what I mean."

Nastasi hadn't heard from anyone that Consuela and Michele Paul had had a tense phone conversation. But if you challenged a witness, it often resulted in a voluntary change of story.

Consuela took a deep breath before saying, "He hadn't come to work the day before. He was supposed to be here. I questioned him about it. As usual, his answers were, well, let's just say frustrating."

"So you were mad at him yesterday."

"Not any more so than usual," Consuela replied, wishing she hadn't.

Nastasi's smile wasn't genuine. "Ever think you'd like to kill Mr. Paul?" he asked.

"Of course not."

"Would be natural," the beefy, gruff detective said. "You must have had that thought now and then."

"I've never wished anyone dead." She

sounded strong for the first time since the questioning began.

The detectives looked at her.

She started to cry.

"It's okay, Dr. Martinez," Shorter said, reaching and touching her arm. "Take it easy. These are just questions we have to ask. Part of the job."

She used the handkerchief to wipe her tears. "I understand," she said, "but please don't think I might have killed Michele. I didn't."

There were a few moments of silence.

"Where were you last night?" Nastasi asked.

"I was at the party, of course."

"After the party?"

"I went home."

"Right away?"

"Yes. I mean, I stopped at my office to pick up a few things. My raincoat. A book. I'd left my purse there, too, locked up."

Shorter asked, "Is theft a problem here at the library?"

"Not at all. I understand it used to be before the new security system was put in place. Locking up your purse is automatic, anywhere, any place."

"Of course," said Shorter.

"Who disliked Mr. Paul as much as you did, Dr. Martinez?" Nastasi asked.

Consuela sat up straight and back, as though the question exerted physical force. "You make it sound as though I hated Michele," she said. "I didn't. Yes, there were times I could have strangled him, if that's what you want to hear. And yes, our relationship was tense at best. But I did not dislike him any more than many others did."

Nastasi slapped the table and stood. "Now we're getting somewhere," he said. "Who are the others who disliked him, maybe enough to kill him?"

The questioning of Consuela Martinez lasted another twenty minutes. During that time she refused to name anyone who held a grudge against Michele Paul. As she was leaving the old Librarian's office, Detective Shorter stopped her. "Who was he sleeping with?"

Consuela turned at the door. "Michele? I never asked."

"You have some pretty attractive women working in your division, Dr. Martinez." He consulted his notebook and read a series of names, including Annabel Reed-Smith.

"I suggest you ask them," she said. "As for Mrs. Reed-Smith, she doesn't work in the Hispanic division. She's researching an article for our magazine."

"Thanks for your time," Shorter said. "We'd appreciate it if you didn't discuss what we talked about with others." The request was de rigueur. Of course she'd talk about it.

After she was gone, Nastasi turned to his partner and asked, "What'a you think?"

"She didn't sleep with him."

"You're right about that. No love lost, though."

"I don't think anybody had any love to lose," Shorter said. "Who's next?"

"The rest of the people from her department. But let's have another talk first with Lapin, the security chief. Besides, I want to get out of here for a while. Libraries give me the creeps."

"Yeah? I like libraries."

"And you weren't brought up in a Catholic school with an ugly old battle-ax who passed for a librarian. She was a book guardian and sergeant at arms, always on me for making noise. She used to tell me to put my hand on her desk and she'd give it a shot with a book."

Shorter grinned. "Must have hurt."

"Yeah, it hurt. I never liked libraries ever since."

"Scarred you for life."

"You being funny?"

"Me? Hell, no. Just feeling your pain."

Annabel subjected herself to the strict security procedures at the entrance to Manuscripts and went to the only vacant reading desk, closest to the main librarian's station. The Book of Privileges wouldn't be available for her until noon—something to do with a minor repair being made to it—but there were other materials she requested that were delivered. As she began to go through them, the chief of the division, John Vogler, came to the desk. Annabel had never met him but knew who he was. He'd been named chief of Manuscripts four years earlier, replacing Jim

Hutson, who'd resigned to devote full time to writing books. Hutson had been considered one of LC's most outstanding scholars, under whose leadership the library had mounted an impressive array of exhibits based upon his years of research into the papers of the Founding Fathers. John Vogler's credentials, too, were extensive and impeccable, but whether he would match up to Hutson's legacy remained conjecture. Perhaps it was Vogler's quirky personality that made it difficult for him to move out from under Hutson's shadow. He defined for his colleagues the term eccentric. It was as though he occupied two spaces at once, where he actually was at any given moment, and where he seemed to be. Some commented on how Vogler always appeared startled in the middle of a conversation that someone was talking to him. Others joked that the little yellow Post-it notes Vogler stuck on his sleeve were to remind him that he'd gotten up that morning. Still, he was treated with the respect due a man of his intelligence and knowledge.

"Mrs. Reed-Smith?" he said, extending a large, rough, red hand.

"Yes."

"I'm John Vogler."

"Hello."

"May I join you?"

"Of course."

Vogler was as big and rough-hewn as the hand he'd offered. Again, so much for stereotypes, Annabel thought. Although he looked like a lumberjack, or dock worker, he was, she knew, a Ph.D. *Dr.* Vogler.

"I spoke with Consuela Martinez earlier this morning. She told me you were the unfortunate soul who came upon Michele Paul's body last night."

"That's right."

"A most unpleasant experience."

"To say the least."

"Dr. Broadhurst tells me he considers the article you're doing for *Civilization* to be important."

"That's good to hear. It'll be useful, I hope, if I get it done."

"Have you heard anything about the murder from the police?"

"No, but I'm supposed to be interviewed by them later today. And they've asked Consuela to help them sort through Michele's work papers at his apartment. She feels a little overwhelmed by the task, so she's asked me to come along and lend a hand. Also, maybe I can find something useful for my article."

"Do they think his research papers have to do with his murder?"

"I don't know, but I suppose you don't say no to the police. Besides, *we'll* want to know what's there. I assume they'll let us bring everything back here to the library."

"After they've eliminated it as evidence. I understand Michele kept a great deal of his research at home." Vogler sighed and rolled his eyes. "He was so paranoid." Annabel started to respond but Vogler added, "Which is probably the kindest thing I can say about him."

Another Michele Paul detractor weighing in?

"Could we go somewhere a little more private, Mrs. Reed-Smith? My office?"

"All right."

He asked one of his reference librarians to remove the materials Annabel had been using until she returned, and led her to his office, a monument to clutter, a small room made more so by the amount of space his large frame consumed. He held out a green vinyl chair with wooden arms for her and sat in a matching chair close to her side. He leaned forward, elbows on knees, closed his eyes, opened them, looked at her and said, "I hope you don't mind my imposing upon you, Mrs. Reed-Smith. It's just that I—well, I prefer not to share too much with my professional colleagues. The staff, I mean."

"All right."

"I suppose you know how unpopular Michele was with our colleagues."

"I've heard bits and pieces."

"The police will probably make a big deal out of my confrontations with him."

Annabel said nothing.

"We actually came to blows a few months ago. Library police had to break it up."

"I didn't know."

"I'm sure it's in the library police's files and they'll turn it over to the investigating officers. You have to realize, Mrs. Reed-Smith, that Michele could be insufferable at times, arrogant and insensitive. The fracas between us actually didn't amount to much. What I mean is, it certainly shouldn't be considered important enough to make me a suspect."

Annabel didn't know what Vogler expected from her in return. Was he trying to reassure himself by telling her? That might be good for your psyche, she thought, but it won't change the facts for the MPD detectives once they learn of it.

"They'll probably dismiss it once they know the circumstances," he said to the room.

Annabel didn't confirm his wishful thinking. Instead, she asked, "Were you the—had anyone else in LC ever had a physical confrontation with him?"

"I really wouldn't know. He accused me of doctoring some of my research, actually *accused* me of that. I couldn't let it pass."

"Of course not."

"He's always known my disdain for him, with his flamboyant ways and flippant approach to scholarship. He should have realized I would take only so much from him, especially after the mess with my wife."

Annabel was now sorry she'd accompanied him to the office. If this intelligent but off-center man wanted to unburden himself, he'd picked the wrong ear to fill. Her résumé might be rich in experience, but a role as priest or shrink wasn't included in the credentials.

Vogler evidently didn't pick up on her discomfort. He continued: "My wife—she's no longer Mrs. Vogler—we've been divorced for seven years. Michele and Candy—her name is Candy—they had an affair. Oh, the marriage was on the rocks when it happened, but still it was extremely hurtful. I didn't mind losing her, but to have a colleague betray you like that was hard to take."

Annabel asked, "Dr. Vogler, why are you telling me this?"

He looked at her strangely, narrowed his eyes, and sat back. "I just wanted you to know that despite things that happened in the past between Michele and me, I didn't kill him."

"The detectives investigating the case are the ones who'll want to hear that."

The smile he exhibited said to Annabel that smiling wasn't a natural act.

"I know that, of course," he said, "and I know that they won't consider me a suspect once they hear what I have to say. My attacking Michele was perfectly justified, as you can see. And I'm certain plenty of people saw me here working in Manuscripts last night and will testify I never went near Hispanic. I had no reason to go there—did I?"

Annabel stood and straightened her skirt. "I'm sure you have nothing to worry about, Dr. Vogler."

"Please call me John."

"And I'm Annabel. I'd better get back. I can see that having two months to write my article isn't going to be nearly enough."

He escorted her to the reading desk, and the two books were again placed before her. Vogler lingered for a moment with his hand on her shoulder, then disappeared in the direction of his office.

You physically attacked Michele Paul because he had an affair with your wife and he accused you of doctoring research? Better block out plenty of time for the police, John Vogler.

At noon, a reference librarian informed Annabel that the Book of Privileges wouldn't be available until two, and she decided to head out for a fast lunch, dropping by the public affairs office on her way. An irate Lucianne Huston could be heard out in the hallway. Annabel paused for a moment, long enough for Lucianne to come steaming from the office, almost bumping into her. The outfit she wore was familiar to TV viewers—tan safari jacket over blue button-down blouse, brightly colored scarf around her neck, tight tan slacks, and highly polished brown boots.

"Hi," Annabel said.

"How friendly are you with the gatekeepers in there?"

"Friendly, I think."

"I need a favor."

"Yes?"

"Could you tell them to cut me some slack? They've got the press on a short leash, which I'm not used to. All the major players at the library have been put off limits for interviews. I've got a news director back in Miami burning up my beeper. And—"

"Slow down," Annabel said, holding up her hand and laughing. "I'm here researching a magazine article. I have nothing to do with—"

A member of the public affairs staff emerged from the office.

"You're supposed to take care of the press, not stonewall us," Lucianne said sharply to her.

"And my priority, Ms. Huston, is to represent the Library of Congress and its interests. We're being as cooperative as possible with you, with all the press, for that matter."

"You call this cooperation? I've had more cooperation from the goddamn CIA and the Kremlin."

"Excuse me." Lucianne's handler walked away.

"I was just going out for a quick bite. Join me?" asked Annabel.

"Sure. And a stiff drink. Then I'm coming back here and raise hell."

"Looks like you already have," said Annabel as they walked toward the main entrance.

"Just getting warmed up," said Lucianne. "If I can get a rebel leader in the mountains of some godforsaken banana republic to talk to me, I'll sure as hell get an interview with a librarian. Besides, I'm a taxpayer. I pay their salaries. So do you. How about a steak place? I need red meat."

"Librarians can be tough-minded, Lucianne—don't go by the cartoons or caricatures."

As they left the building and debated where to eat, Dolores Marwede burst through the doors and started past them.

"Hi," Annabel said. "This is Lucianne Huston."

Dolores hesitated, shoved out her hand to the journalist, said, "Nice meeting you. Sorry . . . I have to run."

"Lunch?" Annabel asked.

"No, I have to—I have to be someplace and I'm late. Thanks anyway."

Annabel and Lucianne watched her almost break into a run.

"Who's she?" Lucianne asked.

"She works in the Hispanic division."

"Did she kill Michele Paul?"

"Did she *what*?"

"When I don't know who killed somebody, I figure everybody did."

"Including me?" Annabel asked.

"Did you?"

"No."

"I'm glad to hear that. I'd hate to lose the only normal person I've met around here."

"Thanks. Steak you want? If we pass a cow you can shoot your lunch on the hoof."

"I've already done that. A pig in Somalia."

"Spare me the details. There's a decent steak house a few blocks from here."

15 Dolores Marwede's apartment, on the top floor of a three-story row house on tree-lined G Street, in the Capitol Hill area, was the only home she'd known since moving from New York nine years ago to take the job at LC.

She'd lived in it alone for the first two years until meeting, falling in love with, and marrying George Bibby, a staffer for a congressman from Illinois. At first, she found his drinking and enjoyment of nightlife to be exciting, and happily joined him on his nightly forays into Georgetown, where they hopped from bar to bar, making and meeting friends, and feeling very much a part of Washington's active young professionals' social scene.

But Bibby's drinking soon escalated from high-octane social to morose serious. They separated, then divorced, Bibby returning to Illinois to work in his father's real estate office, Dolores throwing herself into her work at the library as a way of mitigating the bitterness and loneliness.

"Home early," the elderly woman who occupied the ground floor said as Dolores arrived, breathless.

"Yes, but only for a few minutes, Mrs. Simone. I forgot something important."

"I don't know how you do it," the older woman said, using the sleeve of her sweater to wipe imaginary dirt from a low black wrought-iron fence defining a narrow front patch of grass. "You're always working, always running someplace."

Dolores forced a smile and disappeared through the front door, took the stairs two at a time, unlocked her door, threw it open, and stepped inside the apartment. Although it was a small one-bedroom, sun streaming through a row of windows at the front of the living room gave a feeling of openness. The furniture was pedestrian—she'd bought it all at once from a discount store in Virginia the week after moving in—but Mexican art and artifacts put her stamp on the space. She'd made multiple trips to Mexico for the library, and on vacations, too, and always brought something back to add to her collection, none of it expensive, but each piece and painting had personal relevance.

She poured a glass of orange juice in the kitchen, whose walls and counter were covered with vividly colored tiles purchased in Mexico, then went to the bedroom, closing the door behind her. She opened the door to the room's only closet, got down on her hands and knees, rummaged beneath hanging clothing, and pulled out a shoe box and a manila envelope, which she placed on the bed. A rubber band secured the shoe box. She removed it, took off the top of the box, and peered at its contents. It was filled with small envelopes and a few photographs. She began removing the items one by one, slowly, deliberately, examining each picture, carefully slipping letters and notes from their envelopes and reading them.

After fifteen minutes, she looked at her watch, hastily replaced everything in the box, put on the rubber band, and returned to the living room, where she stood in the middle of the room as though deciding where to put what she carried. If only I had a fireplace, she thought, dropping the box and envelope on a chair, retrieving the glass of juice from the bedroom and pouring its contents down the kitchen sink. She scooped up the box and envelope, locked the door behind her, and went down the stairs, relieved that Mrs. Simone had left.

She walked down G Street, crossed Seventh, and continued in the direction of the Capitol Children's Museum and Union Station carrying the shoe box and envelope as though they were valuable, holding them close to her chest. She fought against a confusion that gripped her, an inability to step aside and rationally view what she was doing. The confusion was unnecessary, she knew, but she was unable to dismiss it, emotions overriding cognition, running out of time but with all the time in the world at her disposal. Her mother had suffered what she called panic attacks: "Just stop it, Mom. What are you panicked about? It's just a mall, nobody here to hurt you." *Stop it, Dolores. It's just a city street. Nobody here to hurt you, nobody who even cares who you are or what you're carrying.* Her thoughts failed to soothe; the panic prevailed.

She reached the splendidly renovated Union Station. Construction was still in progress on Second Street. She paused at the site, next to a large Dumpster. There were no workers, no one watching. She quickly pulled the rubber band from the shoe box, stood on tiptoe, pulled a few envelopes and a photo from the box, dropped these into the Dumpster. Two men in suits approached, talking to each other. Dolores cradled the box in her arms and turned her face from them as they passed, breathing hard, certain they'd noticed her and wondered why she was there, what she was doing standing next to a Dumpster. Had they seen her drop the items into the Dumpster? They might come back, retrieve them, read them.

She got up on her toes again and peered down into the Dumpster. It was almost empty; the envelopes were at the bottom along with scraps of wood and cracked floor tile. The photo had landed on its back; the face in it stared up at her. She looked toward the station's main entrance. People were gathered there waiting for cabs to pull up. Were they all looking at her, asking one another what that woman was doing?

She walked away, back up Second Street, toward the Library of Congress, where tourists congregated on the sidewalk outside the Jefferson Building. She retraced her steps down Second Street until coming to three trash cans with lids in front of a row house. Curtains were drawn over the windows. No one looking out at her. A mother and child passed, laughing as they sang a children's song. Dolores pretended to examine something on the manila envelope until they'd passed, then removed the lid from one of the cans and emptied the contents of the box into it, replaced the lid, realized she still held the empty shoe box, took off the lid again, placed the empty box in with the envelopes and photos and unknown person's garbage, snapped the lid in place, and returned to Jefferson, sweating, certain her smile at the guard was recognized as forced and insincere, and went directly to her tiny office off the Hispanic reading room. She sat quietly for a few minutes collecting herself, then ventured out, carrying the envelope she'd brought from home. The yellow crime scene tape was gone; the stacks and upper gallery were open again. Dolores swiped her magnetic card in the door's slot and entered the stacks. She paused and looked up the narrow stairway leading to the upper gallery, where Michele Paul's body had been. She felt light-headed and grabbed a shelf for support. The wave of weakness passed as quickly as it had come. She walked deep into the stacks. She stopped in an area where file boxes containing donations to the collection rested on shelves. Crudely handwritten labels identified the source of the materials. Dolores knew that the contents of most of the boxes had been given a cursory examination upon their arrival, and would probably sit there for years before anyone found the time to give them a second look.

She opened the top to a box marked AARONSEN COLLECTION, slid her manila envelope beneath the dusty, yellowed papers in it, replaced the top, and returned to the reading room, where Consuela Martinez had just emerged from her office.

"Back to some semblance of normality," Consuela said, indicating where the crime scene tape had been.

"What a relief," Dolores said.

"Dolores, the police have asked me to accompany them to Michele's apartment to look at what library materials he might have had there. Annabel Reed-Smith is coming, too. I thought you might join us. You're familiar with what Michele was working on."

"I couldn't," Dolores said. "It's too . . . too spooky going there."

"I understand," Consuela said. "Are you okay? You look pale."

"I'm fine," Dolores said. "I suppose this is just now hitting home for me. There's a murderer around, probably in this building, Consuela."

The division chief's mouth became a tight line. "I know," she said. "I know it only too well."

Andre Lapin, the Library of Congress's director of security, had held four similar jobs at federal agencies over the past twenty-four years. Like other federal law enforcement officers, including the hundred-plus members of the library's own police force, Lapin had trained for ten weeks early in his career at the Federal Law Enforcement Training Center in Georgia. He was a whippet of a man, compact, thin, active even when at ease. Bushy salt-and-pepper eyebrows formed perfect tents above his eyes.

MPD detectives Nastasi and Shorter had

been meeting with him for the past half hour in his office adjacent to the twenty-four-hour command center.

". . . and so Mr. Vogler attacked Dr. Paul?" Nastasi said.

"It appeared that way," Lapin said. "Always hard to pin down who starts a fight, but I was pretty sure Vogler threw the first punch. Of course, you never know what prompts a guy to hit somebody. In Paul's case . . ."

The detectives cocked their heads and looked at the security chief.

"In Michele Paul's case, I wouldn't be surprised if he'd said something to nettle Vogler."

"What did Vogler say about it?" Shorter asked.

Lapin consulted his file on the incident. "All he said was that Paul insulted him." Lapin looked up from the folder and smiled. "Some insult. Lots of rumors about Paul messing with Vogler's wife."

"That so?" said Nastasi. "Vogler was cuckolded?"

"Can't prove it by me, and that's not the way it's usually described, but that's what I heard. Vogler and his wife divorced."

Shorter, who was writing his own notes,

said, "Any other incidents like the one between Vogler and Paul?"

"Physical assaults? No."

"Did you personally know the deceased?"

Lapin nodded. "Not well, but we had a few conversations over the years. I didn't seek him out. Frankly, I never liked the guy."

"You and the rest of the library," Nastasi muttered.

"True," said Lapin. "Anything else I can do for you today?"

"Yeah," Nastasi said. "What's new with the stalker?"

Lapin rolled his eyes and shook his head. "Still stalking according to the stalkee. Is there such a word?"

Shorter laughed. "I don't think so. We had another complaint filed with us yesterday."

"I've got a plainclothes officer working the main reading room. You can't tell the stalkers without a program. We attract our share of kooks. The main reading room is open to all, even the District's more . . . colorful types."

"Nice way to put it," said Shorter.

"At least we know it's a man," Lapin said. "That rules out the Bride of Christ."

"Say again?"

"The Bride of Christ. She's been coming

here in her white wedding gown for more than a year looking for proof in one of the Bibles in the collection that Christ was her husband."

"That so?" Nastasi said. "How many Bibles do you have?"

"Enough to keep her going another couple of decades. The main reading room librarians are wearing their badges upside down to make it harder to read their names. Have you met Ms. Gomara?"

The detectives shook their heads.

"If I was going to stalk somebody from the library," Lapin said, "I'd pick her. A knockout. A little young for me but . . . Everybody seems a little young for me these days. What's new in the murder investigation?"

"Not much," replied Nastasi. "No prints on the weapon. Tough to pick up prints off that burlap that covered the lead weight. Now it's at the FBI lab. They've got new equipment that might do the trick. Some of your people are meeting this afternoon with ours at the deceased's apartment to look at library materials. It's been searched. Didn't come up with much. He had a black book filled with names, lots of women. I take it that despite being hated around here, there were women who found him charming."

"Oh, yes. He had a reputation of being a ladies' man. Much water fountain scuttlebutt. But Paul kept pretty much to himself. Didn't have any real friends, no confidants at the library as far as I know."

"He lived pretty good," Shorter said. "Nice big apartment. Nice car. Thirty-foot boat. A ton of credit card receipts from when he traveled, which seemed to be often. Didn't skimp when he was on the road."

"By the way," Nastasi said, "have you finished going through background security checks on people in the Hispanic division?"

"No. Maybe by the end of the day."

"How extensive are those checks?" Shorter asked.

"Depends on the employee and what they have access to. Anyone authorized to get close to the rare books, maps, and manuscripts goes through a fairly rigid check before starting work. In some cases, like the Kissinger papers we have, there's material that bears on national security. Employees working in that section have to get a top-secret clearance. Same with anybody working in the congressional research division."

"Let us know when you're done," Nastasi said.

"Shall do."

"You have any info on where Paul got the money to live the way he did?" Shorter asked Lapin.

The security chief shook his head. "Rich uncle, maybe. Moonlighted as a male escort, maybe. Lucky at the lottery . . ."

"Maybe," Nastasi said.

17 Warren Munsch sat at a table outside the San Angel Inn on Diego Rivera, a few blocks from the Hotel Polanco, where he'd been staying since arriving in Mexico City. He'd left his room early that morning carrying his possessions in his overnight bag. Fortunately, the clerks at the desk hadn't seen him leave. If they had, they might have asked whether he was checking out and presented him his bill. That would have been embarrassing. Munsch didn't have any more money.

He'd checked in for only one night, paying cash. The next day he informed them he'd be extending his stay a few days and would settle the bill when he left. Well, now he'd left, and they could go whistle for their money.

He sipped from a mug of hot black coffee the consistency of motor oil and pondered his next move. This morning, as with most mornings of his adult life, he silently cursed what had been and reflected what his life would be if only he hadn't . . .

He flew into Mexico City feeling good despite the thought that he was probably now being sought on a murder charge instead of simple theft. That assumed, of course, that Garraga or Morrie had named him as part of the team. Chances were they had. They were a couple of losers who couldn't be trusted.

He'd left L.A. with plenty of money in his pocket to enjoy a pleasant night in a decent hotel and to book a flight to Cuba the next day. The Hotel Polanco was recommended to him by the cab driver who drove him into the city from the airport. When he checked in, he intended to have a few drinks in some neighborhood bar and get to bed. But as he sat nursing tequila on the rocks and watching a parade of pretty Mexican women, his libido got the better of him. He set off to buy some female companionship. After stopping in a few more bars, and with the tequila clouding what had always been flawed judgment anyway, he found his true love for the evening, a middle-aged lady dressed like a teenager who promised him a trip to paradise.

"You come with me back to my place, huh?" he'd said after buying her a glass of "champagne" for twenty dollars, U.S.

"No, no," she insisted. She lived just down the street, she said, and had plenty of whiskey there for him and a big, comfortable bed.

He never got to enjoy either. He followed her into an alley and to a door she said led to her apartment. When she didn't make a move to open it, Munsch grabbed her and tried to kiss her. The next thing he knew he was attacked from behind by two men who threw him against the building. One of the men straddled him and held a knife to his throat while the second managed to reach into his rear pants pocket and extract the wallet into which he'd put all the cash he'd brought from California. The man with the knife smiled, exposing a mouth full of gold, called him something in Spanish that Munsch thought might have meant fat gringo pig, got off him, and the two men and Munsch's heavenly lover ran from the alley.

He considered going back to the bar in which he'd met her and looking for them, but summoned up his only wisdom of the evening and walked back to the hotel, muttering all the way.

Now, with three dollars in his pocket that had been left as a tip on an adjacent table, and sourness in his stomach, he drank coffee and tried to come up with a way to make a fast score, enough to get to Cuba. He was deep into his thoughts when two men dressed in suits, who'd taken a table shortly after Munsch arrived, got up and slowly approached. They stood on either side of him but said nothing.

Munsch looked up. "Yeah? What'a you want?"

The taller man, who looked American, said, "Warren Munsch?"

Munsch looked at the other man, a Mexican.

"Mind if we join you?" the American said, sitting.

"Suit yourself," Munsch said. "I was just leaving." His heart pounded.

As he started to stand, the Mexican placed his hand on his shoulder, holding him down. The American said, "Let's have a little talk, Warren. Might be worth your while."

Munsch again looked up at the Mexican, who'd unbuttoned his suit jacket to reveal a revolver in the waistband of his trousers.

Munsch said to the American, "So, go ahead. I'm listening. What are you, cops?"

The American shook his head. "Private investigators. You can call me Smitty. My Mexican colleague is Jose."

"Smitty and Jose, huh? What are you, some kinda comedy team?" He sounded confident; inside he was Jell-O.

"We've been looking for you, Warren," said the American.

"Yeah? Why?"

"Someone's anxious to talk to you."

"Like who, an ex-wife?"

"Like someone who wants to know what happened back in Miami when you forgot to pay for a certain painting you walked away with."

"Painting?" He guffawed. "Do I look like an art collector?"

"No, you don't, Warren. What you look like to me is a two-bit hustler. So, what say we go see the man, let him ask his questions, and you can go on your way. Okay, Warren?"

"Hey, look, quit calling me Warren. I don't know you, so don't get familiar."

"Just wanted to be friendly—Warren. I get the feeling you don't intend to cooperate with us."

"What'a you mean, 'cooperate'? Cooperate with what?"

"I'll give you the choices, Warren. Either you come nice and easy with us, or we roll you up like an umbrella and carry you there."

"Get lost. What'a you gonna do, shoot me here in a public restaurant?"

"Maybe. Depends on you. See those *federales* over there?" He pointed to three uniformed Mexican police with automatic rifles slung over their shoulders standing twenty feet away. "They know we're here to make a citizen's arrest. If you, the fugitive, don't cooperate, they'll help us *shoot you right here in this restaurant.*" He'd been speaking softly, but delivered this message in a growl.

"Do I have your attention, Warren?"

"I guess so. What'a you do, pay off those cops over there?"

"You aren't suggesting Mexico's law enforcement officers are open to bribes, are you? If you are suggesting that, Warren, you'll upset Jose."

A glance at Jose's surly face. "I sure wouldn't want to do that," Munsch said, finishing his coffee and standing. "Where are we going?"

"Not far."

"Are you gonna turn me over to the cops?"

"Depends."

"On what?" Munsch asked as they walked away, the two men flanking him.

"On what our client wants to do with you."

Munsch's waitress shouted after them in Spanish.

"He didn't pay," Jose said.

"You didn't pay, Warren."

"Screw you, Smitty. You pay."

Smitty nodded at Jose, who returned to the table and handed the waitress money. As he did, Munsch asked Smitty, "What's in this for me?"

"What do you mean?"

"If I'm gonna talk to this so-called client of yours, I want to get paid."

Smitty grinned. "I like your style, Warren."

"How'd you find me?" Munsch asked as they walked to where the private detectives had parked their car.

"Jose has contacts all over the city, Warren. Took about an hour to learn where a fat gringo named Munsch checked in. You are checked out?"

"Yeah, I'm checked out. I'm paid in full."

"Good for you, Warren. Hate to see you stiff any of our friends south of the border."

18 "Mr. Driscoll on the phone, Dr. Broadhurst."

The Librarian of Congress picked up his phone: "David, good to hear from you again."

"I assume with murders taking place at the library, you've been distracted."

"A fair statement."

"There's been little written about the incident here in Los Angeles. Have they apprehended the killer yet?"

"No, but they continue to investigate. Odd case. Upsetting. About your previous call, David, concerning the Las Casas diaries. We've been putting out discreet feelers on the Hill, and I've had preliminary conversations with private donors who've offered generous support in the past. Is there any news on your end? Have the diaries in fact been located, and are they for sale?"

"There is a good chance that Las Casas's diaries, in one form or other, might become available. I'm flying to Washington tonight. We can meet in the morning."

"I have a—yes, of course. I'll wipe the slate clean. Anyone else you'd like at the meeting?"

"No. Let's keep this between us for now. The others you've contacted, are they likely to make this public in some way?"

"I asked them not to."

"Do they know I'm the source?"

"No, I didn't mention you by name. I kept it on a hypothetical level, a what-if sort of thing."

"Please keep it that way, Cale."

"Of course. What time tomorrow?"

"Eight?"

"Here?"

"My hotel. I'm staying at the Willard."

"I'll be there."

Broadhurst immediately called General Counsel Mary Beth Mullin.

"Mary, you haven't indicated to anyone you've spoken with that Dave Driscoll is the one who's raised the Las Casas issue, have you?"

"No. I referred only to a wealthy collector."

"Good. I'm meeting with David in the morning. He's flying in tonight from California."

"Want me there?"

"Driscoll asked that only he and I meet. I'll fill you in after the meeting."

A minute after their conversation ended, Mullin called back. "Cale, sorry, but I realize I did mention Driscoll to Senator Hale."

"Is he likely to spread that in the Senate?"

"I'll call and ask him not to."

If it isn't too late, Broadhurst thought.

It was vitally important, he knew, that things be done exactly as Driscoll wanted them done. David Driscoll, a rich man by virtue of the brokerage firm that carried his name, was as prickly a personality as Broadhurst had ever encountered. It was said that Driscoll handled big things with aplomb but tripped over bobby pins and paper clips. A tall, imposing, patrician figure, he'd starred in his own commercials for

Driscoll Securities, steely eyes peering into the camera, frosty-white shirt pulled tight around his tie beneath his Lincolnesque face, his voice passing through what sounded like restricted nasal passages: "Other brokerage firms *handle* your investments. At Driscoll Securities, we *nurture* them. You have my word on that."

He'd retired from active leadership of the brokerage house a dozen years ago and traveled the world with his wife, mostly to Latin America, Spain, and Portugal, where he added to what was a superb collection of Hispanic and Portuguese art and artifact.

David Driscoll was a man to be reckoned with, which Cale Broadhurst was perfectly willing to do in order to sustain his generous interest in the Library of Congress. The LC depended upon two types of books: the millions of them in the collections, and the double-entry type that tracked the millions of dollars needed to keep the institution afloat.

Annabel and Lucianne Huston returned to the library after lunch. Lucianne went to the public affairs office, and Annabel to her desk to do some more reading before her appointment at three to go to Michele Paul's apartment.

"Look," Lucianne said to Joanne Graves the minute she was inside and had shut the door, "I need to interview some people from the library. Trying to keep this under wraps is stupid."

"We're not trying to keep anything under wraps, Lucianne," Graves said, her words wrapped in exasperation. "What I am trying to do is approach this in an orderly fashion. And that means no special treatment for individual journalists. You'll just have to wait like the rest of your breed."

"Well, that's just perfect," Lucianne blew up. "I'm sent here on a wild goose chase by that idiot boss of mine, and now some twerp of a librarian tries to keep me from *my* story."

"If you're going to take that tone with me, I'll have to ask you to leave my office. Or else I could have security—"

"Fine! I'll leave. But you'll hear from me again," Lucianne said, stomping out of the office. "And from your boss," she added, echoing the slamming of the door. Frustrated, she decided to corner Cale Broadhurst; maybe he'd have something useful to say.

* * *

Annabel sat at her desk in the Hispanic section and found that she couldn't keep from staring at the empty seat to her right and thinking what an abrupt end Michele Paul's life had come to. And in another hour she would be going to his apartment to, in a way, plunder the bounty of his research for her own article.

She decided to get some air. On her way out of the library, she ran into Lucianne. "Hi again. Did you learn anything new from public relations?"

"No, not a thing. I asked about the John Bitteman disappearance, but they wouldn't tell me anything. Said it was never officially labeled a murder."

"Consuela told me a little about him and his disappearance. Do *you* think there could be a connection between Michele's murder and what happened to Bitteman?"

"I don't know. Bitteman and Michele were rivals, I'm told, both trying to be the first to land the Las Casas diaries or the map. They barely spoke."

"Did Bitteman leave a family?" Annabel asked.

"They say he was openly homosexual. The

police theorized it might have been a gay love affair gone awry."

"I was hoping to see Bitteman's files on Las Casas."

"Good luck. Paranoia seems to run in Las Casas scholars. Bitteman took most things home, too, like Michele."

"But surely he left something."

"Check with your buddy, Consuela. Sure you want to go rummaging through a dead man's apartment?"

"Not on my wish list, but sharing a cramped space with someone who's murdered two days after I got here wasn't either."

The two MPD officers who picked up
19 Consuela and Annabel were talkative types. The driver was in uniform, the other in plainclothes. Getting into a marked police cruiser was unsettling for both women, but the officers' banter soon made them forget what was painted on the vehicle's doors.

They pulled up in front of the Bethesda apartment building that had been Paul's home until his murder, one of hundreds of such buildings in the Maryland and Virginia suburbs, all so similar that they might have been designed and built by a single individual.

The plainclothes detective found the super, who led the officers, Consuela, and Annabel to the top floor, where he let them into Paul's apartment. The super, a portly gentleman who spoke with a Slavic accent, lingered.

"Thanks," the detective told him. "I'll let you know when we're leaving."

"Do you know who killed Dr. Paul?" the super asked on his way out.

"No," the detective answered, "but you'll be the first to know."

"It's a lovely apartment," Annabel said, going to sliding glass doors leading to the terrace.

Consuela agreed.

"You knew this man pretty well," one detective, Simmons, said.

"Yes," Consuela said. "We worked together."

"He was what, a professor?"

"A researcher. Hispanic and Portuguese history."

"Impressive," Simmons said. "Looks like it pays pretty well."

"Where do we start?" Annabel asked.

"In here."

Detective Simmons led them into the largest of three bedrooms, which Paul had set up as his office. On their way, Annabel glanced into the other two smaller bedrooms. One had obviously been where Paul slept. The other served as a storeroom of sorts, with floor-to-ceiling steel shelving on which at least a hundred file boxes, labeled with an electronic labeling device, were neatly arranged.

"Do you think that's all library materials, too?" Annabel asked Consuela.

"We'll have to see." She looked to Simmons: "Can we examine what's in this room, too?"

"Sure. My orders are to let you look at anything you want. We've already gone over the apartment."

"It's going to be awhile," Consuela said.

"Take your time. You've got us for the rest of the day, whatever's left of it."

"Where do we start?" Consuela asked when she and Annabel were alone in the office.

"Those four two-drawer file cabinets, I suppose," Annabel said. "We're looking for anything bearing upon or belonging to LC?"

"Uh huh," Consuela said, opening the top drawer of one of the units.

Annabel pulled out another drawer. Five

minutes after she'd begun, she said to Consuela, "Everything in here is related to his research. I assume the police removed anything of a personal nature for their investigation."

"Looks that way," Consuela said, opening another drawer. "Let's see if we can arrange to have all this shipped back to the library. We'll be days if we have to go through it here."

While the Hispanic division chief conferred with Simmons, Annabel went into the storage room and perused the labels on boxes. It appeared that everything in that room was linked to Michele Paul's professional life, too.

"What did he say?" Annabel asked when Consuela returned.

"He said that's up to us. I'll call Helen Kelly and see if she can arrange for a truck and personnel to get everything out of here. In the meantime, we might as well go through what's in his office. The most recent work he'd been doing is probably there. We can carry some of that back to LC ourselves."

They worked silently, examining each file folder in the drawers, occasionally commenting on what they'd found, and placing selected folders on the floor next to them. One file labeled SEVILLE-REYES caught Annabel's eye. She took it to a black leather sling chair in the corner and began reading.

"What do you have?" Consuela asked.

"Handwritten notes, in Michele's hand, I assume. It's about some artist from Seville named Fernando Reyes."

"Not familiar with him."

"I don't think I am, either, although for some reason his name rings a bell. That's why I picked it up."

"What's it say about him?"

"Sort of a biography, a list of paintings attributed to him, family background, influences, that sort of thing. Looks like Michele did this research fairly recently when he was in Seville, according to dates in his notes."

"He spent a lot of time in Seville over the past couple of years," Consuela said.

"Makes sense," said Annabel, continuing to read. "Michele seems to have gotten most of his material about the artist from someone he refers to as Sebastian. Familiar?"

"No."

"Look at this." Annabel handed Consuela a group of papers attached to one another with a paper clip.

"A list of paintings by Reyes."

"Yes. And a second list of paintings by others, all depicting that famous scene where Columbus presents his Book of Privileges to Fernando and Isabella."

Annabel laid the folder on the floor and went to the living and dining rooms, where the walls were covered with Hispanic art. "There's no painting in the apartment depicting that scene," she said when she returned to the office.

"It says Reyes painted in the nineteenth century," Consuela said. "Aside from the scene, I can't imagine what it would have to do with Las Casas."

"I can't either," Annabel said, inserting the list she'd given Consuela into the folder and adding it to others on the floor.

At five, Annabel took out her cell phone. "I have to call Mac."

"Where are you?" her husband asked. "I called the library. Someone in Hispanic said you'd left for the afternoon."

"I'm at Michele Paul's apartment."

"Why?"

"Going over materials he had here that should be returned to the library. I'm with Consuela."

"How long will you be there?"

"We're about to leave. Consuela and I are carrying back some of the files. They're sending a truck tomorrow for the rest. There's a room full of file boxes."

"Home for dinner?"

"Yes. I'd say about six-thirty."

"I'll have it waiting."

"Don't fuss. How was school?"

"Pretty good. I'm impressed with some of my students this term, at least I was today. Tomorrow's another matter."

"And how's your knee?"

"It's, ah—hurting today. I took a wrong step leaving the building. Must have twisted it."

"Stay off it. We'll order in from the hotel."

"I'll play it by ear. Or by knee. Safe home."

Annabel and Consuela, each carrying an armload of file folders, were driven back to LC by Detective Simmons and his uniformed colleague. They went directly to the Hispanic and Portuguese section, where they spread the folders on a small conference table in a room adjacent to Consuela's office.

"What are you going to do with them overnight?" Annabel asked.

"Lock them in my office, I suppose, unless

you want to stay awhile and keep going through them."

"No, thanks," Annabel said. "I've got to head home."

She went to her desk space on the upper gallery and gathered her belongings. She'd come down the stairs and had said good night to Consuela when Lucianne Huston entered the reading room. "I was looking for you," she said.

"I was out for the afternoon."

"Where did you go?"

"Just out. Part of my research. Did you get the interviews you wanted?"

"The security chief, but he didn't have much to add to what I already know. That Prussian, Ms. Graves, says she's got me set up tomorrow with the lawyer, name's Mullin. I hate interviewing lawyers, party of the first part and that crap. I'm on my way to our D.C. affiliate to file a report for the seven o'clock news. Want to come with me?"

"Thanks, no."

"I'm leading with the Bitteman story. Two murders here, both victims chasing the elusive Las Casas. You know John Vogler?"

"Yes."

"Seems he had a fistfight with Michele

Paul over an affair Paul had with Vogler's wife."

Annabel said nothing.

"Getting juicier all the time. Or at least live. Well, take it easy, and thanks for lunch."

"Sure."

Annabel watched Huston walk toward Consuela's office.

"Lucianne."

The journalist turned. "What?"

"You told me you were sent here because there had been an art theft and murder in Miami."

"Not *because* of that, but it started the process. Why?"

"The artist? Did you say his name was Reyes?"

"That's right. Fernando Reyes."

"Oh."

"Why do I get the feeling this is meaningful?" Lucianne asked.

"Beats me. Somebody mentioned him, that's all. Just a coincidence."

Lucianne's expression was probing.

"See you tomorrow," Annabel said. "I have a husband with a bad knee limping around our apartment getting dinner ready. Got to run."

"If he ever gets tired of cooking for you, send him down to me. I haven't had a man cook for me in a long time."

Fat chance, Annabel thought, smiling and walking away. Get your own man, tiger.

Sue Gomara looked out over the vast main reading room from her position at the central desk. Directly above was the famed domed ceiling, a hundred and sixty feet high, the female figure in its cupola representing human understanding. Surrounding that woman were a dozen other paintings saluting the countries or epochs that had contributed most to the development of Western civilization.

The room itself was inspiring, especially since its reopening in June of 1991 after being closed to the public for more than three years of renovation. The card catalogs, part of the decor for eighty-nine years, rendered out-moded by LC's computer system but still used by some, had been moved to another location. Reader desks now completely encir-cled the raised central desk. All the desks had been wired for laptop computers. Soundproof carpeting, its design based upon the room's architectural elements, had been installed, providing the sort of voluptuous quietude expected of libraries. The visitor's gallery and alcoves on the second-floor-gallery level had been glassed in to further reduce noise.

Peaceful, contemplative, dignified—those were words Sue often used to describe where she was interning to friends who viewed the Library of Congress as only something to add to out-of-town visitors' sight-seeing lists.

Until recently.

Until the breathy, vile calls started a month ago.

Her eyes went to the magnificent John Flanagan clock above the room's main entrance. Five-thirty. Time to pack up that stint, go back to Hispanic to change clothes, and head home.

"Sure I can't buy you a drink?" a colleague at the central desk asked as Sue tidied up her station. Ken Silvestrie had been asking her out ever since he started working the main reading room six months ago. He was attracted to Sue the moment he first saw her, especially her eyes, large, oval brown eyes filled with compassion—and passion?

"Ken," she said pleasantly and quietly, "I told you my boyfriend wouldn't appreciate my going out with you, or anybody else for that matter. Besides, you're working till nine-thirty."

Silvestrie's smile was boyish. "When I get off, I mean. You're not married to the guy, Sue. I mean, what's the harm of us having a drink together? We *work* together. Just a drink to talk—"

Sue laughed, something else he was attracted to, her easy laugh and her large, white teeth.

"Talk business?" she said, touching his arm.

"Yeah, something like that."

"Thanks for the offer but I can't."

"He's always out of town."

Which was true. Sue's live-in boyfriend of the past seven months, Rick Holt, was a junior auditor for the Senate Financial Institutions and Regulatory Relief Subcommittee of the full Banking, Housing and Urban Affairs Committee. Long title, simple job—travel the country and audit federally chartered banks to ensure their compliance with federal regulations. He was gone three weeks out of each month.

There were times when she considered accepting other men's offers of a drink or dinner, but she'd resisted those urges, spawned by loneliness, because Sue Gomara could be as much of a pragmatist as she was a dreamer. She envisioned a future with Rick Holt and wasn't about to jeopardize it. Too, having fallen in love with him meant being able to leave campus housing for a more grown-up life in an apartment. Her parents hadn't been pleased at first, but soon accepted their daughter's decision and continued to help support her college work and career aspirations.

"See you tomorrow, Ken," she said, stepping down from the circular desk and heading for the main entrance.

The reading room was filled to capacity that early evening, and she'd fulfilled hundreds of requests for books since coming on duty at noon after spending the morning in Hispanic. She was tired, yet satisfied with the way the afternoon had gone. Few days disappointed her since beginning her internship in conjunction with her post-graduate library science studies at the University of Maryland.

She kept her eyes straight ahead but took in selected readers' desks with her peripheral vision. Most men and women using the room were serious about whatever it was they researched, and were pleasant, too. Normal people.

But there was the predictable cadre of strange-o's who showed up each day for their own particular reasons. The Bride of Christ sat at the desk she usually grabbed first thing in the morning, poring over yet another Bible. A man with blazing eyes, insane eyes, and who always wore a black cape sat at another desk going through a pile of telephone directories from around the world in search of the name of the person who'd placed a curse on him. And there was the street person Sue had been told by her supervisor to ask to leave a few days earlier because of complaints from other patrons about his body odor. She'd expected she'd need the help of an LC police officer, but was pleasantly surprised when the scruffy man didn't mount a protest and simply left the room. He was back, hopefully having found a working shower.

She wondered as she walked from the main reading room whether one of the men seated at a desk in that vast space, dedicated to knowledge and enlightenment, was the one who'd been making the calls. Was one of those normal-looking persons the pervert?

"Remember," she'd been told during regularly scheduled security briefings, "the person who's likely to try and steal a book, or deface a book, is probably the most normal-looking man or woman in the room. The kooks are annoying but they tend not to be destructive, to property or persons. It's the scholarly gentleman or woman, half-glasses perched on his or her nose, nicely dressed and polite— that's the person to keep an eye on."

After fairly trotting back to Hispanic—she seldom did anything in low gear—and changing into jeans and a U. of Maryland sweatshirt, she went to the main entrance, removed her upside-down badge from around her neck and placed it in her handbag, handed the bag to the officer, returned a "have a pleasant evening," and stepped out onto First Street. It was indeed a lovely evening, cool and dry and with a huge full moon beaming down on the city where the nation's business was conducted.

Damn him! she thought as she walked down First in the direction of Capitol South Metro Station for a train to the Farragut West

Station, not far from her ground-floor apartment near Dupont Circle. The obscene calls had set her whole being on edge, even though the police had assured her that "chances were slim" he was a violent person who would initiate physical action against her: "Obscene callers are *seldom* violent."

How comforting.

And now a murder within the library itself. As far as Sue was concerned, the murderer had to be someone who worked there. The new security system was too formidable for an outsider to gain access to the stacks and to the Hispanic division's upper gallery, where Michele Paul sat. But she also knew that no security system was foolproof. Just thinking of Paul's murder caused her stomach to turn.

She let herself in the apartment. Until the calls, she would have immediately changed into pajamas and robe if she intended to stay in and get to bed early. But the calls had changed that routine. She checked each window to make sure it was locked even though metal ironwork covered them, and double-checked the front-door locks. Rick had been there when the first call came four weeks ago, and he insisted they add a heavy dead bolt to the existing lock.

Feeling relatively secure, she responded to Wendell, rubbing against her legs, fed him, then poured herself her nightly glass of red wine, which she took to the bedroom, gave an extra tug to drapes covering the window, and changed into a gray sweatsuit and sneakers. The TV was in the living room. She turned it on and sat back to watch the evening news, a contented cat on her lap.

International events, and a brewing ethical scandal in Congress, led the newscast. Then, as Sue considered a second glass of wine, Lucianne Huston's face filled the screen.

"I'm Lucianne Huston at the Library of Congress in Washington, D.C. The murder of senior specialist and researcher Michele Paul in this imposing institution of learning has predictably shaken those who worked with him. The police have been conducting nonstop interviews with his colleagues, many of whom I'm told were not particularly fond of the deceased. I've also learned that eight years ago, another researcher from the library was a possible murder victim. I say 'possible' because his body was never found. His apartment had been ransacked and police found traces of blood. This victim, whose name was John Bitteman, was a rival of Michele Paul's—both had devoted their professional careers to attempting to prove the existence of diaries allegedly written by Bartolomé de Las Casas, close friend and sailing companion of Christopher Columbus on his first three voyages from Spain to the Americas. It was also alleged that Las Casas had drawn a map pinpointing where Columbus had hidden millions in gold. Where the investigation into this latest murder leads is conjecture at this point, but we'll continue to report developments as they occur. I'm Lucianne Huston in Washington."

Sue had heard about the disappearance of John Bitteman, but only in snippets. It had happened long ago; she was only sixteen years old. Those who had been there at the time and with whom she talked about it worked in the collections management division, which administered book services through the main reading room, not the Hispanic and Portuguese division. Most had known Bitteman by reputation only.

She went to the kitchen to see what was in the fridge for dinner when the ringing phone stopped her. She reached for it but paused, her hand hovering over the instrument. Was it *him* again?

"Hello?" she said, voice taut.

"Sue. It's Hope."

A sigh.

"Think I was your secret admirer calling?"

"It crossed my mind."

Hope Martin worked as an assistant at the Corcoran Gallery of Art; she and Sue had been friends since meeting there at a fundraiser a year ago.

"Rick out of town?" Hope asked.

"Yes. Denver, I think. Or Chicago. One of those places out there. How are you?"

"Great. Had dinner?"

"No. I was just foraging for something."

"Let's go out. My cupboard's bare."

"I suspect that's the case with mine, too. Where?"

"Zorba's? I'm in the mood for tabouli."

"Okay." The cafe was around the corner from Sue's apartment. "A half hour?"

"You've got it. If you get there first, which I

know you will, grab a patio table. It's warm enough."

Sue changed into slacks, a sweater, and light purple and pink crinkled windbreaker and was out the door when the phone rang again. Go back in and answer it? Hard not to. She picked up on the fourth ring, just before her answering machine kicked in.

"Hello, Ms. Gomara."

The deep male voice spoke slowly, hesitantly, as though he'd stammered at some point in his life.

"Who the hell are you?" Sue said. She'd asked the police to provide a way to trace the calls, but they suggested she see whether the caller persisted. What constituted persisting? she wondered. This was the sixth call, at least, even more when you added the times he reached the answering machine and said nothing.

"Don't be angry with me, Ms. Gomara. This is a friendly call."

Hang up? She wished the answering machine had been activated. She wanted his voice on tape.

"How do you know me?" she asked. The police had told her to say nothing when he called, simply to hang up: "That generally frustrates guys like this. They want a conversation with you. Don't give them the satisfaction."

"That doesn't matter," he said. "I love the way you look, the way you walk. I like beautiful women who are intelligent, too. Such a beautiful woman to be so smart."

"Look you creep, you'd better—"

"Sex and beauty are inseparable, Ms. Gomara, like life and consciousness. The intelligence that goes with sex and beauty, and arises out of sex and beauty, is intuition."

She was about to slam the receiver into its cradle when he said, "Let care kill a cat, we'll laugh and grow fat," and laughed.

Shakespeare? My obscene caller is quoting Shakespeare?

"Cats are such a female thing," he said, and then used a crude sexual term in describing what he wanted to do with Sue.

She hung up and stood shaking, staring at the phone. It rang.

Sue left the apartment and walked quickly to the restaurant. As she passed a phone booth, she stopped, turned, and tried to see the man in it. His back was to her. Two other men walked by, and she stared at them, too.

Who are you?

No more waiting for the calls to "persist." In the morning, she'd demand that the police do something.

She told her friend Hope about the latest call as they sat on the cafe's patio. "Don't wait for the police," Hope said. "Buy one of those recorders that activate whenever the phone is lifted. Get the bastard on tape."

"I will," Sue said. "First thing tomorrow. He quoted Shakespeare."

"The creep?"

"Yes. I think it was Shakespeare, something about killing a cat."

"Your cat, Wendell?"

"Don't even say it."

She returned to the apartment at nine-thirty. The message light on her machine was blinking.

"Sue, it's Rick. Sorry I missed you. Hope you're out having fun. Forgot to give you the hotel I'm staying at in Cleveland." He reeled off the number. "Love you, baby. Pleasant dreams." He ended with a loud kiss.

She tried him at the hotel but he wasn't in his room. She then called the MPD and reported the most recent call.

"We really can't do much tonight," the desk

officer said. "Come on by tomorrow and talk to the officer handling your case."

"And what if this creep decides to break in here tonight and rape me, kill me?"

"Unlikely, Ms. Gomara. These phone stalkers are generally passive types and—"

She yelled at him.

"Okay, okay, calm down, ma'am. We can have a car make a couple of passes by your house tonight, but that's about it. Why don't you buy one of those tape recorders that records phone conversations? They're not expensive. But your best bet is to come in here in the morning and . . ."

The night was spent curled up with Wendell watching old movies on TV and drinking wine. She called in sick in the morning, bought a tape recorder, stopped at MPD headquarters and filed another complaint, which resulted in her case officer promising to put into motion a means of tracking the calls, and spent the rest of the day in bed waiting for the phone to ring.

It didn't. Which was worse than if it had.

ished black wingtip shoes. Broadhurst was in his "uniform"—gray slacks, gray tweed jacket, blue button-down shirt, floppy yellow bow tie, and brown leather shoes with thick soles, adding an inch to his height.

Driscoll had remained standing. Now, he sat, carefully crossed one leg over the other, leaned back, and made a face as though he had bitten into something sour. "So, Cale," he said, "have you made any progress on lining up funds?"

The question threw Broadhurst for a moment because he'd been poised to ask the first question: Are the Las Casas diaries and map really in hand—and for sale?

He answered Driscoll's question: "Yes, although much of it is tentative. I'm at a disadvantage in not knowing how much money will be needed, but I do have expressions of support. Senator Menendez says he's willing to introduce a resolution to fund, at least in part, the acquisition of the diaries."

Driscoll drew a breath. "Naturally, I'm willing to put up the money to buy the diaries, if that becomes necessary. Frankly, I'd prefer that the only other source of money be Congress, not private parties. The people of the United States should be the ones who bring such important documents into the Library of Congress."

The people, and David Driscoll, Broadhurst thought.

"Is there something to buy, David?"

"I believe there will be," he said, his coffee cup at eye level.

"Care to share the source with me?" Broadhurst asked.

A thin smile crossed Driscoll's lips.

"I understand you're reluctant to do that at this juncture, but it will be necessary—eventually."

"Of course. But let's explore this question of sources for a moment. You're no stranger to valuable manuscripts and books coming to the library from—what shall we say?—from unconventional, unexpected sources."

Broadhurst narrowed his eyes.

"The Lucas collection I managed to obtain for you is one good case in point."

"True."

"Precious books, rare maps, indeed entire collections lie submerged for generations, for centuries, then find their way to the surface through a fissure created by need or greed, human tragedy or simple dumb luck."

"And which of the above applies to Las Casas?"

"A little of each, I suppose. You know, putting one's hands on something as valuable as the Las Casas materials isn't easy. It's a very competitive market out there, Cale, not competition in the traditional business sense, but every bit as fierce, perhaps more so."

Broadhurst said, "Are you saying we're facing serious competition for Las Casas?"

"Of course. You didn't expect otherwise, did you?"

"No, but it's a matter of degree. If the diaries and map—Is there a map?"

"I believe so."

"If the diaries and map do exist—and I take it from what you've said that they do—then the matter of origin becomes important. I have the feeling they're not about to be offered through traditional channels." Broadhurst's raised eyebrows asked for verification.

"Let's just say, Cale, that in order to acquire Las Casas for the Library of Congress, I will have had to take unusual steps."

"You'll have to be more specific."

"I'm unable to be more specific."

"We can't expect Menendez to propose a

Senate resolution to purchase materials through less than savory channels."

"I don't think that will be a problem. Two things will be needed from you."

"Should I take notes?"

Driscoll ignored the sarcasm. "First, as I said, if I put up private money, there will have to be congressional involvement. This will be a national acquisition. I'll be putting up the money in the first place—but the final purchasing must be done by the government."

Driscoll waited for a response. Receiving none, he continued: "Second, I'll expect a tangible expression of public recognition from Congress and LC."

"In the form of?"

"As far as LC is concerned, a research center bearing my name within the Hispanic and Portuguese division. And you'd have to accept my appraisal of the material—and, as before, give me a letter saying so, with a generous valuation on what I provided with my . . . shall we say, down payment."

"That would not be my decision to make unilaterally, David. Our Congressional overseers."

"Over whom you have considerable influence."

"And Congress itself?"

"Acknowledgment of my contribution to having secured the diaries and map for the American people."

"Which you would certainly have earned."

"I've already incurred considerable expenses."

"That's to be expected."

"And I happily incur them. My reimbursement will come from having been instrumental in seeing a preeminent institution of learning become the keeper of such monumentally important documents as created by Las Casas during his journeys with Columbus. The diaries are all about having discovered *us,* Cale. Now, we've discovered them. They belong in the Library of Congress, not in some private collection."

"I agree, of course."

"Should I go forward?" Driscoll asked.

"Yes."

"Good. I'm flying home after lunch. I see you have one of the star crusading TV journalists, Ms. Huston, to contend with."

Broadhurst laughed. "Our public affairs people are keeping her in check."

"Michele Paul. His murder still a mystery?"

"Yes."

"It's my understanding that he was reclusive in his work."

"Reclusive and exclusive. He tended to work alone."

"We had met. Has his apartment been examined for any Las Casas or other materials he might have had there?"

"Yes. By Consuela Martinez—she's our Hispanic division chief—Consuela and a writer named Annabel Reed-Smith were there yesterday. They brought some files back with them to the library. A truck and crew are returning today to pick up everything else."

"Annabel Reed-Smith? She has a gallery here in Washington."

"Exactly. She's spending a few months at LC researching a Las Casas article for *Civilization.*"

"I met her once or twice. Beautiful woman, as I recall."

"Very attractive. And knowledgeable. Her husband, Mackensie, and I are friends. Tennis partners."

Driscoll stood and went to the window. Broadhurst followed. They looked down on Pennsylvania Avenue.

"I trust you know how appreciative I am of what you're attempting to do, David."

Driscoll replied without looking at Broadhurst, "It's the least I can do for my country."

On his way out, Broadhurst paused again in the Willard's lobby to soak up a little of its genteel ambiance before returning to the reality of the Library of Congress and murder. He glanced around for friends. Ayn Rand would have winced at Driscoll's parting comment, he thought. Driscoll wasn't doing this for his country. He was doing it to satisfy his own needs, which was fine, Broadhurst knew, continuing to think of Rand, the philosopher and novelist, who believed no one ever did anything that wasn't self-serving, and that good things happened because of self-interest. Driscoll was like any big contributor to a church or synagogue, Broadhurst mused. After a while, he begins to think he owns the place—and later to confuse himself with God. Oh, yes, and he wants to get a receipt for the maximum valuation of his contributions, to smooth the way for deductions with the IRS. I wonder when he and Michele Paul met? Probably at one or another of our social functions. Whatever

Driscoll's motives, a wonderful thing could result, for the Library of Congress and for the American people.

And for me, he silently admitted.

22 Once the two private detectives had put Munsch in the front passenger seat of their car, he realized there was nothing he could do but go along with them, at least for the moment. His mind raced: Maybe they'd let him use a public restroom, or he could pretend to be carsick. Maybe he could talk them out of whatever it was they intended to do with him. Maybe . . . He was tired and confused. If that whore hadn't taken his money; if Garraga hadn't shot the fat security guard . . . Once I get to Cuba—*if* I get to Cuba—things will be different. I'll start doing business in the daylight and . . .

"Comfortable, Warren?" the American PI asked from behind the wheel, sounding as though he didn't care what the answer was.

"Yeah, I'm comfortable," he said, glancing over his shoulder at the Mexican sitting behind him. "Where are we going?"

"You ask one more time where we're going, Warren, and we're going to have to do something to shut you up."

"Pardon me for living. I like to know where I'm going, that's all. Make plans, you know?" The bravado in his voice wasn't matched by the tremors in his stomach.

They slowly lurched through the sluggish traffic of Mexico City before breaking free on a short run of open road leading to the pretty, leafy suburb of Coyoacán. The driver slowed as he passed the Leon Trotsky Museum, then turned onto a road flanked by stately colonial homes. He pulled into a circular driveway in front of a two-story house whose entire front was covered with indigo and terra-cotta tiles. Munsch had valiantly tried to keep his emotions in check during the ride, his nonstop questions and wise-guy chatter his outlet. But now that they'd evidently reached their destination, the dread that consumed him came to the surface. He turned to the driver and held out his hands, palms up, eyes bulging with fear. "Look," he said in a faltering voice, "I don't know you guys and I don't want to know you. All I want to do is get out 'a Mexico and get to Cuba. I don't know what this client of yours is paying you, but I'll do better."

The American PI laughed. "That so, Warren? You're a rich guy, huh?"

"No, I'm not rich, but I've got plans, b-i-g plans. Once I get to Cuba there'll be plenty of scores, believe me. I'll cut you in, give you half."

"Just half?"

"You want more? You got it! So let's just get out of here and go to the airport. Stake me a ticket to Cuba and believe me, you guys will see more money than—"

The driver opened his door.

"Please," Munsch said.

Both detectives left the car and held open the front passenger door for Munsch. He stepped out unsteadily, turned and reached for his overnight bag that had been on the floor beneath his feet. The Mexican roughly pulled him erect.

"You won't need that," the American said.

The detectives each grabbed an arm and

led Munsch toward the front door. But before reaching it, they veered left and came around the side of the house to a rear garden enclosed by a high, fortresslike wall covered with vines bearing yellow and pink blossoms. Beyond the wall, the volcanos of the region rose majestically into a cobalt-blue sky.

Munsch's attention shifted to a corner of the expansive brick patio where a man sat at a white wrought-iron table. He appeared to be going through a stack of mail and didn't acknowledge the trio's arrival until they approached within a dozen feet. He slowly looked up, smiled, and with a wave suggested Munsch join him. Munsch glanced at his two captors; the American nodded for him to do what he'd been told. Munsch sat heavily, his chin tucked into his breastbone, his eyes taking in the man at the table through the top of his head.

Munsch judged him to be in his sixties, maybe seventy. He was slender; he wore pale yellow linen slacks and a shirt-jacket to match. He was bald, his head obviously shaved. Small, tortoise-rimmed glasses perched at the tip of an aquiline nose.

"Thank you for taking the time to join me," he said, his English bearing a trace of Spanish ancestry, the smile remaining on his lips.

"It's not like I had a choice—with all due respect," Munsch said.

"No, I see that you didn't."

He turned to the detectives, who'd remained standing a few feet away, and said in Spanish, "Why don't you gentlemen wait in the car. We won't be long."

It occurred to Munsch as they left that this might be a good chance to escape. The problem was, he realized, he'd never get over the wall, and the only apparent route would take him back around the house to where the two muscles waited. Maybe I can make a deal with this guy, he thought. Seems nice enough.

"I have a few questions to ask you, Mr. Munsch."

"Yeah? Okay. I didn't catch your name."

"My name doesn't matter. What happened in Miami?"

"In Miami? What 'a you mean?"

"We can make this little meeting short and painless, or we can make it long and painful. Miami. The painting you stole with your colleagues. What happened to the security guard?"

Munsch exhaled and sat back. Was this some sort of cop?

"Why was he killed?" the man asked. "You weren't supposed to kill anyone."

"It wasn't me. It was Garraga."

"Garraga?"

"This hot-headed Cuban I brought on the job. Dumb bastard. Drinks too much. The guard comes up on us as we're leaving and thinks he's a hero. Garraga shot him. We could have taken the guy. There were three of us. He didn't have no gun. But Garraga pulls a piece and shoots the guy. I was really mad, believe me I was. Felt like shooting Garraga myself. But I had nothing to do with it."

The man at the table listened impassively, an occasional nod his only response.

"I brought the painting out to L.A. like I was supposed to do, handed it over to some guy who calls himself John Smith, if you like that one. Kind of a big guy with a red beard, wore a white jacket and some big floppy straw hat, like a woman wears. I give him the painting, he gives me the money, and I come to Mexico. I was supposed to go to Cuba but I got mugged, all my money gone."

"A sad tale."

"Tell me about it. Look, Mister Whatever Your Name Is, I had nothing to do with that guard getting whacked. Nothing! Zippo! Nada! All I want to do is get to Cuba and forget it ever happened. You seem like a reasonable gentleman. Stake me to a plane ticket and you'll never hear from me again—except, of course, I'll pay you back as soon as I make a score there. Pay you back in spades."

"This man you gave the painting to, with the red beard and white jacket. Would you recognize him again if you were introduced to him?"

"Sure. How do you forget a character like that? Know him anywhere, spot him in a crowd."

The man stood: "Would you excuse me for a few minutes?" He disappeared through a door into the house.

Munsch couldn't believe he was now alone. Again, he considered attempting to leave but instinct told him to stay put. Maybe that's what they wanted, for him to make a break for it. The older guy at the table seemed receptive to what he'd suggested. Wouldn't even have to be a first-class ticket, although he preferred that. He'd answered his questions. He kept nodding so I must have given the right answers. Just sit tight, he told himself, glancing at the pile of mail on the table. Two envelopes visible to him were addressed to Señor Emilio Sebastian. *At least I know who he is. Just wait it out. Things are looking up.*

Inside the house, Emilio Sebastian sat behind an inlaid leather desk in a large study filled with Hispanic and Portuguese art and artifacts. He'd been on a call placed to the States for the past two minutes. He hung up, went to the front door, and summoned the two men from where they sat in the car. After whispering something to the Mexican, he returned to his study and placed a call to AeroMexico, wrote down what the reservations agent told him, then opened a safe, removed three thousand dollars in American currency, placed it in a number-ten envelope, and returned to the patio, where Munsch still sat at the table.

"Here," Sebastian said, handing the envelope to Munsch.

"What's this?" Munsch asked.

"Money for your trip to Cuba and for your time this morning."

Munsch hurriedly counted the envelope's contents. "Gee, I didn't expect this much, Mr. Sebastian," he said, now wishing there was more to replace what he'd brought with him from L.A.

"There is a flight leaving Mexico City for Havana at seven this evening. I have reserved a seat on it for you."

"That is really nice of you, sir—Mr. Sebastian. I really appreciate it." Munsch stood. "I won't forget this. You can count on that."

"My pleasure, Mr. Munsch. Have a safe and pleasant trip. The two gentlemen who were good enough to bring you here will take you to the airport."

"Okay." Munsch punched the air. "All right! Thanks again."

"Adios."

"Yeah, adios. You watch TV here?"

"Yes. The news mostly."

"Great. Have you picked up on anything about me being in Mexico?"

"No."

"I mean, the local cops aren't looking for me because that drunken idiot Garraga shot that guard?"

"Not that I'm aware of, Mr. Munsch."

"Then my passport should be good, huh?"

"I don't think you'll have any trouble."

"See ya."

Munsch walked with a swagger to the car, where the detectives stood leaning against the Ford.

"Everything all right, Warren?" the American asked.

"Oh, yeah, better than all right. I don't get it, you picking me up like you did, threaten to shoot me, crap like that, then bring me to this Sebastian guy—nice man—who sends me on my way to Cuba." He did a little shuffle to indicate dancing to a Latin rhythm.

"Well," said the American, "you might as well get in. We'll take you to the airport."

"That's right, only my plane doesn't leave until seven. I'd like some lunch."

"We'll drop you some place. You can take a cab after that."

"No, I mean let's have lunch together. My treat."

The PIs looked at each other and smiled, then broke into laughter.

"What's so funny?" Munsch asked.

"You, Warren. You're a funny guy. You're okay."

They ate Mexican food at a roadside restaurant on the highway leading to the shiny new Aeropuerto Internacional Benito Juárez. Munsch talked incessantly during the meal about the Cuban women he would make love to, the businesses he intended to start in Havana, his intention to make friends with Fidel Castro and maybe even end up as some kind of an unofficial advisor to the dictator. His table companions listened with bemused interest, occasionally egging him on to become even more expansive with his dreams and aspirations. Multiple glasses of Mexican beer helped fuel his gregariousness.

They left the cantina at two-thirty, got in the car, and headed for the airport.

"I still got time to kill," Munsch said as they approached the long access road.

"There's plenty of bars and restaurants inside," the Mexican said.

"Too public," Munsch said. "What 'a you say we hit another joint along the road here, have a few more pops?"

"Sorry, Warren, but we're running late for an appointment."

"Whatever you say."

The American suddenly pulled off the road onto a dirt shoulder. "Here's where you get out," he said.

"What 'a you mean?"

"We've got orders not to go into the airport with you."

"Orders? What kind 'a orders?"

"Just get out, Warren. It's not a long walk, take you, what, maybe ten minutes. Walk off that big lunch."

"This is nuts," Munsch said, feeling light-headed from the beer. "I don't feel like a walk."

The American looked Munsch in the eye and said, "Warren, you are one lucky son of a bitch. Don't mess it up for yourself. Just get out here and walk up the road. Enjoy a few more beers, get on your plane, and head for Cuba and all those wild women you're planning to screw. Out! It's been a real pleasure meeting you."

Grumbling, Munsch exited the Ford and was handed his overnight bag.

"You take care, Warren," the American said, slipping the car into gear and roaring away, leaving Munsch coughing in a cloud of yellow dust.

He looked down the road toward the airport, glimmering a half mile away like a desert mirage. He pulled a handkerchief from his pocket and wiped perspiration from his face and neck. Swearing at the detectives who'd refused to drive him to the terminal, he started walking in the direction of the mirage. As he did, two marked patrol cars carrying uniformed Mexican *federales* that had been parked out of sight behind a building across the highway came to where the airport access road bisected the highway and stopped. As the cars' occupants argued about something, a taxi, a vacant green Volkswagen bug, turned off the highway and headed for the airport. Munsch heard it approaching, stopped, and waved at the driver, who came to an erratic stop.

"The airport," Munsch said, opening the passenger door and wedging his bulk into the seat, which was covered with newspapers and a greasy brown bag. The driver complained in Spanish about the short duration of the fare as he shifted into first gear and started moving. The police also went into action, their vehicles' drivers flooring their accelerators in pursuit of the cab. The taxi driver saw them in his rearview mirror, excitedly said something, and pulled to a stop at the side of the road. The patrol cars slid to a stop, one blocking the road in front of the taxi, the other behind it. The cab driver opened his door and jumped out, hands held high. The police ignored him and slowly approached the Volks, handguns drawn and trained on it.

Munsch didn't know what to do.

"Out! Out!" an officer commanded.

"Okay, okay," Munsch said, opening his door and coming out of the Volks. He raised his hands, skirted the front of the taxi, and forced his widest smile. "What's the problem, amigos?" he asked. "Take it easy. I'm a friend, an amigo, *sí?*" He wished he spoke Spanish.

Two officers approached, their handguns aimed at Munsch's head. One pushed him so that he faced the taxi, then gave him another shove so that his hands rested on its sloping hood. They patted him down.

Munsch slowly straightened and turned to face them. "Okay, amigos, I get it. I understand the drill." He started to reach for his wallet but the motion caused the officers to snap commands and wave their weapons.

"Money," Munsch said. "What 'a you call it? *Dinero! Mucho dinero!*" He carefully removed his wallet from his rear pants pocket and held it out for them to see. His mind raced. He'd give them a thousand and keep two. A thousand dollars would buy anybody in Mexico, he reasoned. Just don't take it all, he silently prayed. Leave me enough for the plane ticket.

He pulled out what felt like a third of the bills and waved them in the air, grinning as he did. He shoved them at the officer standing closest to him. "For you, amigo. Take it, share it with your friends."

Another officer came up behind and grabbed the wallet from Munsch's hand.

"Hey, come on, let's not be greedy, huh?" Munsch said.

The rest of the bills were removed from the wallet and placed in the cop's shirt pocket.

Munsch was bombarded with conflicting thoughts. He didn't want to lose all his money. At the same time, he was relieved that he was simply being held up, Mexican style, and not being arrested for the Miami heist and murder.

He picked the cop who looked as though he might be most amenable to a plea and tried to get across that he needed money for an airline ticket, that he would take the cop's name and address and send him more money from

Cuba, that he understood they didn't make much money and needed to rip off gringos— dumb tourists—and that he wouldn't report it to anybody.

"Just give me back five hundred bucks, huh? That's all, just five hundred. How many pesos is that? I'll—"

The officers started laughing as they backed away and stood by their cars. One told the taxi driver to turn around and leave, while another motioned for Munsch to start walking toward the airport. Sadly realizing he wasn't about to receive a refund, Munsch told himself to get away from them as quickly as possible. At least he wasn't being arrested. Get to the airport and maybe find somebody to scam. He thought about his overnight bag but saw it disappearing with the taxi as it sped to the main highway.

He walked slowly at first, looking over his shoulder to be sure he was doing what they wanted him to do. Sweat poured down his face and his breath came hard as he increased his pace, almost running now, stumbling, wanting to cry—why me?—get to the airport and—

The shots crackled from six weapons, a

barrage of bullets tearing into his back and buttocks, sending him pitching forward face-first onto the hard blacktop. But his face didn't hurt. Nothing hurt anymore.

23 Annabel hadn't had a good night's sleep. The pain in Mac's knee had kept him awake, causing him to struggle in search of a comfortable position.

"You should have the surgery," she told him at breakfast. "These things are so easily fixed these days."

He just looked at her. She knew not to pursue it, at least not again that day. He would have surgery only when he was ready for it.

After wincing herself as she watched him limp out of the house to go teach a class at GW, she took a cab to the library. Soon, she and Consuela stood in the deep recesses of the division's stacks. Steel shelving held dozens of cardboard file transfer boxes with BITTEMAN written on them.

"Did anyone go through these after Bitteman disappeared?" Annabel asked the division chief.

"Yes, but that was before I got here. When you said you wanted to look at the Bitteman materials, I pulled out the report that had been written by the people who'd originally examined the boxes. They broke everything down into rough categories, which is helpful. But like so much material in LC, it gets a quick once-over when it arrives and then sits for years until someone decides to take a second look."

"Impossible to analyze it all," Annabel said. "There's so much."

"Twenty million items in storage waiting to be cataloged, and it keeps pouring in. Anyway, Annabel, here's the Bitteman stuff. Help yourself."

"These are the categories they broke it down into?" Annabel asked, pointing to smaller lettering on each of the boxes.

"Yes."

"I don't see—oh, here's a box marked 'Las Casas.' "

"Here's another," Consuela said. "The people who went through them noted that there was nothing especially new and interesting in Bitteman's Las Casas papers, which I found surprising."

"How so?"

"Las Casas was one focus of his professional life. Las Casas did write a book or more after the voyages with Columbus but there was nothing really definitive about any diary and no mention of a map. Everyone assumed all the work Bitteman had put in on the subject would have resulted in more revelations. But I suppose we sometimes expect too much of our researchers. You can spend a lifetime delving into a narrow subject and still come up empty."

"Well," said Annabel, "I'll take a look anyway, although I'm beginning to feel empty."

"I'm pulling together a team to go through Michele Paul's files," Consuela said. "Dr. Broadhurst asked me to do it. Love to have you join us."

"I'd like that," said Annabel. "Anything bearing on Las Casas could be helpful for my article. When are you starting?"

"This morning. Dolores Marwede will be helping, but it's a daunting task for two people."

"Count me in, after I take a look at these."

Annabel spent the morning bringing the boxes labeled BITTEMAN—LAS CASAS to her work space on the upper gallery and going through their contents with more care. The people who'd originally skimmed the materials had been right as far as she could tell by her examination. The boxes were filled with articles written about the Spanish companion to the famous explorer and folder after folder of Bitteman's notes on books and other researchers' conclusions. But there seemed to be nothing of Bitteman's original findings and thoughts. You'd think that a man like him, she mused, devoting almost all of his professional life to one man and one subject, would have come up with something more. But there was good stuff about Las Casas as a writer and as a sailor.

She came down to the main reading room, where Consuela and Dolores had set themselves up at a table in a secluded corner.

"Find anything?" Consuela asked.

"Not much," Annabel said, "although I went through it awfully fast. How's this going?"

"Nothing exciting so far," Consuela said. "A few rare books he took and never returned."

Dolores looked up at Annabel. "You really

didn't expect to find anything useful in John Bitteman's work, did you?"

Annabel shrugged and joined them at the table. "I didn't know him, of course, but I heard he was a dedicated researcher."

Dolores smirked. "John Bitteman was a fraud," she said, continuing to pull papers from one of the boxes on the table. "He made his reputation as a writer and speaker on Hispanic subjects, using other people's original work as a basis for his own. I don't think he had an original idea in his head."

"You knew him pretty well?" Annabel asked, absently picking up papers and glancing at them.

"We worked together," Dolores said.

"Lucianne Huston was here this morning," Consuela said. "She's really trying to make a connection between Bitteman's disappearance and Michele's murder."

"I never took her for a tabloid-TV type," Dolores said.

"It's the Columbus celebration coming up that's driving it, I think," said Consuela. "Nothing like a juicy contemporary murder to bring history alive." To Annabel: "She wanted to talk with you. I told her you were hibernating, but that you'd get hold of her through Public Affairs this afternoon."

"Thanks. Anyone hungry?"

"I am," said Consuela. "Dolores?"

"I brought something from home."

An hour later, as Annabel and Consuela passed through the European reading room on their way back from lunch, Lucianne Huston intercepted them.

"How's it going?" Annabel asked.

"Slow. Got a minute?"

"Sure."

"Got an hour?"

"No."

Consuela said, "Take all the time you need, Annie. Dolores and I will be there whenever you get back."

At Lucianne's suggestion, she and Annabel left the building and sat on a semicircular concrete bench on East Capitol Street, directly across from the Supreme Court. The smell of rain was in the air.

"You went to Michele Paul's apartment to go through his files," Lucianne said.

"That's right."

"Nice apartment." It wasn't a question.

"I take it you've been there," Annabel said.

"This morning. Got the super to let me in. Paul lived pretty well. Fancy apartment, a boat, closets full of expensive clothes."

"He lived nicely, but extravagantly?"

"You know what he was paid?"

"No."

"Seventy-five thousand a year. He was a GS-Fourteen with over twenty years."

"Not a fortune, but enough to carry his apartment, I'd think."

"And build up a savings account of more than three hundred thousand?"

Annabel had been watching one of LC's police officers yell at a pedestrian for jay-walking. Now, she turned to Lucianne and asked, "How do you know that?"

"I have a friend in the police department here."

"You seem to have friends everywhere."

"In this business, you're only as good as your little black book. The police are running down his finances. Routine in a murder investigation. They traced an account to New York. That's where he had most of the money."

"Did it ever occur to you that someone in his family might have left it to him?"

"If so, that someone died just before Paul

did. He deposited a check for a hundred thousand in the New York account the day before he was killed."

"Who was the check from?"

"They're tracing that now. What do you think of John Vogler?"

"A nice enough man. I don't know him. I've only had one conversation with him."

"I think he's a fruitcake."

Annabel laughed. "I haven't heard that term in a while. Why do you say it?"

"Just my reaction. The police are looking hard at him as a suspect."

Annabel nodded. "That's understandable, considering his past relationship with Michele Paul. He's evidently a considerable scholar. I hear nothing but good things about him; he's a little eccentric, maybe."

"They haven't written off your buddy Dr. Martinez, either."

"Preposterous! No one would ever think Consuela is capable of murder. Why are you telling me this?"

Lucianne ran her tongue over her lips, smiled, and said, "Because I think we have a common failing."

"And what is that?"

"We're both always looking for something.

I wanted no part of this story when my boss assigned it to me. It was based on a rumor that these so-called diaries and a map might be discovered and offered for sale through some kooky underground rare books network. And there was that theft of a painting in Miami and the guard who died. But when I got here and tried to get some decent material on the diaries, I came up empty, except for what little you told me on camera. Then, the leading scholar on the subject gets his head bashed in, and soon I learn another leading Las Casas scholar disappeared under mysterious circumstances eight years ago, probably murder. The most recent victim, the charming Dr. Paul, is hated by half the world, at least the half who knew him. And then, Annabel . . ."

"And then *what*?"

"And then you ask me yesterday about the painting that was stolen in Miami. Why?"

"Why did I ask?"

"Uh huh."

"Because—because—look, Lucianne, I know you have a job to do, a story to report. I respect that. You say we're both looking for something. You're right. You're looking for your story, and I'm looking for material on which to base a magazine article. That hardly makes us soul mates."

"Oh, I think it does, Annabel. I think you're the sort of person who can't resist digging into a murder."

"Why would you say that?"

"Who you are, that's why. Former matrimonial attorney, and a damn good one, I hear, married to one of D.C.'s top criminal defense attorneys. Or 'former,' as he says. You ended up helping track down a precious Caravaggio painting stolen a few years back from the National Gallery. And you and your husband, who has a bad knee but still cooks for you—lucky you—got up to your necks in a series of murders last year at the Watergate right after you moved in. I can go on."

"I should be flattered that you have so much interest in me and my husband. I'm not."

"Just routine, that's all. The more I know about the players, the better chance I have of coming up with the story. Besides, you seem wired in pretty solid with everybody at the library. The top guy, Broadhurst, and your husband play tennis together, at least when your hubby's knee doesn't hurt. You get invited to Broadhurst's private little cocktail parties. Same with Consuela Martinez, who picks you to help go through Michele Paul's apartment. What have you learned about John Bitteman?"

"Probably not nearly as much as you have," Annabel said, standing and straightening her skirt. "I have to get back inside. I'm helping—"

"Helping go through Michele Paul's files."

"That's right."

"Any chance of filling me in on what you find?"

Annabel couldn't help but smile. Despite Lucianne Huston's aggressive personality, bordering on offensive, she liked her.

"I might," she said.

They walked to the corner.

"I have to go back," Lucianne said. "Free for dinner?"

"Yes, but—"

"Know what I'm missing?"

"What?"

"A home-cooked meal. Invite me for one of your husband's dinners."

Annabel sustained her smile. "Sure," she said. "I'll call and see if he's up to it. I'll leave a message for you with the PA office. Allergic to anything?"

"People who get in the way of a good story. Oh, and anchovies. Can't stand anchovies."

24 Annabel spent the rest of the afternoon helping Consuela and Dolores go through the boxes from Michele Paul's apartment. They worked quietly for hours, the only intrusion an occasional comment concerning something found in the boxes or question about a file.

During a break, Annabel asked, "Did either of you read about an art theft in Miami about a week or so ago?"

"No," Dolores said.

"A painting by an artist named Fernando Reyes was stolen from a small museum there. It depicted Columbus giving King

Fernando and Queen Isabel his Book of Privileges."

Consuela laughed softly. "Not a very creative choice of subjects." She asked Dolores, "How many paintings do you think have been done of that scene?"

Dolores shrugged. "A hundred? Why do you ask, Annabel?"

"When Consuela and I were going through material at Michele's apartment, I ran across a file devoted to this artist, Reyes. I wondered why Michele Paul would have such interest in him. Reyes was never a major artist and worked long after Columbus's time."

"Then the real question is, why would someone want to steal one of his paintings?" Consuela asked.

"Exactly," said Annabel, "unless . . ."

The other two looked at her.

"Unless there was something else to steal besides the painting. Something else in the painting, or that the painting led to."

"Like what?"

"I have no idea. Just thinking out loud." She looked up at the clock. "It's five. Lucianne Huston is coming tonight for dinner. I told Mac I'd do the shopping on my way home."

"You and Huston are friends?" Dolores asked.

"No," Annabel said, standing and stretching against a kink in her back, "but she sort of invited herself. I like her."

"Careful what you say," Consuela said lightly. "Your dessert'll end up on the evening news."

"I have the feeling that could happen no matter what I say. Sorry to run out on you. See you both tomorrow."

". . . we don't often have dessert," Mac Smith said as he, Annabel, and Lucianne sat at the dining room table, "usually only when we have guests."

"I'm glad I prompted you to have it tonight," Lucianne said. "This mocha cake is wonderful."

"From our own bakery right here in the Watergate," Annabel said. "More coffee?"

It had been a pleasant evening. Mac and Annabel had expected the highly charged journalist to dominate the conversation, but that wasn't the case. She was quiet and unassuming, showing intense interest in her host and hostess's lives and careers, and the story of how they met and conducted their courtship. But she did have, of course, her own stories to tell, especially about some of the most harrowing assignments she'd been on around the globe.

They took their second cups of coffee in the living room, fortified by small snifters of brandy. Lucianne went to the sliding glass doors leading to the terrace and said, "Beautiful view."

Mac opened the doors and they stood outside looking down at the Potomac. The air was clean from an hour of rain earlier.

"How's *your* investigation of the murder going, Lucianne?" Mac asked.

"Better, it seems, than the police's."

"I'd love to hear about it," he said. "I'm always interested in a murder investigation."

"Like quitting smoking but still wanting one years later?"

"Something like that."

"Mind if I smoke? I've been on my good behavior all evening."

"If it isn't too chilly out here."

"I'm comfortable."

"I'll get a sweater," Annabel said, going inside. When she returned, Mac had brought three fresh glasses of brandy to the terrace and arranged chairs around a small green metal table.

"I told Mac about our conversation this afternoon," Annabel said, "that you feel wanting to know things is something we have in common. I'm not sure I agree with you about me, that I have some genetic need to delve into murder, but then again, maybe I do. So, let's discuss the murder of Michele Paul and see what we can teach each other."

"Okay," Lucianne said, lighting her second cigarette, "what about this artist, Reyes?"

Mac and Annabel glanced at each other before Annabel said, "Michele Paul seemed to have an inordinate interest in him."

"Why do you think that is?"

"I don't have an answer for that," said Annabel.

"What do you base it on?"

"Papers in his apartment. He did a fairly exhaustive study of the artist."

"Interesting," Lucianne said. "I spoke with a contact I have in the Miami PD this afternoon."

"Lucianne knows a few people, Mac," Annabel said, a smile in her voice.

"Doesn't surprise me," said Mac. "What did your Miami source have to say?"

"This conversation stays out here on this lovely terrace," Lucianne said. "I'd hate to have something I've uncovered end up on somebody else's newscast."

"No guarantees," Mac said. "If you want to make sure no one hears it from us, don't tell us. That's a rule I learned years ago when I was still trusting prosecutors."

Lucianne laughed. "Fair enough. My guy in Miami tells me that the person behind the art heist is named Warren Munsch, a small-time loser with a minor league rap sheet. Mr. Munsch, it seems, took the painting to Los Angeles, then headed for Mexico City. They know that because he booked flights using his own name. No master terrorist he."

"Where did he go from there?" Annabel asked.

"They lost track of him. The original information came through a Mexican source, some private detective there who operates as an informer for stateside police departments. According to this source, Munsch went to Mexico City with the intention of getting on a plane to Cuba. He's got a lot to run from. A security guard was killed during that theft."

"Let me get this straight," Mac said. "Munsch steals a painting by a second-rate artist, kills a guard in the process, and takes the painting to California. I assume he stole it on someone else's instructions."

"I doubt if he has his own art collection," Lucianne said, lighting up again. The small ashtray was filling rapidly.

"No, I'm sure he doesn't," said Mac. "How much was the painting worth?"

"Not much," Lucianne answered. "The guy who runs the museum said it was used more to set a background scene, not displayed as a work of art."

Mac looked at his wife. "You made a comment when we were preparing dinner, Annie, that maybe there was something else stolen along with the painting, something more valuable."

"Like what?" Lucianne asked. Then, she answered herself. "Like something hidden in the painting. Or behind the painting? Like a map?"

"Las Casas's so-called map?" Mac added.

"Can you hide something like a map *behind* a painting?" Lucianne asked.

"Sure," Annabel said. "I mean, I don't know the techniques used, but stories come out now and then about art conservationists discovering a valuable painting behind a less valuable one."

"And you say Michele Paul had been researching this artist, Reyes?" Lucianne said.

"Yes."

"More brandy?" Mac asked. When he returned from the small bar in the living room, Annabel was in the process of asking her own questions.

"You told me that you were sent on this assignment to the Library of Congress based upon some rumor that big money was being offered for the Las Casas materials through the rare books underground."

"That's right."

"Have you learned any more about that? When? Where? By whom?"

The journalist sipped her brandy.

"We've been open with you," Annabel said.

"I know, and I appreciate it. Ever hear of a part-time, rich collector of rare books and manuscripts named David Driscoll, the investment guru?"

"Sure," Annabel said. "He's one of the world's foremost collectors of Hispanic documents and artifacts. I've met him. In fact, I once tried to buy a Mayan mask from him that he'd put up for sale. I don't think he really wanted to sell it because he asked ten times what it was worth."

"He lives in L.A., doesn't he?" Mac said.

"That's right," Lucianne said.

"David Driscoll is also one of the Library of Congress's leading benefactors," Annabel said. "Why did you ask about him?"

"My boss back in Miami told me it's Driscoll who's spreading money around in search of Las Casas. Driscoll gets on to some obscure sources—and sometimes dubious stuff. Early on in his collecting career, he bought some of that dubious material but in recent years, maybe the last ten or so, his acquisitions and donations check out, or at least turn out to be worth quite a lot. It's peculiar, a guy who traffics in the shade but who comes up with previously unknown or lesser work that turns out to be very valuable. I called his house in L.A. Whoever answered said he's out of town."

"He's in town—this one," Annabel said.

"I didn't know that," Lucianne said. "I'd like to interview him."

"He was in for a morning meeting with Dr. Broadhurst. At least that's the scuttlebutt. I think he went back to California. Shall I put on another cup of coffee?"

"Not for me, thanks," Lucianne said, standing. "I'd better get back to the hotel. This has been great. You're a good cook, Mac."

"Thanks. I muddle through."

Annabel walked Lucianne to the elevator.

"Do me a favor?" Lucianne said after pushing the Down button.

"If I can."

"Keep being my eyes and ears inside the library. See what this David Driscoll and Broadhurst met about. Let me see the material Michele Paul had on Reyes. Tell me if—"

"Thanks for coming to dinner," Annabel said. "We enjoyed having you."

The elevator arrived and the doors slid open.

Lucianne said good night, stepped inside, and the doors closed.

Mac was cleaning the kitchen.

"She wants me to be her on-site spy at LC," Annabel said.

"You said no, of course."

"I said we enjoyed having her for dinner. What did you think of the globe-trotting Ms. Huston?"

"I liked her, like her style."

"She's certainly attractive."

"That, too."

"How's your knee?"

"Lousy. I'm calling Giles in the morning, make another appointment to discuss options."

"Good," Annabel said, knowing the only viable option was surgery.

"Mac."

"Yeah?"

"Were you flirting with her tonight?"

"Of course not. I don't flirt with other women."

"You laughed louder and longer than her stories warranted. I mean, it's okay as long as it's just flirting."

"I'm an old man with bad knees. My flirting days are over."

She turned him from the sink and wrapped her arms around him, gave him a lingering kiss. "I always wonder whether you're flirting when a woman as attractive as Lucianne Huston is around. Not insecurity. It's a compliment—to a handsome husband."

"Glad you feel that way. About being handsome, not about me flirting."

"I'll finish up. You take Rufus out and get back here quick."

"Am I being seduced?"

"Uh huh. You know I've always had a thing for old men with bad knees."

Annabel came to the conclusion after the dinner with Lucianne Huston: She'd spent enough time thinking about Michele Paul's murder. It wasn't her business despite what Lucianne had claimed, that they were kindred spirits in search of an answer. Not true, Annabel told Mac while cleaning up the kitchen: "I can see two months slipping by with me not even close to having the research I need for the piece."

"Good for you," he'd said. "Ms. Huston is paid to dig into murder, you're not."

"Exactly."

And so the following morning, Annabel

went directly to her work space on the upper gallery and settled in for a day devoted to researching Bartolomé de Las Casas. She'd emptied her briefcase on the small desk and was about to compare material from two books published shortly after Columbus's second voyage to the New World when John Vogler called on the number Annabel had been assigned.

"Yes, Dr. Vogler?"

"I'm sorry to intrude on your work, Mrs. Reed-Smith," said the chief of Manuscripts, "but I urgently need to speak with you."

"Later, perhaps?" said Annabel. "I've fallen terribly far behind in my research and—"

"It will only take a few minutes. Please? It's very important to me."

"Now?"

"If it would be convenient for you."

"All right. Your office?"

"No, somewhere outside the library. There's a small bagel shop a block away on Pennsylvania Avenue. It's called Chesapeake Bagel, in a string of restaurants."

"I know where you mean." Annabel had noticed it when she had lunch with Dolores Marwede.

"I'll go there now," Vogler said.

Annabel considered taking another stab at postponing but decided she'd rather get it over with, whatever *it* was.

Vogler had wedged his considerable frame into a chair at a small table at the rear of the bakery. He bumped it as he stood, causing coffee from a full cup to spill over its sides. He was obviously agitated as he invited Annabel to sit: "Coffee? Tea? Would you like something to eat?"

"Thank you, no. I really have to get back. What is it you need to speak to me about?"

"Michele Paul's murder."

Remembering her resolve, she said, "I'm trying not to spend any more time thinking or talking about the murder, Dr. Vogler. It's getting in the way of my work."

"Oh, I can understand that," said Vogler, "and I agree. But this is terribly important to me. The police—they interrogated me for hours yesterday. It was brutal."

"I'm sorry to hear that, but they have a job to do."

He ignored what she'd said. "They're making so much of the confrontation I had with Michele and the business with Candy, my wife."

Annabel wasn't surprised.

"It's even worse than that," he said, leaning across the table and fixing her with pale blue, watery eyes. "Someone has told them—the police, I mean—that I was seen in Hispanic at the time the murder occurred."

Annabel's eyebrows went up. "Were you?"

"Of course not. You remember, I'm sure, when I told you I hadn't been there that night, went nowhere near it."

"I remember you telling me that," Annabel confirmed, not adding that having told *her* didn't mean anything. "Who told the police you were there?"

"I don't know. They wouldn't reveal the name to me, which I consider a breach of my Constitutional rights."

"Dr. Vogler," Annabel said, "I would love to help you but there's nothing I can do. Why are you telling *me* this?"

"You were there that night. You discovered the body. Was it you who—?"

"Was it me who told the police you were at the scene? It wasn't."

"Do you know who it might have been?"

Annabel shook her head.

"Would you try and find out for me?"

"I—no, I'm afraid that isn't my responsibility. Look, Dr. Vogler—"

"John."

"John, I'm certain that if what you told the police was completely truthful—and I'm sure it was—you have nothing to worry about. Now, excuse me. I really have to go."

He stood, again threatening to tip over the table. "Of course," he said, offering his hand. "You've been very gracious taking time from your busy schedule."

"Think nothing of it."

"Mrs. Reed-Smith."

"Annabel."

"Yes, Annabel. If you do hear who might have told the police this lie about me, you will let me know?"

Annabel left without answering.

Her concentration impaired by Vogler's call and their meeting, Annabel walked back to LC with conviction, determined to shut the rest of the world out from her upper-gallery space for the rest of the day. She almost made it. As she passed Consuela's open office door, Lucianne Huston, who was on the phone, stretched the cord to reach the door and motioned for Annabel to join her. Annabel waved back and was about to continue on her way when Lucianne's words to whoever was on the other end of the call caused her to stay.

". . . can we get a statement from somebody in Mexico? Yes, someone who knows the details of how he was killed. There's got to be somebody who doesn't spout the official Mexican line, damn it. I may want to go there. . . . Of course I'll let you know. . . . Right. I'll check in later. Uh huh. Okay. All right, Bob."

"Hi," Annabel said when Lucianne hung up.

"Great dinner last night. Your husband's quite a guy."

"No debate."

"They found the man who pulled off the art theft and security guard killing in Miami. Masterminded it, you might say."

"Where did they find him?" Annabel asked.

"Just outside the Mexico City airport. When Mexican police tried to arrest him, he ran. They shot him."

"He's dead?"

"Very."

"How did you find out?" Annabel asked.

"My boss in Miami. The Miami cops were notified by the Mexicans."

She motioned for Annabel to join her in the office. Annabel stepped inside and Lucianne shut the door.

"You've taken over Consuela's office?" Annabel said.

"Anything to get away from my keepers in Public Affairs. Consuela offered. At least somebody around here makes sense."

"You're too hard on Joanne and her people, Lucianne. They're doing their job."

"And keeping me from doing mine. Want to know where that hundred thousand to Michele Paul came from?"

"I'd like to say no but go ahead."

"David Driscoll. Turns out he'd been sending checks to our Michele Paul for years."

"It's not a surprise, is it? I mean, your sources said it was Driscoll spreading money around in search of the Las Casas materials."

"But to Michele Paul? Paul worked for this library. If he was feeding Driscoll information about Las Casas, he violated his agreement with the Library of Congress—didn't he?"

"I don't know what agreement Paul might have had with LC."

"I do. He was an employee, paid by LC. His research belonged to LC, just like engineers inventing something on GE's time. What they come up with belongs to the company."

"You're *assuming* Paul was selling his research findings to Driscoll."

"What else did he have to sell?"

"Hmmm."

"Driscoll lives in L.A."

"And?"

"And this two-bit thief Munsch steals a painting with Columbus as its theme and heads to L.A. with it. Munsch was no art collector. He had to have stolen the painting at someone else's behest."

"That's what Mac said. David Driscoll?"

"Got any better ideas?"

"Do you know what I decided last night after you left our apartment, Lucianne?"

"That you wouldn't invite me back?"

"That I didn't want to spend another minute thinking about the murder."

"That'll teach you to invite a journalist for dinner."

Annabel nodded and smiled. "I think I'll stick to that decision, at least for the rest of the day."

"Okay, but remember what you promised, that you'd let me know if you pick up anything I can use about the murders."

"Murders, plural? Oh, John Bitteman. I didn't promise anything. But if some startling revelation jumps up and bites me, I'll pass it along, if I can."

"Can't ask for more. Best to Mac. See ya."

Returning to her work area, Annabel decided that she'd have to tell someone at the library about her conversation with Lucianne, and made up her mind to call Cale Broadhurst later in the day.

It was said that you could set your watch by Abraham Widlitz. The **26** seventy-two-year-old art restorer and conservator rigidly adhered to a schedule ingrained in him ever since emigrating to Hollywood from New York City in the late 1940s.

Like so many young men and women seeking fame and fortune in L.A., Widlitz carried with him a change of clothing and a talent, in his case a considerable skill at drawing. He landed work at Columbia Pictures, where he served an apprenticeship in the set design department for small pay, supplemented by the excitement of being close to the glamour of the burgeoning film industry and its famous players.

His technical skills were appreciated at the studio; he stayed there forty years, until someone in the increasingly youthful hierarchy decided he was too old to understand and contribute to modern films and sent him out to pasture with a decent pension and four decades of memories. His wife of thirty-six years, Sylvia, whom he'd met when she was a secretary in the set department, died four months after his forced retirement, leaving Widlitz to fend for himself, which he did quite nicely.

Unlike many widows and widowers, his routine didn't change following his mate's death. He just kept doing what he'd done for the past fifty years, up at five, a light breakfast, an hour devoted to the plants and flowers he and Sylvia took pleasure in cultivating, a walk to a neighborhood convenience store for the morning paper, a second cup of tea with honey while reading the news, a phone call to their only child, Philip, an orthodontist in Pittsburgh, then boarding an RTD bus for the ride downtown to where he had opened his small art restoration and conservation studio in El Pueblo de Los Angeles a year after leaving Columbia.

This morning, like all other mornings, he stopped at a bakery before entering his building to buy for his lunch one *churro,* a Mexican doughnut, and then on to a street vendor's *puesto* where he purchased a peeled mango and papaya.

Abraham Widlitz was a familiar figure in the lively, multiethnic neighborhood, although few knew him through conversation. Aside from never failing to extend pleasant greetings to others in the area, he kept to himself, seldom leaving his small studio until it was time to retrace his route home.

He went to work immediately in the outer room of the two-room studio on a small, damaged oil a customer had picked up in a thrift shop. The painting was of a garden and featured a frog in the lower left-hand corner; the client collected anything depicting frogs, including coffee mugs, jewelry, bric-a-brac, and pictures. A tree overhanging the frog had suffered water damage and Widlitz carefully repainted its leaves.

He completed the task by noon, and after consuming the fruit and doughnut went into the back room where he'd spread the Reyes painting on a large flat surface. He'd started work on it the previous day, going over every inch with a jeweler's loupe, through which he examined the pigments the artist had used, seeking visual evidence that the scene of Columbus kneeling before the king and queen might have been painted over another work of one sort or another. Heavy coats of varnish had been applied to the entire painting; Widlitz judged the most recent to be no older than fifty years, probably done when the painting was last put up for sale. He also noted that the original, finely woven canvas had been lined with an equally fine canvas with an aqueous adhesive.

He worked in one corner, carefully removing the varnish—he now realized there were at least three distinct and separate layers—until exposing what appeared to be two lines that were not part of the painting itself, unless, of course, they had been drawn by the artist while making initial sketches. If so, the lines evidently had not been incorporated in the finished work.

He extended the square until it became three inches by three inches. As he worked, he muttered to himself about the artist's crude brush work and clumsy rendering of the figures in the painting. Abe Widlitz realized years ago that he would never become an artist of note—dozens of classes at local colleges and studios convinced him of that. But he knew good art when he saw it, and this painting didn't qualify.

The task was tedious and tiring for the aging craftsman. Ordinarily, such a project would be attacked over many weeks. But Widlitz knew from previous experience that his client was not a patient man. He'd handled a number of projects for Driscoll, put off by his abrasive, demanding demeanor but appreciating how quickly and generously the multimillionaire paid for the work Widlitz performed on his behalf.

He continued using solvents to remove the varnish in the painting's corner until the area had been expanded to approximately two square feet. From what he could ascertain, the only material contained beneath Reyes's painting was, with few exceptions, preliminary pencil sketches of the scene.

At precisely five, he put away the materials he'd used that day and sat down at his desk to pay bills that had arrived in the mail that morning. At 5:45, he washed the few dishes he'd used, put on his jacket, adjusted the blinds on the windows, and prepared to depart the studio, leaving just enough time to catch the 6:02 bus.

He set the burglar alarm, opened the door, and came face-to-face with two men in suits and two uniformed officers from the LAPD.

"Abraham Widlitz?" one of the suits asked.

"Yes."

"We have a warrant to search these premises." He showed Widlitz a piece of paper and his badge.

"Search?" said Widlitz. "Why would you want to search my studio?"

"Excuse me." The man led his plainclothes partner inside and snapped on overhead lights. One of the cops in uniform escorted Widlitz back into the studio while the other officer remained in the hall.

"Please, would you explain to me why you are here?" Widlitz said, hands outstretched. "What are you looking for?"

"My partner and I are with the LAPD art squad, Mr. Widlitz. We've been told you sometimes turn your back on who really owns some of the paintings you work on."

"That is not true."

"If it's not, we'll find that out. In the meantime, why don't you just sit down and relax. If our information is wrong, maybe we'll see something we like and buy it from you. If our information is right, we can all go down to headquarters and have a little heart-to-heart about art and artists. How's that sound to you?"

"Am I allowed to make a phone call?"

"Your lawyer?"

"My son. He will know what to do."

"Sure. Call your boy." He surveyed the larger, outer room. "Lots of stuff here, Mr. Widlitz. Business must be good."

Widlitz didn't respond as he dialed the number in Pittsburgh with a hand that trembled in rhythm to his heartbeat.

"So, where are we?"

27　Detective Marcus Shorter took a bite of his burrito and washed it down with a sip of Coke. He and his partner, Frank Nastasi, had spent the morning in the old Librarian's office interviewing a dozen people from LC, including the two researchers who occupied work spaces adjacent to Michele Paul; Dolores Marwede for the second time; members of the public affairs department; General Counsel Mary Beth Mullin; the intern, Susan Gomara; and John Vogler for the third time. It was Nastasi's day to choose where to eat lunch, and he had opted for

Burrito Brothers, nestled in the string of inexpensive restaurants on Pennsylvania Avenue, a block from the library.

"Where are we?" Shorter repeated, pulling a pad from his jacket pocket on which he'd made notes that morning. "Let's see. Kelman made no bones about not liking the deceased, but he's got an alibi the night of the murder. I have a feeling it'll check out. Same with Ms. Warren." He laughed. "Another hour with her and we'd know everything we'd ever want to know about burying people."

"Go figure, a pretty little thing like her loving buried bodies. She admits she went out with Paul a few times—"

"Twice. For drinks."

"But no sex, right?"

"Right, and no alibi either, home alone all evening, but a call to her father in Denver around eight. We'll have her phone records this afternoon."

"Had a relationship with the guy, though," Nastasi said. "Maybe they did get it on and he failed the test, ticked her off."

Shorter shrugged and finished his burrito. Nastasi's was long gone.

"The intern—what's her name? Gomara?—cute kid. Said the guy verbally abused her but

I'm sure she didn't whack him in the head. Too sweet, and for real. I'm not sure she could even lift the weight that whacked Paul."

Shorter consulted his notes. "She was working in the main reading room until nine-thirty. Checks out."

Nastasi nodded. "Let's leave this burritoville before I eat another."

They paid and slowly walked back to the Jefferson Building, continuing to discuss the morning's interviews as they went.

"That Ms. Graves from Public Affairs is an impressive piece of work," Nastasi said, stopping to prop a foot on a bench to tie a shoelace that had come undone. "What 'a you think of Mrs. Smith?"

"I like her," said Shorter as they resumed their walk. "Her husband was a big-shot attorney in D.C. years ago."

"Yeah, I know that. He got off a scumbag I collared. He was good, smooth as silk. Should we look at her again? She found him."

"No. She's off my screen. I keep going back to Vogler. He swears he never went that night to where the murder took place, but Marwede swears she saw him there. He sure had motive."

Nastasi nodded and—he knew he ate too

fast—belched against his fist as they reached the main entrance.

"What do you think Broadhurst will do about the money this Mr. Driscoll was sending Michele Paul?"

"No idea. When he said he'd follow through on it, he tried to act like it was nothing but he was shaken. You read that, too?"

"Uh huh. Maybe Paul got greedy and wanted more."

They flashed their badges at the library security guard but were made to go through the metal detector anyway, and went directly to what had been their home since the murder, the handsomely appointed, genteel old Librarian's office. Waiting there for them was John Vogler, chief of the manuscripts division.

"What can we do for you, Dr. Vogler?" Nastasi asked.

"I'd like to speak with you."

Shorter checked his watch. "We have a few minutes before our next interview. Come on in."

Sue Gomara knocked on Consuela Martinez's closed office door.

"Yes, Susan?"

"I don't want you to think I'm unhappy or

anything," Sue said, "but I was wondering whether I could do something else in Hispanic besides the Cuban newspapers."

Consuela smiled. She'd been waiting for the young woman to assert herself and ask for greater responsibility.

Sue continued with her pitch: "I could still do the newspapers some of the time, but not all of the time. Maybe you could get another intern to help out—if that's possible."

"What sort of things would you like to do?" Consuela asked.

Sue shrugged, said, "I don't know, like maybe go through one of the collections, catalog it, feel like I'm helping to do something important."

"Keeping track of the Cuban newspapers *is* important."

"Oh, sure, I know that, but . . ."

"I think it's a fine idea that you branch out a little."

"You do?"

"Yes, I do. Tell you what. We have dozens of collections sitting in the stacks just waiting for someone to go through them carefully, make notes on what's in them, that sort of thing. Make up a preliminary inventory, a simple report."

"That would be great, Dr. Martinez. I'd love that."

"Okay."

Consuela pulled a printed list of collections that had been donated to Hispanic over the past few years and jotted down a list of names of the contributors. She handed the paper to Sue.

"Start with the first three on the list, Koser, Aaronsen, and Covington. They're small collections, not much more than a box for each."

"Which one should I do first?"

"Your choice. Lay out the material, break it down into categories that make sense, note what each section contains, and put the materials back in file folders marked with the name of the subject."

"I really appreciate this, Dr. Martinez."

"And I'll appreciate the good job I know you'll do."

Sue eagerly went to leave but Consuela stopped her with "But you'll still have to handle the Cuban newspapers."

"Oh, sure, I can do both. Thanks again."

After the fourth ring, Cale Broadhurst picked up the phone himself, his secretary having left her desk for a moment. "Broadhurst."

"Hi, Cale. This is Annabel Smith. Do you have a moment?"

"Of course."

"Thanks. I just had a talk with Lucianne Huston, and she told me something she knows that I thought you should know."

"Okay." Feeling blood rush to his head, Broadhurst asked, "What despicable rumor is she peddling now?"

"Apparently one of her more reliable sources informed her that Michele Paul was receiving large sums of money from David Driscoll. I know she assumes that Paul was selling information about rare books he had found to Driscoll, who would then buy them for the library."

"Is she going to make this public?" Broadhurst asked nervously.

"I think so."

"Well, thanks for calling me. I guess I better talk to Ms. Huston before she does permanent damage to the library." As he hung up, he couldn't strike the image of a gleeful Lucianne Huston—*"Reporting from Washington, money and murder at the library"*—from his mind.

Los Angeles' "art squad" was, as in all major cities, small and not considered terribly important in the overall scheme of law enforcement. Stealing an expensive piece of art from someone who obviously had enough money to buy it in the first place didn't rank up there with drive-by shootings, racial unrest, rape, and arson.

Still, the few detectives assigned to the task in Los Angeles took their job seriously. While investigating the studio of Abraham Widlitz, they methodically looked at every piece of art in the studio while the owner tried in vain to reach his son in Pittsburgh: "Daddy's at a dentists' convention in Florida, Papa Abe," his sixteen-year-old granddaughter told him, "and Mom went to a garden show." Widlitz didn't want to upset his granddaughter. "Nothing important," he said in a tremulous voice. "I'll call again."

He'd sat at his desk while the police continued their examination of the contents of the studio, answering an occasional question but spending most of the time thinking about calling an attorney. He hesitated to do that because he felt it might make him appear guilty. As far as he was concerned, he hadn't done anything wrong in accepting art from clients despite knowing they might have obtained their "finds" from less than honest sources. It wasn't his responsibility to determine the provenance of any work of art. He was just a craftsman.

The detective who seemed to be in charge asked Widlitz for his records.

"Those are confidential," Widlitz protested weakly.

The detective laughed. "You're not a lawyer or a doctor, Mr. Widlitz. You can cooperate with us, which would be in your best interests, or we can do it the hard way, take you downtown and subpoena your records."

"Am I under arrest?"

"Depends on what we find here. Do we see the records or not?"

Widlitz gave them what few records he kept, which they packed into an empty leather catalog case they'd brought with them. Widlitz was told he was free to go, but that he was not to leave Los Angeles.

"What about my work?" he asked.

"Look at it this way, Mr. Widlitz. We're giving you a few days vacation while we take a closer look at what's here in the studio. We'll let you know when you can come back."

Abe Widlitz's final words as he left were "I have a lawyer."

"That's good. Have a nice evening, sir. We'll be in touch."

Having operated on a tip from an informer that Widlitz was in the business of fencing stolen art, the two detectives spent the next day comparing lists of stolen art contained in a publication used by art squads around the world, the *Stolen Art Alert,* produced monthly by the International Foundation for Art Research, with the canvases in Abe Widlitz's studio. They came up empty. They then went through their own reports of stolen art from the Los Angeles area and attempted to find a match. There was none.

At the end of the day, they sat in their cramped two-man office and went over their findings, or lack thereof.

"Joey called," one said, referring to the snitch who'd sent them on their fruitless search of Widlitz's studio. "The little twerp wants his money."

His partner's laugh was half snarl. "Tell him he owes us. You want to call Widlitz and tell him he can go back to work?"

"Sure. Nice old guy."

"Don't get soft. Behind that 'nice old man' facade could lurk a serial killer. Call him before his lawyer decides to sue the city."

As his partner made the call, the chief of the art squad started writing a report on their activities on the Widlitz case. He was interrupted by a homicide detective from down the hall. "How's everything with you two Rembrandts?" he asked.

"All right. You?"

"Good. O'Connell wanted me to give you this." He tossed a file folder on the desk and sat down.

The art squad chief opened it and began reading.

"It's that security guard murder they forwarded us from Miami," the detective who'd delivered the report said. "The perp evidently stole that painting and killed the guard in the process. This guy, Munsch, brought the painting with him to L.A. after the heist, then ended up in Mexico, where our esteemed colleagues south of the border gunned him down by the airport."

"Yeah, we'll put it on our list," the art squad chief said, closing the folder.

His partner, who'd just hung up after informing Abe Widlitz he was free to return to his studio, absently opened the file.

The homicide detective said, chuckling, "You guys ever find a stolen Picasso or Andy Warhol and consider selling it on the side?"

"Sure, we find stuff like that every day. That's how we got rich and live in Beverly Hills, drive a Jag and a Bentley, and—"

"Un momento," the other art squad detective said. "Look at this." He pointed to an item on the list they'd made of what was in Widlitz's studio.

"Yeah?"

"It could be the same piece, that one

rolled up on the table in his place. Columbus on his knees giving something to a king. Yeah, it *is* the same. Artist, Reyes."

The art squad chief looked up at the homicide detective. "How long has this been kicking around?"

"Few days."

"Nice you finally got around to bringing it to us."

"You say it's the same one?" the homicide detective asked.

"Sure looks like it." To his partner: "Widlitz didn't have any record of who brought it to him, did he?"

"No."

"Maybe we should call that nice old man again and have another talk—down here!"

"You want a cup of coffee, a soft drink, maybe?"

"No, thank you. I have told you what I know about that particular painting. It was brought to me by Conrad, who asked me to see whether there was anything under it, another painting, perhaps a map."

"Does this Conrad have a last name?"

"I don't know it."

Widlitz sat with one of the art squad detectives and the lead homicide investigator on the Miami case in an interrogation room at LAPD headquarters in Parker Center, on Los Angeles Street. The arrival of the police at his home had upset him. Now, being where criminals were questioned completely unnerved him. He was on the verge of tears; everything he said in response to their questions was delivered as a pleading.

"Tell us what Conrad looks like."

"What can I say? He is of medium build and height, I think. He has a red beard—neatly trimmed—and wears a white jacket and a straw hat."

"A real fashion plate."

Widlitz threw up his hands. "That is all I know about him."

"No idea where he lives?"

"No. I swear."

Widlitz's determination to protect David Driscoll as the real source of the Reyes painting was fading fast.

"This Conrad, he's the one who paid you for the work?"

"I haven't been paid yet. I haven't finished the work."

"Did you find anything behind the painting?"

"No. There is nothing behind it."

The art squad detective left the room and conferred with his partner while looking into the room through a one-way mirror. The homicide detective had taken up the questioning and was leaning over Widlitz, causing the older man to shrink into a ball in his chair.

"He's not being straight with us," the chief told his partner.

"I know. This Conrad works for somebody else. We're being too nice to him."

"We mention the security guard murder in Miami, maybe suggest he's an accessory to murder?"

"Yeah. Let's do that."

Ten minutes later a frightened, panicked Abraham Widlitz told them his client was David Driscoll.

"*The* David Driscoll?"

"Yes."

The detectives looked at each other.

"This Conrad works for him?"

"I don't know. He delivers things for him. He delivered this painting."

"He's delivered other paintings to you?"

"Yes, a few. Murder? Please, I know nothing about murder. I want to speak to a lawyer."

"That's probably a good idea, Mr. Widlitz. Excuse us."

They conferred outside the interrogation room with an assistant district attorney they'd called in.

"There's nothing to hold him on," the DA said.

"Possession of stolen property" was offered.

"You think he knew it was stolen?"

A shrug. "Let's assume he did."

"What's to be gained?" asked the DA. "You think he has more information to offer?"

"Maybe not, but I'd just as soon not have him contacting Driscoll until we've been able to hash this out with Miami. Twenty-four hours?"

"All right, but no more than that. And no more questions until he has an attorney present."

29 Dr. Broadhurst was engaged in quiet contemplation. The question on his mind was whether to call an emergency meeting of the Joint Committee on the Library of Congress to discuss Paul and the Driscoll matter. His thoughts were disturbed by his secretary reminding him that someone from Public Affairs would bring a writer from *American Heritage* for an interview in fifteen minutes, and that a final draft of a speech Broadhurst was to give that night at American University was ready. She handed it to him.

"Thank you, Pamela. Have the writer come in as soon as they arrive."

He read quickly through the draft, making a few minor changes. Fifteen minutes later a public affairs specialist arrived with her journalistic ward. The interview lasted a half hour. The moment they left, Broadhurst's secretary handed him a message slip, explaining, "Public Affairs wonders whether there's any possibility of you finding a few minutes to speak with Lucianne Huston?"

"I wanted to have a word with her anyway, but off the record. See if you can arrange that."

Minutes later, his assistant returned. "Ms. Huston can't promise not to use anything you say to her. She thinks this story is too important. 'The American public has a right to know what goes on in the institutions it finances,' she said."

"Then tell her that I can't talk to her right now."

Annabel had received a call from *Civilization*'s editor, Rich Wilson, that morning before leaving home: "I'll be in D.C. today, Annabel, flying down later this morning to meet with the good folks at Public Affairs. Thought we might catch up for a few minutes while I'm there."

"Sounds good to me," she'd said. "When will you be free?"

"Having lunch at one. How about twelve, twelve-thirty at their office?"

"I'll swing by."

She spent the morning in the manuscripts reading room poring over materials published in the early fifteen-hundreds that might shed light on the relationship between Columbus and his friend and sailing companion, Bartolomé de Las Casas. The exercise didn't prove productive and she had the manuscripts returned to their vaults at noon.

She took the underground walkway from Madison to Jefferson and went to Public Affairs.

"Is Rich Wilson here?" she asked an intern manning the reception desk.

"In there," the intern said, pointing to the employee kitchen.

Annabel went to the door. Wedged in the small kitchen was what seemed to be the entire public affairs staff, their attention focused on a TV on the counter tuned to Lucianne Huston's cable network. Annabel spotted Wilson in a far corner and gave him a wave, which he returned. Someone said, "Quiet!" as Lucianne's face filled the screen.

"This is Lucianne Huston reporting from the Library of Congress in Washington, D.C. What started as a simple murder—if any murder can ever be branded simple—of a leading researcher at this institution has turned into a brewing scandal complete with mysterious payoffs to the murdered researcher, Michele Paul; a stolen painting in Miami, where a security guard was gunned down; the shooting death of the person who stole the painting in Mexico by police there; and the unsolved disappearance eight years ago of yet another researcher at this institution, John Bitteman. Bitteman and Paul were both scholars in search of the mysterious, alleged diaries of Bartolomé de Las Casas, a companion of Christopher Columbus on his voyages in search of a new world.

"I've learned that Michele Paul had been receiving money for years from one of America's richest men, David Driscoll, founder and now chairman emeritus of Driscoll Securities, a passionate collector of Hispanic art and artifacts, and a leading benefactor of the Library of Congress. Why he paid hundreds of thousands of dollars to the murder victim is a question still to be answered.

"Authorities at the Library of Congress, its Jefferson Building behind me, have been uncooperative in my search for answers to the many riddles surrounding Michele Paul's murder. Their silence speaks volumes to this reporter.

"I'm Lucianne Huston reporting live from Washington."

The staffers gathered in the kitchen looked at one another in bewilderment as someone removed a videotape from the VCR and squeezed out of the room. The others followed, buzzing about what they'd just seen. Rich Wilson came to where Annabel stood outside the kitchen.

"Is all of what she reported true?" he asked.

"Who knows? There are more rumors flying around this place than cards in the card catalog. The reporter, Lucianne Huston, had asked me about David Driscoll, so I suppose there's some truth to what she says about him."

"That's a bombshell."

"More like a land mine someone just stepped on. Where there's one, there's bound to be others."

They moved to an empty cubicle.

"Annabel, will this have any bearing—I mean, an adverse bearing on the article you're writing or the issue itself?"

"I don't know. At the moment, the murder is *over*bearing. But the article will be about Las Casas, not Michele Paul. I do know that the library is being turned upside down by all that's happened. Lucianne Huston is in the process of painting it to be the devil's crib itself."

"She's pretty good at that. Fill me in on how your article is going."

"Sure."

After giving Wilson an idea of her approach and some of the better bits from her research, Annabel went to the Hispanic reading room and looked in on Consuela Martinez.

"Come in, come in," Consuela said. "How's everything going?"

"Despite my best intentions, much too slowly. You?"

"Doing my best, which isn't very good. What's new with the investigation?"

"Lucianne just gave a live report on it on the noon news."

"Really? What did she have to say?"

"Lots." Annabel recapped what she'd seen on TV.

"Wow! I'd heard something about David Driscoll having paid Michele for some information, but now it's definite?"

"According to Lucianne. Did you ever have an inkling that something like that might have been going on?"

"Absolutely not. If I had, I would have immediately brought it to the Librarian's attention and probably taken pleasure in doing it, I'm ashamed to admit."

"Why do *you* think Driscoll would have paid Michele, Consuela?"

"Pretty obvious, isn't it? It had to have been for something Michele was giving Driscoll. His research. I mean, what else would he have to offer? Unless . . ."

"Unless?"

"Some personal reason? Blackmail of some sort?"

"Perhaps."

"No, it had to be professional, Annabel. Michele must have been using his research findings to point Driscoll in the direction of rare Hispanic finds, books, manuscripts. There's no question about it, David Driscoll has come up with more important discoveries in recent years than any other single collector."

"And donated a number of them to LC."

"Yes, which makes his having paid Michele that much more unfathomable. If Michele knew where to locate these treasures, all he had to do was tell us and we would have gone after them."

"Except Paul wouldn't have augmented his income that way."

"True, and if we'd gone after those materials as an institution, it would have had to be done in a public way. Having David Driscoll act as the go-between avoided having those items end up on the auction block and driving up the price. Is someone contacting Driscoll?"

"From LC? I don't know. Cale may be. I understand that Huston, too, is trying to reach Driscoll, and I'm sure the police will want to see him."

"This thing is exploding, Annie."

"It certainly has that potential. I'm going to grab a sandwich in the cafeteria."

As she was leaving, Consuela said, "Oh, you asked me whether I knew someone named Sebastian."

"That's right. His name came up in

Michele Paul's notes regarding the artist Reyes."

"I realized later that I do know of someone by that name. I've only heard of him, never met him. He's Mexican, lives in Mexico City last I heard. He's a collector of Mexican books and art although you won't find him at any of the usual gatherings of collectors. From what I know of him, he's a crook wired into the higher echelons of the Mexican government and power elite. Here, I dug this out. It says he's suspected of laundering drug money and using his import-export business to bring in drugs from Cuba."

Annabel took the small, faded newspaper clipping from Consuela, read it, and handed it back. "Lovely fellow."

"Why would Michele Paul be involved with someone like that?"

"I didn't say he was, just that he noted the name Sebastian a few times in his file about Reyes. I'll be back in an hour. I think I'd better hunker down for the afternoon in that lovely space you've given me and get some serious work done."

The cafeteria was busy when Annabel arrived and she joined a long line at the sandwich section. She was eventually served and sought out an empty table. There weren't any. But then she spotted Sue Gomara.

"Mind if I join you?" Annabel asked.

"Oh, sure. Please do."

Annabel noticed that Sue was dressed for duty in Hispanic—jeans and a plaid shirt.

"Back to Cuba, Sue?"

"What? Oh, the newspapers. No. Consuela gave me a new assignment, going through some small collections and logging what's in them. I'm definitely moving up in the world."

"One small step toward becoming the Librarian of Congress," Annabel said. "Good for you. Sounds like something you'd enjoy."

"Better than filing Cuban propaganda. I mean, keeping track of what Cuban newspapers are saying is important."

"No need to explain. Congratulations on your new responsibilities."

Annabel started on her sandwich.

"Did you know Michele Paul real well?" Sue asked.

"No. I just met him a few times. You probably had more contact with him than I did."

"I really didn't like the guy, but you know that. It's horrible what happened to him, his head bashed in and all. Have you heard anything more about who did it?"

"No. The police are—"

Sue guffawed. "The police! I don't think they can find their way to work."

"Pretty harsh assessment," Annabel said. "You've had some dealings with them?"

"I sure have, and every one of them has been bad. I've been getting obscene phone calls for over a month now, but every time I report it, the cops sort of shrug it away. I suppose I'll have to be killed by this nut before they'll take it seriously."

Annabel said, "I was an attorney in my former life. Obscene callers are generally passive types."

You could tell by her face that Sue was thinking, Not you, too.

"That must be terribly upsetting. He'll probably become tired of calling and stop," Annabel said, finishing her sandwich. "If it keeps up, tell me. Mac may have an idea or two. Thanks for sharing the table with me. Have to get back."

"I'll be there soon."

Annabel was alone in the space on the upper gallery that afternoon, with the exception of Sue Gomara, who sat at her small desk going through the contents of a file box at her feet.

"Made any discoveries yet?" Annabel asked.

"No, only I suppose it's all interesting to somebody. This guy Koser collected a lot of strange things. He was big into Haiti."

"I love Haitian art. My husband and I have bought a few pieces over the years. What other collections will you be going through?"

Sue glanced at a note on her desk. "Aaronsen and Covington. I'm almost done with the Koser box."

At four, Annabel remembered that Mac had had a two o'clock appointment with his orthopedic surgeon, Giles Scuderi. She called the apartment.

"Just came through the door," he said. "How are you?"

"Fine, but the question is how are *you*? What did Giles say?"

"What he always says, that I need surgery."

"And?"

"I told him to go ahead and schedule it. He assures me that my knee will be good as new. It's an outpatient procedure. He's getting back to me with a date."

Annabel broke out in a self-satisfied smile. "Great," she said.

"I suppose so. What's new at LC?"

"Lots, although I'm trying to stay focused on my research. Lucianne Huston did a report on the noon news. She claims David Driscoll was paying Michele Paul really big bucks, ostensibly for his research findings."

"No surprise. She talked to you about it and to us at dinner."

"But it's a different story when it's broadcast around the world. Everyone's on edge."

"Stick to your guns, Annie, and stay out of it."

"Wish I had a few guns. Not easy, but I'm trying. Should be home by six."

"I'll be here. Love you."

"Love you, too, Mac."

She worked at her desk for a while until a kink in her back prompted her to get up and stretch. She wandered over to where Sue Gomara had just started on her second box, the one marked AARONSEN COLLECTION.

"How goes it?" Annabel asked.

"Great. I finished the first one; I'm starting this one now."

"Good for you. I'd take my time, Sue, so you don't overlook anything."

Annabel started for the stairs but stopped when Sue called, "Mrs. Reed-Smith, look at this."

Annabel returned to the intern's side and looked at the envelope she held. Written on it was *Las Casas.*

"What have we here?" Annabel said, perching on the edge of the desk and opening the envelope. Inside were five computer discs; each had *Las Casas* written with a black felt-tip pen on its label.

"These might be helpful for the article you're writing," Sue said.

"I imagine they will be," Annabel said, more to herself than in response to Sue. "The Aaronsens collected material on my guy?"

"Yup, looks that way. Underneath these other papers."

Annabel had no idea who the Aaronsen family were, or their approach to collecting Hispanic and Portuguese manuscripts and books. But they evidently had quite an interest in the man who'd been consuming Annabel's days and nights since starting her research. What good luck, she thought as she replaced the discs in the envelope and stood. "I think I'll pop one of these in my laptop and see what's on it. As the line goes, Sue, you might have made my day."

"Great!"

At five-thirty, Annabel returned the disc she'd been looking at on her laptop to its envelope and started down to the reading room.

"Anything good on the discs?" Sue asked as Annabel passed.

"Ah, I think so, Sue. I have to talk to Consuela. Thanks again for finding these. They're . . . they're very interesting."

Consuela was in her office preparing to leave for the evening. With her was Dolores Marwede.

"Got a minute?" Annabel asked.

"Sure," the division chief said.

"I was just leaving," Dolores said. "I have a date."

"Good for you," Consuela said.

"Yeah, nice guy. He's a librarian at the Smithsonian. Have a good evening."

Annabel waited until Dolores was gone before saying, "You're not going to believe this, but Sue found this envelope in the Aaronsen Collection." She handed it to Consuela.

"What's in it?"

"Computer discs labeled *Las Casas.* There are five of them. I took a look at what's on one."

"Aaronsen? As I recall, that family's interest was exclusively on slavery tracts and pamphlets from the West Indies, nineteenth century. *Las Casas*?"

"I don't know anything about the Aaronsens, Consuela, but I do know that the disc I looked at is filled with notes about the diaries."

"Fascinating."

"I also think . . ."

"Yes?"

"I also think the notes might have been written by Michele Paul."

30 Broadhurst's attempt to reach David Driscoll that morning had been frustrating in the extreme.

"Mr. Driscoll is out of the country, Mr. Broadhurst," the man who answered the phone at Driscoll's Los Angeles estate said.

"Do you know how I might reach him?"

"No, sir."

"When do you expect him back?"

"I don't know that."

"Please leave a message that I called."

"Yes, Mr. Broadhurst, I will."

David Driscoll's whereabouts remained unknown for the rest of the day.

* * *

Broadhurst hadn't been the only one interested in contacting David Driscoll that day.

"Mr. Driscoll's office."

"Hi. This is Lucianne Huston, NCN, News Cable Network. Is Mr. Driscoll there?"

The secretary in Driscoll Securities' chairman emeritus's office said, "I'm sorry but he's not, Ms. Huston. Is there something I can help with?"

"Probably not. I'm working on a story about what the economy will look like in the year two thousand. Leading financial experts are giving their forecasts, and I was anxious to include Mr. Driscoll."

"I'm sure he'd be pleased to participate, Ms. Huston, but I'm afraid he's out of the country."

"Back to Mexico again?"

The secretary laughed. "Yes, as a matter of fact. I enjoy your work on television very much."

"Thank you. I suppose you've been following my coverage of the murder at the Library of Congress."

"Some of it. A terrible tragedy. Mr. Driscoll was extremely upset when he heard."

"I'm not surprised. His support of the library is well known."

"A real passion with him."

"When is he due back?"

"He didn't say, although probably in a day or two. He seldom stays there long unless he's traveling with his wife."

"Will he be checking in with you today?"

"I don't think so. He spends very little time here. He's retired, you know."

"I hope I'm that active when—and if—I ever retire," Lucianne said, injecting a laugh for effect. "I'll just have to try again."

"Please do. It was a pleasure talking with you."

Lucianne hung up and dialed Baumann's office at NCN in Miami.

"Bob, Lucianne. I've been trying to reach Driscoll but he's in Mexico."

"I'd be more comfortable if you had a statement from him, Lucianne."

"I don't need a statement from him. My source with the police here in D.C. is solid gold. No doubt about it. Driscoll was sending this Paul person money and lots of it over the years, including a hundred grand the day before he was murdered. I want to go out to L.A. this afternoon and be there when Driscoll returns."

"How long will that be?"

"A few days at the most. Driscoll's the key to this story, Bob. One of the country's filthy rich paying off a murdered researcher, for whatever reason, at the Library of Congress. Smells. Driscoll's rumored to have been waving money around the rare books and manuscripts underground looking for lost diaries by Las Casas. Researcher is hit at his desk. Security guard is shot in Miami during the theft of a third-rate painting that's delivered to—where else?—Los Angeles. The lowlife who stole the painting is gunned down by police in—where else?—Mexico. Another Hispanic researcher at LC, as it's affectionately called, disappears eight years ago, no trace. Was Driscoll paying him, too? Did Driscoll do more than just give these guys money?"

"Like what?"

"Like maybe kill them, or have them killed to keep his payments quiet."

Baumann whistled into the phone: "Payments for what? Pull back, Lucianne. You don't go around accusing somebody like David Driscoll of murder unless you have the video of him standing over the body, blood on his hands with a crazed look in his eyes. Look, I'll run it by our esteemed leader."

"Why?" she exploded. "You're the news director, *you* make the decisions."

"I told you, Lucianne, that our leader happens to be a friend of the Library of Congress's top guy, Broadhurst. Driscoll is a big supporter of LC, as you call it. Right?"

"Right."

"So I'm not letting you go further on Driscoll until I have a talk with the guy who signs our checks. You're at the hotel?"

"Right."

"Cool it, Lucianne. Go get a pedicure and a stiff drink. My treat. Relax."

"I don't get pedicures, Bob. They're tough to find in Somalia."

"I'll get back to you."

"I can't wait."

Two LAPD detectives sat in an unmarked car a few houses down from Driscoll's. They'd called the house and received the same message as Lucianne Huston, that Driscoll was "out of the country." Naturally suspicious, they decided to spend a few hours watching the house on the chance they'd been lied to. After four boring hours, during which no vehicle or person came to or left the house, they decided to return to headquarters. They started the engine when a car arrived, a white BMW convertible with its top down. Its driver, wearing a white jacket and full-brimmed straw hat, and sporting a neatly cropped red beard, got out of the vehicle and went to an intercom mounted next to a pair of black iron gates.

"That's the guy Widlitz described," one of the cops said. "Our Conrad. We should have a little talk with him."

"Let's see what he does, where he goes after this."

The electronically operated gates swung open and Conrad Syms drove into the compound. Ten minutes later he emerged and turned right, followed at a discreet distance by the detectives. He drove south on the San Diego Freeway until exiting for Hermosa Beach, and pulled into the parking lot of Woody's Comedy Club, a one-story building close to the water. The detectives pulled up next to him as he was getting out of the BMW.

"Conrad?" one of them said. "LAPD." They displayed their credentials.

"So, what do you want from me?"

"You related to David Driscoll?"

"What? Come on!" He started to walk away but they blocked his path.

"Look, dimwit, we can talk nice and friend-ly here, or we can take you in for wearing an illegal hat."

"Illegal hat? What are you guys, audition-ing at Woody's?"

They moved in unison, one on each side of him, pinning him against his car. "What is your last name?" one asked.

"Syms."

"Conrad Syms?"

"Yeah. How come you asked about Driscoll?"

"Know a gentleman named Abraham Widlitz?"

"Jesus, what's this all about?"

"It's about a murder in Miami, which we're led to believe you were an accomplice to."

"Murder? Miami? Ah, come on, guys, you've got to be joking."

"So how come you're not laughing, Conrad?"

"I don't know anything about any murder. I've never been to Miami. Look, I'm here to audition for a comedy flick. I'm an actor."

"I bet you are."

"I told you—"

"And we're telling you that we have a lot to talk about. Be a nice boy and put the top up on your fancy car there, lock it, and come with us."

"Am I being arrested? I want a lawyer."

"No, Conrad, you are not being arrested. You're being invited to a party. If you want to bring a lawyer as your date, be our guest."

The only people, it seemed, who weren't looking for David Driscoll that day were Annabel Reed-Smith and Consuela Martinez. After Annabel had taken the envelope containing the discs to her friend, and the door to the office had been closed, they continued talking about Sue Gomara's discovery.

"And you think these discs were not Aaronsen stuff, that they belonged to Michele?" Consuela asked.

"From what I've read, yes. The question is, how did they end up in the Aaronsen file box? When was that collection donated?"

Consuela consulted a card. "Almost three years ago."

"What do we do with the discs?" Annabel asked. "I'd like to be able to go through all of them. From what I saw on the first one, there might be a wealth of material for my article."

"I've got to let Dr. Broadhurst know."

"Of course."

"I'd like you to come with me."

"If you wish."

Consuela dialed the Librarian's number. His secretary answered and said Broadhurst had left for the evening for a dinner with a trustee and a speech at American University.

"It'll have to wait until morning."

Annabel's brow furrowed.

"You're thinking?"

"I'm just thinking, realizing, that once we deliver the five discs to Cale, I won't have an opportunity to go through them."

"Not necessarily true. They're library property."

"And they'll most likely become police property."

"Not forever."

"Long enough to deny me what's on them that might contribute to the article. The police will want to examine their content to see whether there's any material relevant to the murder. That could take months. They can sit on them for as long as they want. Consuela, would you be willing to let me take these discs home with me tonight?"

"Oooh, I don't know, Annie."

"I'll understand if you say no, but I'll also

be eternally grateful if you do. If Cale was in his office right now, and we were to bring them to him, I wouldn't even think of doing this. But unless you're going to turn them over to someone else tonight, they'll sit here until morning. Are you planning to give them to someone else?"

"No. I think Cale should be the first, and only, person to have them."

"But I've already seen them, Consuela, and I can make good use of them. I just want to make notes of anything on them that's helpful to my article."

Consuela thought for a moment before saying, "Only because it's you, Annie."

"I owe you."

"No, you don't. But what if you come across material that bears on the murder?"

"I've been thinking about that. I suppose I'll make note of anything of that nature, too, and share it with you tomorrow."

Consuela narrowed her eyes; a small smile crossed her lips. "Are you sure, Annie, that you want to see what's on those discs only because you're searching for Las Casas material for the article?"

Annabel's eyebrows went up. "Why else would I want to take them home?"

"To see whether there *is* anything on them about the murder?"

Annabel didn't answer, but Consuela read her face.

"Once a lawyer, always a lawyer. Take them home, Annie, but be back with them first thing in the morning. If there is anything on them referring to Michele's murder, I'd hate to be charged with obstruction of justice."

"Me, too. See you tomorrow. And thanks."

Annabel wondered as she left the building whether the security guard would ask to see what was in the envelope. He didn't. She walked quickly up First Street in the direction of the Supreme Court Building in search of a cab.

"The South Building, the Watergate," she told the driver.

Mac and Rufus were on the terrace when she arrived. It was a lovely, warm evening in Washington, the sun seeming to stay high in the sky longer than usual, a gentle breeze from the west displacing the city's legendary humidity with dry air. She noticed immediately as man and beast crossed the living room to greet her that Mac wasn't limping.

"How's the knee?" she asked.

"Great. I may not need that surgery after all. The magnet's working."

"What magnet?" she asked, slipping out of her shoes and heading for the kitchen.

He came up behind her and kissed her neck. "The one I'm wearing. I stopped in a drugstore and bought one. See?" He pulled up his pants leg to display an elasticized bandage. A small lump pressing against it was, Annabel assumed, the magnet. "Feels good already."

"That's . . . that's great, Mac."

"Drink?"

"I don't think so. I'm in for an all-nighter."

He laughed. "Trying to relive your under-grad days?"

"No, trying to make sense of something and I only have one night to do it."

"Tell me more."

A club soda with lemon in her hand, and a dry Rob Roy in his, they went to the terrace and sat at the table. Mac positioned the large multicolored umbrella to shield them from the sun, which had suddenly decided to make its lovely dive for the horizon.

Annabel told Mac about how Sue Gomara had discovered the envelope containing five discs and how she, Annabel, had taken a look at one of the discs on her laptop. Mac listened intently, a nod or grunt of understanding his only intrusion into her monologue.

"I'm sure these discs weren't part of the original collection donated by this Aaronsen family. Other things in the box were dusty, yellowed. The envelope was new, the discs pristine. Someone put the envelope in that box recently."

"Maybe it was Michele Paul," Mac offered.

"Why would he do that?"

"To hide the discs for whatever reason he may have had. Cale Broadhurst told me the last time we played tennis that one of the biggest problems at the library is finding the time and manpower to go through donated collections. He said some collections sit for years before anyone gets around to really seeing what's in them. Sounds to me like a perfect place to hide something."

"Unless an intern is given the order to go through them. Let's say you're right, Mac. Let's say that Michele Paul put the discs there to hide them. *Why?* All his other research was neatly filed in his apartment. If he had wanted to conceal the discs, I don't think he would just plop them in a box in the stacks."

"You're probably right, Annie. The discs might or might not have relevance to his murder. They could be important for your article."

"I'm sure they are, which is why I'm determined to go through all five of them tonight before they're turned over to Cale. Speaking of that, I'd better get started."

"Go to it. I'll whip up something for dinner."

"Order in from the hotel. Something simple. Crab bisque and a salad?"

"Okay. Anything else I can do to help?"

"Yes. Keep the coffee coming and give me an occasional neck massage."

"You're too easy, Annie."

Annabel worked steadily at the computer in the bedroom they'd set up as an office, the soft strains of Mozart and Haydn, and Rufus's body wedged beneath the desk at her feet, keeping her company. Mac stayed up, too, popping in occasionally to deliver a fresh cup of coffee and to knead his wife's lovely neck.

At three, Annabel got up from the computer for the first time and went to the living room, where Mac had dozed off in a recliner. Her presence woke him.

"More coffee?" he asked sleepily.

"No. I need to talk."

He smiled, stood, and stretched. "Find something of interest?"

"I think so."

They sat side by side on the couch.

"Mac, I was wrong."

"About what?"

"About the discs. I don't believe the material on them is Michele Paul's research."

"Oh? What's brought you to that conclusion?"

"Some of the entries on them. They mention Michele in the third person."

Mac laughed. "Maybe he was like some of those athletes and politicians who refer to themselves in the third person."

"I don't think so. If he was that sort of person, he had some pretty harsh things to say about himself."

"A masochist who speaks in the third person?"

"Mac."

"Sorry. Go ahead, I'm listening."

"Much of the material on the discs—I've gotten through three of the five—is devoted to possible sources of information that might lead to the Las Casas diaries. Some concern the mythology of the diaries, why some experts consider them a possibility, why others are convinced they're a myth."

"That's all good for you and your article."

"Yes, it is, it's virtually the theme—and I've been making good notes for that purpose. I've also copied off sections onto another disc of my own."

His eyebrows went up. "Think twice about that, Annie."

"Just for my recollection when I'm writing the article. I don't have time to make all the notes I need. I'll erase it when I'm done."

Mac excused himself to go to the bathroom. When he returned, Annabel was back in the office.

"Look at this, Mac." She brought up a file from the second disc.

He read over her shoulder as she scrolled down. It was a long series of rambling thoughts on the Ovando family of Seville, Spain. Don Nicolás de Ovando, Annabel knew, had been appointed governor of the islands and mainland of the Indies, a post Columbus had coveted. Shortly after Ovando set sail for the Indies, Columbus petitioned and was granted money to launch his fourth voyage to the New World. According to the notes on the screen, he felt that Ovando and his predecessor, Francisco de Bobadilla, had deliberately withheld gold and other valuable consideration due him, and was anxious to return to the scene of his first three voyages to stake his claim.

The computer notes went on to mention that a separate diary prepared by Bartolomé de Las Casas, said to have been written during those three previous voyages, contained information detrimental to Columbus's claims of having been cheated out of vast riches. Ovando wanted those diaries and offered a large sum to anyone delivering them.

"Did this Ovando ever get the diaries?" Mac asked.

"Not as far as I know. I've done my own research on Ovando. There's no record of his ever taking possession of them."

"What do those initials mean?" Mac asked.

Annabel turned, looked up at him, and smiled. "My question exactly," she said, scrolling back to the beginning of the notes. "There are sets of initials all over the discs. Here. I've been making note of them."

She handed her husband a slip of paper on which she'd written "MP," "LC," "DD," "JS," "DM," "BE," "CX," and "WA."

"MP?" Mac said. "Michele Paul?"

"Could be. If it does refer to him, it reinforces my belief that he didn't write these notes."

"A reasonable assumption. What about 'DD'? Would that be David Driscoll?"

"The initials fit."

"What about the rest of them?"

"I don't know. Except for 'LC,' of course."

"Others?"

"I originally thought some of them might refer to names out of Columbus's past, one of his sailing companions, a member of his family. I went through all the names in my database but came up empty."

"Are you finished for the night?" Mac asked.

"No. I have the other discs to get through. You go to bed."

"Not on your life. If you can stay up all night, so can I."

"Mac, it's not a contest."

"Just want to show I can keep up."

"Keep up? With me?"

"Uh huh."

"Why?"

"A newfound spirit of proving age doesn't matter. If John Glenn can blast off into space, I can stay up all night with my young wife."

Annabel shook her head. "I'm only five years younger than you."

"I'm aware of that. Go on, get back to work. I started on that speech I'm supposed to give next month at the D.C. Bar. I'd better get back to work, too."

He kissed her on the cheek and started to leave. Annabel watched as he took a step, grimaced, then continued through the door favoring his right leg.

"What happened to the magnet?" she called after him.

He stopped, turned, and said, "I took it off. Better get it back on. It works miracles."

Her thought before returning to the subject that had consumed her all night was, Get that damn leg operated on, and do it fast! It's got you talking like an old man.

He looked back over his shoulder. "Oh, yes, my love: If you come across anything pertinent to Michele Paul and the payoffs, log when, where, how long between presumed delivery of whatever and the payoff.

As they were supposed to have said in the Watergate case, follow the money."

But not thinking like an old man. She placed disc number four into the CPU, drew a deep breath, and went back to work.

32 David Driscoll entered Hacienda de los Morales, his restaurant of choice whenever in Mexico City. He navigated the crowded main room and passed through French doors to lush gardens behind the restored fifteenth century mansion. The table for two he'd reserved in a secluded corner was the only vacant one in the garden. A chair was held out for him. He was seated and served a "Mexican," rum and tequila with honey and lime juice—a drink he'd grown fond of when visiting Havana's La Bodeguita del Medio, where Ernest Hemingway ordered doubles. Two waiters hovered near-

by, keeping anxious eyes open for any subtle signal that he wished something else.

He wore a double-breasted navy blazer with gold buttons bearing his family crest, white shirt with pinched collar, solid blue tie, and gray slacks. It was as informal as David Driscoll allowed himself to be, even in the three o'clock heat of the day.

He sat stiffly, eyes straight ahead as he sipped his drink. Nor did his posture change when Emilio Sebastian appeared at the French doors, saw him, nodded, smiled, and approached the table. His floral shirt and white slacks contrasted with Driscoll's buttoned-up apparel. A waiter pulled out the chair across from Driscoll.

"Buenos días," Sebastian said.

"Emilio."

Sebastian ordered a Bloody Mary. "It's a pleasure to see you again, David. Your trips to Mexico seem to be less frequent."

"I come as often as always, Emilio. I simply don't inform you of my every visit."

"Of course." Sebastian looked up through white blooms of the soapberry trees and exclaimed, "A perfect day. We must drink to that, David. How many more perfect days will we have the time to enjoy, huh?"

"When can I have the diaries? Where are they?"

"Well, we seem to have hit a snag," said Sebastian, moving his elbows off the table—a gesture of retreat.

"What do you mean, a snag? Can I get them or not?"

"Yes, you'll have them, but . . ."

"But what?"

"Some additional expenses have come up, and we've experienced some delays."

"Delays?" Driscoll asked, ignoring the matter of additional money.

"Yes, the books are in fragile condition, so they have to be transported with extreme care. We can't just mail them."

"But you told me we'd have them by now. Wherever they are, you could have walked them to Los Angeles by now," Driscoll said, his anger and frustration becoming clear to Sebastian.

"I promise you, I'll do everything I can to get them for you as soon as possible. If you could just get me another—"

"You want more money now? Pay your expenses from what I already paid you," Driscoll said loudly, causing several patrons of the restaurant to turn their heads toward the corner table. "Anyway, why did you have him killed?" he asked, quietly now, his thin lips barely moving now.

Sebastian's puzzled look was exaggerated. "Have *who* killed?"

"You know who I'm talking about."

"Oh, yes, the thief from Florida. What was his name, Munsch?"

"Why did you have him killed?"

"I had him killed for . . . well, for you, of course."

Driscoll glanced at the waiters and motioned impatiently for them to leave. They misunderstood and approached.

"Not *now.* Leave us alone," Driscoll said.

They retreated, casting furtive glances at each other.

Driscoll's body remained stationary as he turned his head to Sebastian. "Don't you ever say that again. Do you understand?"

Sebastian smiled. "If you do not wish me to say it, I won't. But that is the truth."

"I told you to find him and question him, that was all."

"And I did find and question him, David. An unsavory type, but that was to be expected considering what he did for a living."

David Driscoll hated losing patience,

detested people who allowed their emotions to dictate their actions. One of his favorite movie characters was E. G. Marshall in *Twelve Angry Men,* who never broke a sweat in the stifling, excited jury room. But he recognized he was losing patience at this moment. He controlled his voice. "I am not interested in your character analyses of Mr. Munsch, Emilio. I *was* interested in how much he knew of who'd ordered the painting stolen. I was interested in whether he could link me to my man, Conrad. I distinctly told you that should you feel he could provide a link to me, you were to get him out of the country. I provided money to do that. I didn't mean in a box!"

Sebastian's drink was served by a waiter who wasn't sure he should be there and who immediately withdrew. Sebastian raised his glass. "You have nothing to worry about, David. Sending Mr. Munsch out of the country would only provide you with temporary relief. My solution was infinitely more permanent."

Driscoll waved for the waiters. "Walnut soup," he said, "and an endive salad with duck."

His sudden order took Sebastian by surprise. "The same for me."

Driscoll now adjusted himself so that he leaned closer to Sebastian. "I have never been in the business of having people murdered, Sebastian."

"Of course you haven't, David, but I am having trouble understanding your concern. The man was a common thief and murderer—a security guard died during the theft, did he not?"

Driscoll didn't respond, and Sebastian continued.

"You provided three thousand dollars for me to give to this reptile so that he could fly to Cuba and enjoy the good life. Why should he be rewarded for his vile deeds, David? The money is in more worthy hands. Our police aren't paid very much, as you know. Three thousand dollars is a great deal of money for them. They are hardworking family men. But most important, you never have to worry about Mr. Munsch again. He told me he was certain he could identify your man, Conrad. He seemed proud that he could. It was my judgment—and you paid me for my judgment, David—it was my considered judgment that he posed a significant threat to you. I acted in your best interests. An expression of appreciation would be more appropriate."

Conversation during the meal was one-sided. Sebastian left the subject that had brought them together and talked of the political situation in Mexico, of its soccer team's prospects in the World Cup, the young woman with whom he'd recently been involved, new restaurants he'd discovered, and other banal topics to which Driscoll barely responded.

"Dessert?" Sebastian asked.

"No. I must leave."

"As you wish. We should do this more often." Sebastian grabbed the check from the waiter and laid cash on it.

"That wasn't necessary," Driscoll said.

"If it had been, I wouldn't take such pleasure in doing it. You know, David, you never did tell me why you wanted that particular painting. Hardly a worthwhile addition to your collection."

"It's no concern of yours."

"A shame about your contact at the Library of Congress. A brutal, premature ending to a good life. You didn't order that, either, did you."

Driscoll merely stared at him.

They stood in front of the restaurant, where both men had cars and drivers waiting. As Driscoll was about to climb into his limo, Sebastian grabbed his elbow and urged him back. "David," he said, "there is nothing to worry about. Justice was served when our police were forced to shoot Munsch as he tried to escape. There is no one now who can link you to what happened in Miami." Sebastian's laugh verged on being a girlish giggle. "Your worries are over. Keep in touch. Smile, my American friend. It's a beautiful day. How many more will there be?"

Driscoll said to his driver, "Airport." He closed his eyes and took a series of deep breaths. Sebastian had been right, he decided. With Munsch dead, justice had indeed been served, and there was no one who could link him to the theft of the Reyes painting in Miami and the unfortunate shooting of the security guard there.

But his eyes snapped open.

There's always someone, and I've just left him.

33 Dr. Cale Broadhurst waited in the anteroom to Senator Richard Menendez's office in the Russell Senate Office Building. He'd been there for fifteen minutes, the senator's delay due to an unexpected floor vote.

Broadhurst had spent most of the morning at LC huddling with members of his management team, including Mary Beth Mullin; a representative from Public Affairs who knew from experience with Broadhurst never to refer to that office's activities as putting a "spin" on something; Broadhurst's chief of staff, Helen Kelly; and a senior staffer from

Congressional Relations. Those in attendance were treated to a rare burst of anger from the Librarian.

"I've only been Librarian for three years. I came here expecting to spend my days and nights helping guide this institution to even greater prominence than it currently enjoys, and to find the money to do that. I expected rocky going in some areas, and turns in the road that would require some skillful maneuvering. But I did not expect to have a scandal like this Driscoll and Michele Paul matter taking center stage. Does anybody here remember what Harry Truman said about this special place? He said in a letter to one of my predecessors, Luther Evans, on the Library's hundred-and-fiftieth anniversary, 'It,' this institution, 'has stoutly defended the freedom of mind, and the right of the quiet voice of truth to be heard.' *Quiet voice of truth!* Instead, we have the shrill voice of a TV reporter telling the world that our people sell out their research for personal gain, and maybe get murdered in the bargain. Some security guard in Miami is killed and that death is linked to us. A small-time hoodlum from Miami is killed by police in Mexico and *that* incident is woven into this scenario created by the media, Ms. Huston its spear carrier. Or thrower."

"Has Driscoll been directly confronted about this, Cale?" Public Affairs asked.

"He's out of the country. Mary Beth has been trying to reach him."

"Lucianne Huston has been trying, too."

"And we'd better get to him before she does," Broadhurst said.

Helen Kelly asked, "Is anyone besides Ms. Huston suggesting that David Driscoll might have had a . . . well, had a hand in Paul's murder?"

"If so, it had better not be anyone from this place," Broadhurst snapped. Then he realized the pettiness of his outburst.

"The police are obviously examining that possibility," Mullin said.

"It's a ridiculous notion," Broadhurst said, getting up from behind his desk. "Preposterous. I have to leave. Senator Menendez has asked for a meeting."

"There's lots of talk in Congress about this," LC's Congressional Relations rep said. "Some administration haters on the House Administration Committee are floating the possibility of a hearing."

"That's all we need with the budget being debated," Broadhurst said. "Remember what else Truman said? 'The buck stops here.' In this case, it stops in this office, with this Librarian. But for now, you're all carrying the buck with me. Let's meet again this afternoon. Thank you for coming—and for your support."

The senior senator from Florida burst through the door, followed closely by two aides. He smiled broadly as he slapped Broadhurst on the shoulder and said, "Come in, come in. Sorry I kept you waiting. The Rules Committee threw us a last-minute curve. They seem to enjoy doing that these days."

His office was spacious and handsomely appointed. Signed photographs covered the walls, interspersed with copper metalwork from Michoacán, Mexico, and a grouping of *milagros,* votive offerings to the saints created from hammered tin and inlaid with semi-precious stones. The fourth wall, dominated by windows, displayed a map of Florida, a U.S. map, and the senator's family coat of arms.

He hung his jacket on a corner coat tree,

invited Broadhurst to take a seat, and folded himself into a high-backed leather chair behind a massive desk.

"Good of you to come on short notice," he said. To a young female aide who lingered just inside the door: "We'll need a few minutes alone, Ellen."

She backed out of the office, closing the door behind her.

"Well, Cale," Mendendez said, "I'm sure you know why I felt it necessary to get together."

"The TV report on David Driscoll," Broadhurst said.

"That's right. And now this."

He slid that morning's *Washington Post* across the desk. The paper was open to a page on which a long article appeared concerning the intrigue surrounding Michele Paul's murder, the money paid him by David Driscoll, and questioning any possible correlation between Paul's murder and the disappearance eight years ago of John Bitteman. Broadhurst pushed the paper back to Menendez. "I've read it."

"Is it true?" Menendez asked.

"That David Driscoll had been sending sizable sums of money to Michele Paul?"

Broadhurst said. "We're investigating further. Unfortunately, it seems to be."

"How did you learn about it?" asked the senator.

"The police came to me after they'd investigated Michele's finances."

"When did the police contact you?" Menendez's tone had been friendly, pleasantly inquisitive. This question was hard-edged.

"Yesterday," Broadhurst answered.

"It didn't occur to you to contact me immediately?"

"No," Broadhurst said, uncomfortable with the tenor the meeting had taken. "I took immediate action, of course. We've been trying to find Driscoll. He's out of the country. I wish I were. I have my entire staff looking into it, going back over Paul's work, checking to see whether anyone was aware of what was going on."

"You approached me, Cale, and asked for help in obtaining funds for those Las Casas diaries. I took immediate action. I started the ball rolling by having my staff draft a special spending resolution laying the groundwork with key colleagues should the diaries turn up. The fact that someone of Driscoll's stature was involved added to my comfort level in pursuing it. Now, I turn on my TV and read my newspaper and see serious accusations being made against him, and, by implication, the library, and a murder in the wings."

"If it bothered you, Senator, imagine my reaction."

"Why was Driscoll sending money to Paul?"

"We don't know," said Broadhurst. "David might have been making use of Dr. Paul's research to locate important collections or manuscripts or books. It hardly seems likely that pure research would be so valuable to a collector but . . . you never know. Hopefully, we'll get a straight answer to that from Driscoll—once we catch up with him."

Menendez sat back, his brow furrowed, eyes trained on an ornate chandelier hanging directly above his visitor. He said, "I know this is asking for speculation on your part, Cale, but is it even remotely possible that the money Driscoll was sending Michele Paul had something to do with his murder?"

"It's inconceivable to me, Senator, but the murder was, too. That's a personal view. David Driscoll and I have been acquainted for a long time, going back long before I became librarian. You know as well as I do of his generosity to the library over many years, especially in the past ten years or so. That said—and I stress it's my personal reaction to your question—I don't know. I wish I did."

Menendez said, "Again, I ask about the money. If Paul was being paid by Driscoll, that would be a serious breach of Paul's responsibility to the library, would it not?"

"Of course," said Broadhurst.

"Do you have any further information that others on your staff might be doing the same thing?"

A nervous laugh came from the Librarian. He didn't know. "No. Michele Paul was undoubtedly an isolated incident, an aberration. Most librarians do not get rich, ethically or otherwise."

Menendez ran his tongue over his lower lip, swiveled left and right, then came forward, elbows on the desk. "These Las Casas diaries and map are now tainted."

"Tainted? They haven't even been found yet."

"With scandal. I'm sure you can understand the position I'm in. I can't very well push for a resolution to release funds to buy them if they come through a now sullied source like David Driscoll."

Broadhurst shifted in his chair and exhaled audibly. "I never thought I'd hear the name David Driscoll and scandal mentioned in the same breath." He sensed the meeting was about to end. "When I've had the opportunity to ask Driscoll why he's been sending money to Paul, I'll be better able to answer your questions."

"When you have those answers," Menendez said, "I want to be informed first."

"Before the police?"

"First. In the meantime, I'm putting on hold any further consideration of funding the purchase."

"Which is certainly understandable," said Broadhurst.

"Before we break this up, is there anything else threatening to erupt at the library, something that might further contribute to what I'm sure you'll agree is a brewing scandal?"

Broadhurst paused before responding. Should he mention the unknown person who'd been phone stalking the young intern in the main reading room? The drunk who'd been escorted from the Jefferson Building by library police, and who threatened legal action for violation of his civil rights? The recent technical snafu in the digital library project?

"Not to my knowledge," Broadhurst said.

"Good."

Menendez stood, opened the door, and summoned two of his staff into the office. All beautiful smile, he turned to Broadhurst: "Thanks for coming. I think it was a useful meeting."

Broadhurst walked down First Street to the Madison Building, passing a familiar homeless woman in whose paper cup he often dropped coins. He ignored her. He crossed against a traffic light and went directly to his office.

"No visitors or calls, please," he told his secretary.

He hung his tweed jacket on a coat tree, went to the large globe and gave it a vigorous spin, then sat behind his desk. He picked up the phone and dialed Mary Beth Mullin's extension.

"Any luck?" he asked.

"No."

"Get some people working the phones and call any place he might be, California, Alaska, Mexico, the South Pole, any place. I want to talk to him now!"

Despite not having slept the previous night, Annabel arrived at LC feeling energized and purposeful, as a person sometimes does on too little rest. It's the second day that terminal fatigue usually strikes. She walked through the door of the Jefferson Building at eight-thirty and was in her space on the upper gallery before Consuela or any of the other Hispanic Portuguese staff members showed up.

She plugged in her laptop and inserted the last of the five discs taken from the envelope found in the so-called Aaronsen Collection. She'd run out of time at home; another fifteen pages were still to be read and notes taken.

She was so intently focused on the screen that she wasn't aware of someone standing behind her until that person cleared her throat. Annabel turned to look up at Dolores Marwede. Was she reading the computer screen over Annabel's shoulder?

"Oh," Annabel said, shifting in her chair in an attempt to block the screen.

"Early start, huh?" Dolores said.

"Yes. I feel the clock ticking, the deadline for my article looming larger and closer."

"I heard you've found computer discs in one of the collections that might bear on Michele's case."

"Actually, Sue Gomara came up with them."

"Is that what you're looking at now?"

"Yes. I'm waiting for Consuela to arrive so I can give them to her."

"What's on them?" Dolores asked, pulling the chair from what had been Michele Paul's desk to Annabel's side.

"A lot of research notes, nothing especially enlightening so far."

"From what I hear, you told Consuela you thought the discs might belong to Michele."

"The grapevine is in full flower. Do you know if Consuela is here yet?"

"I didn't see her when I came in, but she should be."

Annabel popped the disc from the drive, slipped it into its paper sleeve, added it to the envelope containing the other four discs, and stood. "I'll go down and check," she said.

She walked away, aware of Dolores Marwede's eyes following her as she stepped aside to allow Sue Gomara to pass—"How was the stuff on the discs, Annabel?" "Ah, fine, Sue. Interesting."—and went downstairs. Consuela Martinez had just arrived. There was no need to say anything. Annabel stepped into the office, closed the door, and laid the envelope on the desk.

"Were they helpful?" Consuela asked.

"I'm not sure yet. I do know that what's on those discs is disturbing."

"How so?"

"Consuela, I thought these discs belonged to Michele Paul."

"And?"

"I don't believe that now. I think they were the product of John Bitteman."

"Bitteman? What makes you say that?"

"I compared some written materials I had from Bitteman's files with the material on the discs. They track. The discs didn't come from Michele Paul's hand because they're filled with disparaging comments about him."

"What sort of disparaging comments?"

"Oh, snide remarks, mentions of professional inadequacy, claims that someone known as 'MP' stole his research, things like that. He never mentions Paul by name. It's always initials. The material is filled with initials. I have no doubt that 'MP' stands for Michele Paul. But all those negative references aren't what concern me, Consuela. It's what's on the final fifteen pages that really captured my attention."

Consuela's wide eyes urged Annabel to go on.

"Bitteman—and I'm convinced it's Bitteman's writing—says he knew all about MP's deal with 'DD'—"

"David Driscoll."

"Yes."

"Go on."

"And says he intends to go to LC."

"LC? Library of Congress?"

"Or Librarian of Congress. He says he intends to go to LC and expose Paul's financial arrangement with Driscoll."

"He lays that out?"

"Yes. Portions of what Bitteman wrote are almost like a legal brief, building a case against Paul."

"You're the lawyer, Annie—the ex-lawyer. Is it a strong case?"

"I'm not sure because I don't understand parts of it. I thought you might help."

"If I'm able, sure."

"Bitteman—and I'm certain everything on the discs was written by him—has a couple of pages of charts."

"Charts?"

"Yes. Here. Put this in your computer," Annabel said, taking one of the discs from the envelope on the desk and handing it to Consuela. When its table of contents appeared on the screen, Annabel reached over Consuela's shoulder and scrolled down to CHART, hit Enter, and the file became visible. It was arranged in four columns, with a heading at the top of each: "Material," "Value Pre-MP," "Venue," and "New Value." Beneath the first heading was a list of dozens of books and what appeared to be manuscripts, each having to do with Hispanic or Portuguese subjects.

"We have these books here in LC," Consuela said.

"I know. I've run across a few in my research."

Consuela concentrated on the list. "I distinctly remember this one," she said, touching it on the screen. "David Driscoll donated it. I recall it because of talk about it here in the division."

"Talk?"

"Not exactly controversy, but some questioned its valuation. It's a nice book, Annie, of genuine but modest value, worth maybe what's in the second column alongside it."

"What about the fourth column, 'New Value'?"

Consuela nodded. "I think that was what Driscoll claimed it really was worth, ten times that first number." She looked up at Annabel. "What does this mean?"

"Look at 'Venue.' "

Consuela read from the screen: " 'Society of Latin American Scholars, 11/89.' It must refer to the society's annual scholarly meeting. It's always held in November."

"Any idea why that entry would be there under 'Venue'?"

"No. Oh, wait. We've had a speaker from

LC at the meeting every year since I've been here, probably a lot longer than that. November, 1989. I attended that session. Michele Paul was one of the speakers."

"Do you have a record of when Driscoll donated that particular book to the library?"

"Give me a minute."

After rummaging through a file cabinet, Consuela handed Annabel a printed form, its spaces filled in by hand.

"August 1990," Annabel said. "Nine months after the meeting. Do you recall what Michele spoke about?"

"Not specifically. He tended to ramble, go off on myriad tangents."

"Did he mention that book?"

"Possibly. As I said—"

"Look at the other items in the first column. Recognize any of those?"

"Sure. Oh, I see what you're getting at. Just about all of these were Driscoll contributions to the library."

"Were his other donations ever considered overvalued?"

"Yes, but that's not unusual. People donating things to charity often inflate their value for tax purposes."

"Inflate it ten times?"

"It does seem excessive."

Annabel pointed to another item on the list, a map, and said, "According to Bitteman's calculations, the map was worth six thousand dollars 'Pre-MP.' The new value he assigns it in the fourth column is a hundred and twenty five thousand dollars. That's more than twenty times its original value. Look at what Bitteman lists as the venue— *Hispanic Insight*, 6/90."

"A magazine, well respected in the field."

"I assume you have back copies."

"Sure."

She placed a call to one of the reference librarians, who delivered it within minutes. Annabel went to the index. "Look," she said, handing the magazine to Consuela, "Michele Paul has an article in this issue."

The two women huddled together to read the article's lead.

"He's talking about that map on the list," Consuela said. "He's claiming it's vitally important to—listen to this: '. . . and when the map is found, as one day it certainly will be, scholars will finally be able to ascertain with some certainty Columbus's and Bartolomé de Las Casas's movements on land once they'd reached and colonized Hispaniola.' "

"Date when Driscoll donated the map to LC?"

A phone call from Consuela to LC's vast map division provided the answer: "October 1997."

"Four months after the article ran."

Consuela's nod confirmed the math. She removed the disc from the computer and handed it to Annabel.

"I have a feeling you'll find the same thing to be true with everything on this chart, Consuela. It looks like Michele created an artificial market value for items Driscoll donated to the library."

"For tax purposes?"

"Probably. It could be that Driscoll already possessed the items he intended to donate, picked them up for the proverbial song, their true worth. Then Michele, with his reputation as a Hispanic scholar, went out and hyped the items, which made them far more valuable than they actually were. Consuela, do you know the date of John Bitteman's disappearance?"

"Not offhand, but I can find out."

As the division chief prepared to place another call in search of information, there was a knock on her door. Annabel opened it to Dolores Marwede.

"Sorry," Dolores said. "I didn't know you were still here."

"I won't be much longer."

"Come in," Consuela said, waving to Dolores.

Dolores entered and closed the door. Consuela asked Dolores while waiting for someone to answer her call, "You were here when John Bitteman disappeared. Remember when that was?"

"Eight years ago," Dolores answered. "Why?"

"Do you have a more specific date?" Annabel asked.

"No. It was summer, I think."

"July?"

"I—I really don't know."

Consuela reached a friend in the personnel office and asked the same question. When she hung up, she said to Annabel and Dolores, "July fourteenth, 1991."

"Why the interest in John Bitteman?" Dolores asked.

Annabel looked askance at Consuela.

From her perspective, what she'd confided in Consuela should have been kept between them, at least until the discs had been turned over to the Librarian of Congress . . . or the police.

"Consuela, I wonder if . . ."

The division chief sensed Annabel's discomfort and quickly said, "We can get into this later. In the meantime, I have a meeting with Dr. Broadhurst. You'll have to excuse me."

Dolores and Annabel started to leave the office.

"Oh, Annabel, stay just a minute, won't you?" Consuela said.

When Dolores was gone, Annabel asked, "Are you taking the discs to Dr. Broadhurst now?"

"Yes. I called his secretary from home and told her it was urgent that I see him first thing this morning." She looked at her watch. "We're due there right now."

"We?"

"Absolutely. You're the only person who knows what's on these discs."

"Do you want me to tell him that I think they belonged to John Bitteman, and that Bitteman disappeared two days after he wrote notes about exposing Michele Paul's dealings with David Driscoll?"

"Two days after?"

"Yes. Bitteman disappeared on July fourteenth. The computer file index on those final fifteen pages says he wrote them on July twelfth."

"Which led to his disappearance."

"Or murder."

"We'd better go. Dr. Broadhurst is a stickler for punctuality."

"With what we're about to tell him, he might prefer that we be late—a couple of years late."

". . . and I find this extremely distressing," Broadhurst said after Annabel and Consuela had explained the purpose of wanting to see him. "You say the material on these discs came from Bitteman?"

"I can't be absolutely certain of that, Dr. Broadhurst," Annabel said, "but I believe it to be the case."

"And Bitteman knew of what was going on between Michele Paul and David Driscoll?"

"According to what he wrote two days before he disappeared. He threatened to bring what he knew to what he referred to as

LC—Library of Congress, or Librarian of Congress. That would have been Jim Billington."

"Yes," Broadhurst confirmed.

"Dr. Broadhurst," Consuela said, "is the story true about Mr. Driscoll paying Michele substantial sums of money over the years?"

Her question caused overt discomfort in Broadhurst. He got up from his chair and went to the sliding glass doors opening onto the terrace, hands shoved in the pockets of his tweed jacket, shoulders hunched beneath it. Consuela looked at Annabel and grimaced.

Broadhurst turned and said, "We're attempting to contact David Driscoll as we speak. If the police are correct, he was sending Michele Paul money over time—not big money in his terms but big to Michele Paul—but I want to hear it directly from David. As you know, the press is spreading the story all over hell and creation."

He said to Annabel, "Based upon having read what's on those discs, do you think they should be turned over to the police?"

"Of course," she replied, "although I suggest a copy be made before they're taken out of our hands. I . . . I copied some of the material on a disc of my own, but not all of it, just selected sections I felt might be helpful to my article."

Broadhurst pondered her suggestion. "You're right, of course. Can you take care of that? I'll want a printout, too."

"I'll have it to you by the evening," Consuela said.

"Good," the Librarian said. "Anything else I should know about what's on those discs?"

"I don't think so," Annabel said, "but if something else strikes me, I'll let you know."

"Good. Thank you for bringing this to my attention."

Consuela and Annabel returned to the Jefferson Building using the underground walkway, its umbilical cord to the Madison.

"What do you think?" Annabel asked as they walked.

"I think he's in a tough position, Annie. Michele Paul's murder was troublesome enough for the library, but now it's mushrooming into a full fledged scandal—Michele being paid by David Driscoll to turn over his research, a possible tie to another possible murder eight years ago, discs mysteriously showing up in the stacks—when does the next shoe drop?"

"Consuela, was there ever any question of Michele's sexual orientation?"

The question brought a short, harsh laugh from Consuela. "God, no. His reputation as a womanizer was well known. Of course, he never married, hardly a basis for questioning his sexual preferences. No family that I know of. Why?"

"John Bitteman was an acknowledged homosexual. Obviously, there was bad blood between him and Michele Paul. Bitteman's comments about Michele on the discs are vitriolic, intensely personal at times. I just wondered if their relationship went beyond the professional."

"No," Consuela said. "That's out of the question."

"Just thought I'd ask. Want help with copying the discs and printing out hard copies?"

"Thanks, no, Annie. You've got your article to do. I'll get Sue Gomara or Dolores to do it. Shouldn't take very long."

"Okay, try Sue. But if you need an extra hand, just yell."

They parted in the Hispanic-Portuguese reading room, Consuela disappearing into her office, Annabel swiping her magnetic card in the door's slot and going up the narrow stairs to her space. Sue Gomara was at her desk wading through Cuban newspapers again. She dropped that task and turned to Annabel.

"The stuff on the discs was good?" she asked, beaming.

"Very good, in its way. Thanks again."

"Good thing I looked through the Aaronsen box. You never know."

"A very good thing. Nice motto for a research librarian. Why don't you go down and check in with Consuela. I think she has an assignment for you."

"Really? Okay, I will."

Annabel had turned on her laptop while talking with the intern. As Sue started to leave, Annabel stopped her. "Sue, were you here at my desk this morning?"

"At your desk? Me? No. Why?"

"I was sure I'd removed this disc from the computer before I went with Consuela to meet with Dr. Broadhurst." She held up a disc on which she'd copied sections of the five discs taken from the Aaronsen collection.

"Wasn't me," Sue repeated.

"Did you see anyone else here?"

She shook her head. "Not really. Dolores was around for a while, but I didn't see her at your desk. She was in the stacks. I wasn't here the whole time."

Annabel forced a smile. "They call such lapses a senior moment these days," she said lightly. "I must have forgotten to take the disc out. Go see Consuela. You might enjoy what she has in store for you."

Annabel stared at the laptop, her face creased as she tried to resurrect whether she had, in fact, taken the disc from the computer and placed it to the side. She was sure she had, but how sure could you ever be of something like that?

She put aside the question and got to work on material for her article. By one, the night without sleep had caught up with her, although the morning's work, during which the structure of the article had suddenly become clearer, buoyed her spirits if not her tired body.

She called Mac's office at the university.

"Holding up?" he asked.

"Fading fast but I'll make it. You?"

"Feel great. We ought to pull all-nighters

more often, and not just reading discs. What was the outcome of giving the discs to Consuela?"

"We met with Cale. Since I was the only one who'd read everything on them, Consuela wanted me with her. He was upset."

"I don't wonder."

"He's still trying to get through to David Driscoll."

"Did he confirm the reports that Driscoll was paying off Michele Paul?"

"He said the police have confirmed it. Consuela is having copies of the discs made before Cale turns them over to the police."

"I'm glad he's giving them the discs. It's obviously not clear what bearing they might have on the murder, but there could be something there."

"I agree. How's the knee?"

"Pretty good. I think the magnet is working. I don't like the bulge it makes in my pants but that's a minor price to pay to avoid the knife."

Avoid the knife! He could be too dramatic at times.

"See you at dinner?" she asked.

"Sure, only let's make it an early one. I

have a feeling we won't be seeing the ten o'clock news."

"Or the nine o'clock. Love you."

"Me, too."

She smiled and hung up.

Consuela had set Sue Gomara up with a computer in a cramped meeting room off her office. The intern peered intently at the screen as she brought up each individual file from a disc, then replaced it with another disc on which she copied the file. Annabel looked in on her.

"How's it going?" she asked.

"Okay," she said, not taking her eyes from the screen. "Some of this stuff is interesting."

"Don't get bogged down reading everything," Annabel said. "I know that Consuela needs the duplicate discs as quickly as possible."

"Yeah, she told me that."

"Good. I'm going out for a sandwich. Want me to bring back something?"

"No, thanks, I had lunch."

When Annabel came out of the office, John Vogler was coming from Consuela's office. From the anguished expression on his face, it had not been a pleasant meeting. For a moment, he seemed startled to see Annabel. He said nothing and walked away. Annabel poked her head into Consuela's crowded space. "Feel like a sandwich?" Annabel asked.

"I feel like a large margarita. Make that a triple."

"Something else happen since this morning?"

Consuela answered by jerking her head toward the door.

"Vogler?"

A sigh was the only response to the question. "You buying?" she asked.

"Absolutely."

They walked to Bullfeathers and sat at the long bar. Midday temperance won out; it was soft drinks for both, and crab salads.

"Dr. Vogler did not look happy when he left your office," Annabel commented.

"Is he ever?" was Consuela's response. "He's an enigma. Beneath that neurotic outer shell is a very decent man, but, boy, is he a wreck over the murder investigation."

"So I've noticed."

"He wants me to go to the police and tell them he wasn't anywhere near Hispanic the night Michele was killed."

"Do you know that he wasn't?"

"No, and I told him that. He said someone informed the police that he *was* there, and that they consider him the prime suspect because of past incidents he had with Michele. You know about his wife, don't you?"

"Only because Vogler told me about it himself."

They raised their glasses in a halfhearted toast to nothing special.

Their conversation dealt mostly with the events of the past twenty-four hours— Annabel having stayed up all night going through the discs; of her initial belief that the material on them had been written by Michele Paul, but having come to the conclusion that they were, in fact, John Bitteman's property; that Bitteman had written of learning about Paul's deal with Driscoll and had threatened to expose the scheme to, in all likelihood, the then Librarian of Congress; and of that morning's meeting with LC's current leader.

"I wonder what new revelations our lovely Ms. Huston will conjure up on her next newscast," Consuela said.

"At least we won't be surprised with whatever it is. I heard she winged off to Los Angeles."

"Oh? Chasing David Driscoll?"

"Probably. But he's not there. Or is said not to be. My money is on her. She'll find him and get something from him. She's good at that."

"Do you think—?"

"The only thing I'm thinking at the moment, Consuela, is that I've gotten too old to stay up all night. Pardon me if my head suddenly ends up in this salad."

Consuela patted her friend's arm. "If it does, I'll have to tell Lucianne Huston, and she'll have it on the evening news. Finish up and let's get back to my office. Among Sue Gomara's new duties is keeping the coffeepot going. I know you're not a fan of institutional java but Sue makes the world's strongest coffee. One cup and you'll stay up for a week."

Lucianne Huston didn't bother book-
35 ing a hotel in Los Angeles. She
grabbed the first available flight from
Washington, got off the plane, and took a
taxi directly to Parker Center.

"Detective Davis, please," she told the
desk sergeant.

"Who wants him?"

"Lucianne Huston, NCN."

He cocked his head and smiled. "Yeah, it
is you."

"I'm relieved to hear it," she said, going to
a corner and sitting, her carry on bag at her
feet.

A few minutes later LAPD homicide detective Sam Davis emerged from a door behind the desk, came up to Lucianne, stopped a few feet away, and laughed.

"What's funny?" she asked, not getting up.

"Seeing you, Lucy. You always bring a smile to my face."

"You know I hate being called that," she said, standing and closing the gap between them. She kissed his cheek, causing him to look nervously at the desk sergeant.

"Still the handsome, dashing foe of all evil," she said, stepping back and making an exaggerated point of looking him up and down.

Davis was a strapping middle-aged man, forty-five years old, an LAPD veteran who'd been assigned to, and solved, some of the city's high-profile cases. And in Los Angeles, many cases quickly became high profile, even if the profile was altered by cosmetic surgery. Local media had given him a lot of play as a celebrity; he'd become known as a hunk, a homegrown heartthrob whose appeal to the opposite sex soared when his divorce from his wife was reported three years ago.

"And still the globe-trotting reporter," he said. "I saw you last night on the tube. Things must be slow at the network, Lucy—Lucianne. The Library of *Congress*?"

"More exciting than you think."

"Let's go outside. Leave your bag."

"With cops around? I'm not that crazy."

They walked up Los Angeles Street until reaching the Otani Hotel at the corner of First Street. Lucianne looked up at it. "Returning to the scene of the crime?" she asked.

"Sleeping with me was a crime? I thought I was supporting the First Amendment."

"I considered it more a matter of search and seizure."

"I was good, wasn't I?"

"You were—good. Time for a drink?"

"Sure. I went off duty two hours ago but hung around to catch up on paperwork. Your timing's impeccable, as usual. Another fifteen minutes and I'd have been on my way up the coast. Two days off starting tomorrow."

They settled in the Rendezvous Lounge in the center of the main lobby.

"So, here we are," Davis said after they ordered from the kimono-clad waitress, "déjà vu all over again. Another case of looking for inside information, Lucianne, or tired of sex with the wimps of your profession and looking for something better?"

"Your modesty is overwhelming."

"Just fishing for the *real* reason you're here. I'd rather it be the second one, but—"

"I'm looking for information."

"Ah ha," he said, smiling and nodding his approval. "The lady has learned to be candid with her sources. Ask away, only it's your treat this time."

"It was last time, too, in a different way. Sam, I'm out here following up on a murder case at the Library of Congress."

Davis looked at her quizzically. "What would I know about a murder in Washington?"

"Maybe more than you think. Is the name David Driscoll familiar to you?"

"Sure. Richer than God and aspiring to the title. Why? Oh, that's right, you reported something about him having paid money to someone at the Library of Congress. The guy who was murdered?"

"Uh huh. I'm out here hoping to interview Driscoll. He's in Mexico, I'm told. Let me fill you in."

She ran through what she knew of Driscoll's connection with Michele Paul and laid out the details of the theft of the Reyes painting in

Miami, the shooting of the guard at the museum, and Warren Munsch's flight with the painting from Florida to Los Angeles, disappearing
in Mexico only to be gunned down by Mexican
authorities.

"So?" Davis said when she was through.
"Are you suggesting that Driscoll had something to do with all that?"

"I'm suggesting that I'd like to know
whether LAPD has anything on it. Look, I
know from cops in Miami that your people
were informed that the painting headed this
way, and that this slob, Munsch, who was
wanted for the theft and guard shooting, was
here, too, before skipping across the border.
No bells ringing?"

Davis shook his head.

"But you will find out for me, won't you?"

"For a lousy drink?"

"Dinner's on me, too. Spago. Morton's.
Your choice—provided you give me something I can use."

"It's a deal. The Belvedere at the
Peninsula Hotel. Got your credit cards with
you? It'll run you a couple of hundred."

"Nickels and dimes, my friend. But first the
info, then dinner."

Davis ordered another round and pulled

out a small cell phone. He settled back in his chair and made three calls, making notes as he did. Lucianne watched, a bemused smile on her face. When he completed the third call, he flipped the phone closed, returned it to his pocket, and said, "This is worth six dinners. The painting ended up with an art restorer named Abraham Widlitz. The art squad—yeah, we have an art squad—they pulled a raid on Widlitz's studio looking for stolen art. They came up empty *except* for the painting that was stolen in Miami. Piece of junk, according to our art experts. Widlitz told them the painting had been brought to him on Driscoll's behalf by a guy named Conrad, only it turns out that's his first name, Conrad Syms. Mr. Syms is some sort of a gopher for Driscoll and was picked up after leaving Driscoll's house. He confirmed he took the painting to Widlitz on Driscoll's orders. How am I doing?"

Lucianne looked up from notes she was taking, grinned, and replied, "Not bad. What else?"

"What do you mean, 'what else'? I've just handed you your story."

"What's the disposition so far?"

A shrug from Davis. "They want to bring

Driscoll in for questioning but, as you say, he's out of the country."

"He's an accessory to murder," Lucianne said.

"He's a rich and powerful guy. Sits on a dozen boards, big arts benefactor."

"Including the Library of Congress."

"I'm hungry."

She placed an American Express card on the bill.

"Where are you staying?" he asked.

"Haven't figured that out yet."

"Stay at my place. I'm leaving in the morning."

"Visiting an elderly spinster aunt? Or a nubile young starlet?"

"None of your business."

"True, but I'll have the answer before the night is over."

Davis laughed and stood. "Yeah, I'm sure you will. But you'll have to drag it out of me."

"Oooh, sounds like fun. I can't wait to get started."

36 Upon returning from lunch, Annabel spent a few minutes with Sue, who sat at a computer in a semi-isolated corner behind the Hispanic division's reference librarian's desk. She'd started making copies of each file on the five discs and printing out a hard copy of each.

"How's it coming?" Annabel asked, sipping from a mug of the intern's coffee, which, as promised, seemed to instantly jolt her awake.

"Pretty good, only I have to get over to the main reading room. My shift starts at three."

"I can do some," Annabel offered.

"No need," Sue said, reading a printout of the file she'd been copying. "Dolores said she'd take over for me." As she said it, Dolores arrived.

"Hi," Annabel said.

"Hi," Dolores said, slipping into the chair Sue had just vacated. "Where do I start?"

Sue filled her in on where she'd left off, then said, "Got to change into my fancy librarian duds."

Annabel couldn't help but smile as she watched the intern run off to change wardrobes, tripping over a chair because her eyes were on a clock on the wall.

"Great kid," Annabel said, peering over Dolores's shoulder as the next file to be copied appeared on the screen. The words, of course, were familiar to Annabel, who had read them at home the night before. "If you get bored, give a yell and I'll do some."

Dolores sat up straight and looked up at Annabel, as though her presence was startling. "What? Oh, sure, thanks, Annabel. I appreciate it."

Sue bounded out of the room she used as her dressing room and came to Annabel and Dolores.

"How do I look?" she asked, pirouetting.

"Like the next Librarian of Congress," Annabel said.

"I wonder who the youngest one ever was," Sue said.

"A lot older than you," Dolores said, never taking her eyes from the screen as she scrolled through the text. Annabel was tempted to suggest that if Dolores kept reading what she was supposed to be copying and printing, she'd be there forever. But she held her tongue. It wasn't her concern how or when the discs were duplicated and their material printed. That was up to Consuela. Sue left for her other LC life, and Annabel went to her space on the upper gallery to resume work on her article.

Dr. Cale Broadhurst had a last-minute, unscheduled lunch that day, too, with Mary Beth Mullin. After his meeting with Consuela Martinez and Annabel Reed-Smith, the Librarian canceled the date he had on his calendar with a former George Washington University colleague and asked Mary Beth to break her own previous engagement.

Seated at an isolated table at the University Club, where Broadhurst had been a member for years, they explored the legal ramifications of the Driscoll–Michele Paul connection.

"Are you sure Mrs. Reed-Smith is correct in what she says is on the discs?" Mullin asked the Librarian. "It sounds like speculation to me."

"I don't think so," Broadhurst said. "We'll know precisely what's on those discs after they've been duplicated, and we have a hard copy to read. But it seems prudent to me that we *assume* the material on them bears on Michele Paul's murder. I suppose that's a decision the police will have to make. I'm glad we're having copies made. At least anything of value to the library will still be in our hands."

She nodded.

"But I'm not as concerned about that as I am about the public relations ramifications for the library. If David Driscoll, one of its leading benefactors, has been corrupting its professional staff for years, *and,* if that same David Driscoll was involved in some way with Michele's murder, *and,* if the murder was linked to John Bitteman's disappearance—we'll be further smeared, this time on every tabloid TV show and in every supermarket rag. The World's Great Unsolved

Mysteries, direct to you from your nation's library. By releasing the discs to the police, Mary Beth, we might as well hold a press conference to announce to the world that you don't have to check out murder mysteries from our librarians, all you have to do is hang around and see the real thing." He said it through tight lips, small muscles in each cheek contracting in anger.

"When will you have the hard copy, Cale?"

"Consuela promised them to me this evening."

"Good. May I make a suggestion?"

"I welcome all the suggestions I can get."

"Don't worry about what handing over the discs to the police will mean, Cale. There's really nothing else that can be done until you speak with Driscoll."

A rare smile creased Broadhurst's face. "The timing is dreadful, Mary Beth. Senator Menendez was in the process of seeking funds to buy the Las Casas diaries, but now this Driscoll matter has surfaced, he's backed off. Can't say I blame him. I assume the trustees will, too."

"I'm not sure I agree," she said, her tone soothing. "No matter what the source of the Las Casas diaries, and no matter how flawed the individuals involved, people will turn a blind eye on how they're obtained. No one will stand on principle and let something as important as those diaries slip away."

"I hope you're right," Broadhurst said grimly, signing the bill.

"Know what I'm thinking, Mary Beth?" he said as they parted on the sidewalk in front of the club.

"What?"

"If David Driscoll did anything to sully the reputation of the Library of Congress, I just may commit the next murder."

Mullin watched him walk away, seeming even smaller than he actually was. Two things crossed her mind as she hailed a passing cab: She ached for her boss, and what she'd said inside represented unfortunate reality. Events would steamroll ahead with the force of an avalanche, and those standing in the way couldn't do a damn thing to stop it.

"Dr. Broadhurst, a number of people called while you were gone," his secretary told him upon his return, "but I think you'll want to see this one first. He says it's urgent that he speak with you this afternoon." The slip she handed him said *David Driscoll—2:15—Urgent—Call at 555-9100.*

"A local number?"

"The Willard. He said he'll be there all afternoon awaiting your call."

It was the same suite Driscoll had occupied when he and Broadhurst last met at the venerable landmark hotel. Driscoll had been brusque on the phone: "I'll only be in Washington until early this evening," he'd said. "It's important we talk before I leave."

"David, do you mind telling me why—?"

"When you get here, Cale."

Broadhurst was left with a loud click in his ear.

The Librarian arrived at four-fifteen. A tray of hors d'oeuvres and a bar setup had been delivered from room service just prior to Broadhurst's arrival. Judging from Driscoll's demeanor on the phone, the Librarian of Congress expected a tense, confrontational atmosphere. Instead, Driscoll greeted him with an outstretched hand and broad smile. "Come in, Cale, make yourself at home. Single-barrel bourbon, if I remember correctly. Blanton's. The best. Help yourself. The scallops are excellent. They do something special with them. It's the lime juice, I suppose."

A drink was the last thing on Broadhurst's mind, but he poured some bourbon over ice and tasted a scallop. "Yes, quite good, David. To be honest, your call this afternoon took me by surprise. I've been trying to reach you since—"

". . . since that whore of a reporter, Lucianne Huston, started with her trash on TV about me. Is that what you were about to say?"

"Yes."

"Sit down, Cale. Let me refresh your drink."

"Thank you, no, I—"

"I insist. I'll join you. It's been a hell of a day."

Drinks in hand, they sat across from each other at a small dining table. The multimillionaire peered out a nearby window, drink in hand, eyes narrowed against his thought of the moment. Broadhurst sat silently, content to wait for what his friend of many years had to say.

Driscoll slowly turned, smiled, raised his glass to Broadhurst, and said, "Here's to those, Cale, who enjoy making mountains out of molehills."

Broadhurst didn't respond as Driscoll continued.

"I presume all the irresponsible reporting that's been going on has caused you some grief."

"Yes, it has. The timing was bad."

"Is there ever a good time for such things? I'm certain you know the high regard in which I hold you and the library."

"Of course I do, David. Your friendship and generosity to the library have always been deeply appreciated."

"I've done it—I do it—because I believe that without knowledge, without centers of knowledge like LC, the future of this nation is questionable."

Broadhurst looked down into his drink and pondered where the conversation was headed. He'd heard Driscoll pontificate many times before, wrapping the Republic and its future into the contribution of institutions like the Library of Congress, feigning modesty but seeking adoration, publicly eschewing gratitude but privately lobbying for greater recognition from the library, its benefactors, and Cale Broadhurst. Was that what he was looking for this day?

"I believe," Driscoll said, "that if a man isn't willing to take a chance, to put himself on the line, he isn't much of a man. Agree?"

"I suppose it depends upon the cause."

"Ah hah, exactly. What greater cause can there be than the quest for perfect knowledge, Cale? 'And this gray spirit yearning in desire to follow knowledge like a sinking star, beyond the utmost bound of human thought.' Tennyson."

"Yes, Tennyson."

Driscoll straightened and became more animated.

"Do you realize, Cale, what possession of the Las Casas diaries would mean to the elevating of man's knowledge?" He didn't wait for a response. "It could rewrite the history books if Las Casas's diaries contradict Columbus's writings about his voyages. Was Columbus really Spanish rather than Italian? A Spanish Jew? What were his ideas of geography? Was he as benevolent to the natives he encountered on his voyages as his writings would have us believe, or was he a cruel conquerer? What did Las Casas say about these things, and more, Cale? And the map. My God, think of it. Did Columbus plunder those natives and stash millions in gold for himself instead of enriching his benefactors in Spain as he was expected to do? If Las Casas's writings are ever unearthed, Cale, how we view who we are and how we came to be here could forever be changed."

What about the payments to Michele Paul, David? Why did you give him money? Did you have anything to do with his murder?

There would be time later to ask those questions. For now, yes, let us talk about Bartolomé de Las Casas, he mused.

"Are you closer to obtaining the diaries, David?"

"The most daunting quest in a lifetime of questing for the truth."

It took Broadhurst a moment to realize Driscoll was referring to himself.

"Cale, let me be blunt with you. I took unusually daring steps to try and obtain the diaries and map for you." Broadhurst started to say something but Driscoll held up his hand. "No, no need to thank me, at least not at this juncture. I do not believe a map ever existed."

Have I been summoned here to be informed of his failure? Broadhurst quietly wondered.

Driscoll went on: "But as you've known all along, the map was the least likely to surface. I followed, at great personal sacrifice, the most promising route in search of the map. I was informed by a very reliable source that it existed behind a painting created in Seville that was brought to this country. It turned out not to be true."

Was that "very reliable source" Michele Paul?

"Was our Dr. Paul your source, David?"

"There you go, Cale, believing what you read in the papers."

And from the police.

And on the discs.

"David, I certainly don't wish to be argumentative, but are you telling me there is no truth to the allegation that you'd been paying large sums to Michele Paul in return for . . . his research?"

Driscoll's smile dismissed the question as not being worthy of a reply.

"It's important that I know," Broadhurst said, displeased with the pleading tone that had crept into his voice. "It isn't just the press reports, David. The police traced Michele's financial records."

"So I've heard—on television."

"If it's not true," Broadhurst said, injecting optimism into his tone, "if there's been some mistake, some misinterpretation of the information, I assure you that I, and the library, will stand with you to correct this erroneous report. But if—"

"Yes? But if *what*?"

Broadhurst, uncomfortable with the palpable tension in the space between them, stood and went to the rolling bar, on which he placed his half-empty glass.

"Cale," Driscoll called from where he continued to sit.

Broadhurst faced him.

"Yes, David?"

"It is irrelevant whether I helped support Michele's work. He was a brilliant researcher. People like that need all the financial help they can muster. You should applaud my becoming his patron. And I hasten to remind you that a good number of the 'finds' delivered to the Library of Congress—which certainly enhanced your stature as Librarian, and of Librarians before you—resulted from the arrangement Michele Paul and I enjoyed."

Broadhurst stared intently at Driscoll. Yes, and some, while valuable, had not benefited the library all that much. Driscoll had gotten out of his chair and stood at the table, his chin jutting out in defiance of what Broadhurst would say next. The Librarian wanted to ask about John Bitteman, about what role Driscoll played in Michele Paul's murder, about so many things. He would have if the phone hadn't rung.

Instead, he watched and listened as the founder of the nation's largest discount brokerage firm said, "Yes, Constance, I'm here with Cale Broadhurst. . . . They are? What do they want? . . . All right, put them on."

After thirty seconds, Driscoll said, "I'll be returning to Los Angeles tonight. I'll be happy to meet with you tomorrow—with my lawyer. What was that? No, there's no need to have someone meet me tonight when I arrive. I'm a man of my word, Detective. My lawyer and I will be at your office at ten. Oh, and please, do not harass my wife. She isn't well. Thank you."

Broadhurst looked away as Driscoll hung up, pretending he hadn't heard. When he again looked at Driscoll, he saw a man whose defiant stance had been replaced by a sagging humility.

"Thank you for coming, Cale," Driscoll said.

"Is there anything I can do?" Broadhurst asked, meaning it.

"No, thank you. A misunderstanding, that's all. Easily resolved. Rest assured, Cale, that I continue to pursue those diaries. I have my exclusive sources. I assume you want me to do that."

"I . . . yes, of course, David. We'll all be in your debt once more if you're successful. Safe trip home. My best to Constance."

Broadhurst returned to the Madison Building and rode the elevator to his office floor. Waiting anxiously for him was Mary Beth Mullin, who followed him into his office.

"Cale," she said, "there's something vitally important I must discuss with you."

"Yes?"

"Public Affairs received a call a half hour ago from Lucianne Huston. She called from Los Angeles. It's about David Driscoll."

37 "Annie, it's Consuela. Got a minute?"
"Sure."

Annabel checked her watch. Five-thirty. Wow. She raised her head wearily from the notes. Almost time to pack up and go home.

She came downstairs into the reading room and went to Consuela's office, but on impulse stopped first to say hello to Dolores, who was still working at duplicating files and printing out the discs. She was so intensely focused on the task that Annabel said nothing.

Consuela, who was on the phone when

Annabel arrived, waved her in, cupped her hand over the mouthpiece, and said, "Only be a minute."

Annabel browsed a copy of the library's latest annual report until Consuela ended her phone conversation with "No, not a problem at all. I sort of expected it. See you later."

"Hi," Annabel said.

"Hi. Getting anything done up in your rabbit warren?"

"As a matter of fact, yes. Once I realized how to structure the article, I've been able to focus my research, aiming a rifle instead of a shotgun. I see you've still got Dolores hard at work."

"Sure have. Annie, can I impose upon you again?"

"I'm not aware you already have. What's up?"

"Can you come to the meeting tonight when I deliver the discs and hard copy to Cale?"

"What time?"

"I told him six-thirty."

"Sure. Nothing on the home-front agenda tonight except Mac and getting to bed. Staying up a few extra hours won't kill me—I don't think."

"I'll order in dinner. Preferences?"

"Keep it light. A heavy meal will sink me, literally. I might as well go back upstairs and keep working. Yell when you want me."

Despite Annabel's determination to continue working on her article, the road to hell being paved with such intentions, she found it hard to concentrate. She turned on her laptop computer and inserted the disc on which she'd copied sections of the five discs found in the Aaronsen collection. "Damn," she muttered as the screen filled with words. "I *know* I took this disc out when I went with Consuela to see Broadhurst."

She fast-forwarded through the pages until reaching the copy she'd made of the final fifteen pages from the fifth disc. Then, using the cursor, she slowly scrolled down through the pages, brow furrowed, tongue running over her lips as she went. She repeated the process three times, frequently stopping to make notes. As she was about to start a fourth reading, she realized she hadn't told Mac that she wouldn't be home for dinner. She called; he answered on the first ring.

"I'm going to be late, Mac. A meeting with Cale and others."

"About?"

"The discs and what's on them. They're being duplicated and printed out now. The meeting won't start until that process is completed, so I can't give you a definite time."

"You must be exhausted."

"No, the adrenaline kicked in, and I had a cup of coffee after lunch that would wake the dead. Consuela is ordering dinner. Why don't you pop down to the hotel, have a drink and dinner, and get to bed. Don't wait up for me."

"I'll do what you suggest about a drink and dinner, but I'll be up when you get here."

"Okay, but it may be late."

"Just don't stick that pretty neck out too far, Annie. You're there to research an article, not end up knee-deep in a murder case."

"Take care of your own knees, darling."

Annabel willed herself to get back to focusing on the article.

While she worked, Mac took Rufus down in the elevator for a walk, returned to the apartment, made a few phone calls, and started out the door to go to the Watergate Hotel's dining room for dinner. The buzzer from the front desk of the South Building stopped him.

"Hello?"

"Mr. Smith, you have a visitor."

"Oh? Who?"

"Ms. Huston. Shall I send her up?"

"Really?" He paused to think. "Tell her I'll be down in a minute."

Lucianne was pacing the large lobby when Mac stepped off the elevator. "A pleasant surprise," he said, shaking her hand. "What brings you here?"

She smiled and said, "Couldn't it be that I simply wanted to stop in for a friendly visit?"

"Sure, but unlikely. This isn't Mount Pleasant, Iowa. Friendly visits are usually preceded by a phone call."

"I didn't have time. I just got off a plane from Los Angeles."

"I was just heading to the hotel for dinner," Mac said. "Buy you a drink?"

"Sure, dinner, too, if you're in the mood for company."

They left the lobby and headed down into the mini-mall of shops that linked the buildings in the Watergate complex.

"Where's your wife?" Lucianne asked.

"At the library."

"Working late?"

"Yeah. The deadline for her article is coming up fast and she's feeling under the gun. So to speak."

"I tried to call her there but didn't get any answer on the number I have. I assume you know how to reach her. What's new there on the murder and David Driscoll?"

Mac stopped walking, turned, and asked, "Is that why you showed up at the apartment, to see if I can reach Annabel for you?"

"That's one reason. I came to see you, too."

He grunted and resumed walking.

"You're limping," she said.

"A trick knee, that's all. I'd say it's an old war or football injury, but the fact is it's just an old man's wear and tear."

"Make up something exotic."

"Maybe I will."

They sat at a table in the Potomac Lounge and ordered drinks. Lucianne took in her surroundings before saying, "The famous Watergate, symbol of the Washington power elite."

"And occasional scandal," Mac added.

"Speaking of scandal . . ."

"You never quit, do you? I'm sure you know more than I do."

"And you're probably right, although I was hoping your wife's insider status at the library would add, well, insider information."

"Sorry to disappoint."

A tourist couple recognized Lucianne and stopped to tell her how much they enjoyed her work on television and asked for an autograph, which she graciously provided.

"What were you doing in Los Angeles?" Mac asked after the tourists left the table.

"Tracking down Driscoll."

"Successfully?"

"I didn't find him, but I was successful in other ways."

Their drinks were delivered. She raised her glass: "Oogy wawa!"

Mac laughed. "What's that?"

"Zulu for 'cheers.' Learned it the last time I was in Africa."

"I'll try to remember it next time I go on a binge there."

"Impresses the natives, knowing their language. Sure there's nothing new on this end about the murder?"

"I'm sure, but tell me about your success in L.A."

"Okay, I will. No, I'll do even better than that. I'm sitting here with one of D.C.'s top criminal attorneys. Let me—"

"*Former* criminal attorney."

"But still itching to get back in the saddle. Am I right?"

"No, but it doesn't matter. Go on. I'm listening."

"Pretend you're back in court, in this case defending someone like David Driscoll."

"All right."

"And pretend I'm your chief investigator. Okay, here's what I've learned from impeccable sources. David Driscoll hires a two-bit hustler in Miami to break in and steal a painting from a small museum of sorts, Casa de Seville. The artist was named Fernando Reyes, a hack, I'm told. While this petty thief—his name was Warren Munsch—does the deed, a security guard at the museum is shot and killed. A part-time maintenance worker at the museum left a skylight open for Munsch and his cronies, two of them, to gain access to the museum. The Miami police pick up the maintenance worker, who turned in Munsch's two accomplices. They, in turn, ratted on Mr. Munsch."

She checked Mac for a reaction.

"I'm with you so far."

She pressed on. "Munsch took the Reyes painting to Los Angeles and delivered it to one of Driscoll's gophers, a so-called actor named Conrad Syms. Syms then took the painting to an art restorer named Widlitz, Abraham Widlitz."

"To have it restored?" Mac asked.

"No, to see whether there was something hidden behind it."

"Such as?"

"Such as a map."

"By Señor de Las Casas?"

"Exactly. I just got that information yesterday from my source."

"Was there a map?"

"No. Mr. Widlitz was questioned extensively by the L.A. police. Nothing behind the painting except crude preliminary pencil sketches by the artist."

Mac held up his hand, said, "Driscoll went through all this and came up empty?"

"Yup."

Mac's hand went up again. "You're sure that David Driscoll was behind this?"

"Absolutely sure."

"Doesn't play for me, Lucianne. A man of Driscoll's wealth and stature doesn't go out and hire a two-bit Miami thug to steal a two-bit painting."

"Not directly. Leaves plenty of layers between him and those who dirty their hands. Mr. Syms, aspiring movie star, tells the police that he acted on Driscoll's behalf, and Widlitz confirms the painting came from Driscoll. Pretty strong evidence against your client?"

"I've dealt with worse."

"Okay, now in our little role-playing exercise, I'm now the prosecutor. Here's the scenario I come up with. It's been established that Driscoll was paying Michele Paul on occasion lots of money for Paul's research findings. This titan of industry and patron of the arts uses Paul's research over the years to identify and uncover rare books and manuscripts, which he generously donates to the Library of Congress. This makes him a big man in the eyes of those whose approval he seeks, people like Dr. Broadhurst and others of that genteel, academic ilk. Making money is fine, but it doesn't buy you the cultured status you yearn for."

"Fair enough. What are you as the prosecutor going to do, charge my client as an accessory to the Miami security guard killing?"

"Yes, but I'm not stopping at that."

"What other charges do I have to defend? Lay it all out, Ms. Prosecutor. Remember, we have disclosure laws."

"I wouldn't think of withholding anything from a lawyer of your stature, Mr. Smith. After years of coming up with interesting items to donate to the library, Driscoll decides to go after the really big one, the Las Casas diaries and map, if they even exist. Michele Paul tells Driscoll he can help him locate the diaries and map, and Driscoll sends Paul a big check. Paul tells Driscoll the map may be behind this second-rate painting in Miami. That spurs Driscoll into action. He hires Munsch and his gang of bumblers, through intermediaries, of course. The painting is stolen, the guard gets offed, and things start to unravel for your client."

"We've already gone over that," Mac said, shaking his head at the waitress, who'd asked if they'd like more drinks.

"True," said Lucianne, "but Driscoll can't stop there. Let's say Michele Paul decides he wants more money than he's been getting from Driscoll. Let's say he tells Driscoll he intends to reveal their arrangement to the Librarian of Congress and others who wouldn't be too happy with the news. Paul must have known about the bungled Miami heist and could identify Driscoll as an accessory to that theft and murder. So, your client, David Driscoll, has to get rid of Michele Paul."

Mac laughed. "David Driscoll—my client— didn't come into the Library of Congress, Ms. Prosecutor, and hit Michele Paul over the head. Not his style."

"Of course it isn't, but again, people like Driscoll can always find someone else to do their dirty work. He did in Miami; no reason he couldn't have paid someone in the Library of Congress."

"Prove it!"

"I was hoping to get some help with that from you and your wife."

"You'd like the defense to help the prosecution make its case?"

She nodded.

"Nice try."

"Driscoll is going to be brought in and questioned when he gets back to L.A."

"If I were his attorney, I'd be with him."

"I'd love another drink."

"One's my limit, at least tonight."

"I don't set limits on myself."

"So I've noticed."

"What I haven't figured out is the connection between Michele Paul's murder and the disappearance of that other Las Casas researcher, John Bitteman."

"Maybe there isn't one."

"Has to be. That's why I want to talk to Annabel. I assume she told you about discs some intern found in a collection back in the stacks."

"You know about them?"

"Yes."

"Another impeccable source?"

"Of course."

"From inside the Library of Congress?"

A noncommittal shrug.

"Well, Ms. Huston, I am duly impressed with your ability to get people to confide in you."

"What was on those discs, Mac?"

"How would I know?"

"My source tells me your wife ended up with them."

"Maybe all your sources aren't as impeccable as you think."

Lucianne smiled. "I'm pretty good at reading people, and judging from my read on you at this moment, I think my source was better than impeccable."

"Think what you wish."

He signaled for a check.

"My treat," Lucianne said.

"Good. I think I'll skip dinner here in the hotel, go back and make myself something simple."

"Am I invited back with you?"

"No."

They stood. Lucianne extended her hand, which Mac took.

"I'm not offended at being disinvited for dinner," Lucianne said.

"And no offense intended. I just think we've run out of things to talk about."

"Maybe you're right, but there'll be more— things to talk about."

"Undoubtedly."

He walked away, paused at the entrance to the lounge, looked back and saw her standing next to the table, hands on her hips, head cocked, a smug, knowing smile on her lips. Another tourist came up to her and handed her a napkin on which Lucianne scrawled her signature. For a moment, Mac considered going back and extending the evening with her. There was something strangely compelling about being close to someone who managed to know so much about things she wasn't supposed to know anything about. He'd enjoyed the what-if exercise, the role playing, being cast as a criminal defense lawyer again.

But the pleasure was fleeting. He quickly returned to the apartment, prepared a cheese-and-cracker platter for himself, and settled down to watch Lucianne Huston's all-news network, NCN, hoping Annabel would call, and soon.

Annabel was immersed in what was
38 on her computer screen when
Consuela Martinez entered her
space on the upper gallery. It was six thirty.

"I think we're ready," Consuela said.

"Running late."

"For some reason it took longer than I thought for Dolores to copy and print all the discs."

Annabel removed her disc of selected files, slipped it into her blazer pocket, and turned off the laptop.

"Put this in your locker," Consuela said, handing Annabel an envelope.

"What is it?"

"The duplicate discs. The safe in my office isn't working. I've been after Maintenance for a week to fix it, but they never seem to get around to it."

Annabel took the envelope from Consuela, placed it in her locker, added her laptop and some files, and locked it, the key going into the other pocket of her blazer. She followed Consuela down to the reading room, where Dolores Marwede waited.

"You can go home," Consuela told Dolores. "Thanks for staying late and doing such a great job."

"I didn't mind," Dolores said. "But I'll be here for a while. I dropped a project to dupe the discs. I'd better finish it up before I leave."

"Sorry," Consuela said.

"Not a problem."

As Dolores walked away, Sue Gomara arrived.

"How's things in the main reading room?" Annabel asked.

"The same. I saw a guy I thought looked like he could be my stalker—'telephone harasser,' the cops call it—but I asked him something and listened to his voice. Not him."

"Is that still going on?" Consuela asked with a sigh.

"Yeah. Well, time to change back into my grunt clothes and get to work here."

"Go home," Consuela said.

"Boyfriend's out of town again, so I might as well stay instead of going home to my dark, cold apartment, eat leftovers, take another call from that creep and go to sleep crying my eyes out." Her dramatic delivery, hand over her heart, eyes rolled up into her head, caused Annabel and Consuela to laugh.

"You laugh," Sue said, joining them, "but wait'll the creep starts calling you. Actually, I'm staying for the continuing ed lecture."

"What's that?" asked Annabel.

"Weekly programs to keep people up to date on what's going on around the library," Consuela said. "We're too compartmentalized these days, left hands not knowing what right hands are doing. Cale Broadhurst initiated the series, people from different divisions telling others what's going on in their areas. It's been useful."

"Dr. Vogler from Manuscripts is speaking tonight," Sue said.

"Should be good sport," Annabel said, visualizing Vogler sharing his knowledge with others. "Have fun."

Consuela and Annabel walked to the stairs leading down to the walkway linking the Library of Congress's three buildings. Consuela carried the envelope containing the original discs; Annabel held the pages Dolores had printed.

"The more I read what's on those discs, Consuela, the more convinced I am that John Bitteman was the author," Annabel said as they walked, "and that Michele Paul had something to do with Bitteman's disappearance eight years ago. At least they provide a motive."

"Let's say you're right," Consuela said as they reached the Madison Building and headed for the elevators. "Let's say Michele killed Bitteman. The bigger, more timely question is, who killed Michele Paul?"

Annabel was surprised to see that a group had been assembled in Broadhurst's office when she and Consuela arrived. She'd met General Counsel Mullin and security director Andre Lapin before, and was introduced to the four others. Broadhurst welcomed them, announced they represented the final two arrivals for the meeting, closed his door, and got to the point.

"As most of you know, I called this meeting in anticipation of receiving computer discs and a printout of what's on them. These discs contain, according to an informal report I received from Mrs. Reed-Smith, information that could have a bearing upon Michele Paul's murder. The discs will be turned over to the proper authorities once we've had the opportunity to examine and evaluate their contents.

"Ms. Martinez took it upon herself to have a duplicate set of discs made so that we could preserve whatever research was on them that might benefit the library. A photocopy of the printout was also produced. Much of what's on the discs deals with the elusive Las Casas diaries. I see you and Annabel have those things with you."

"Actually, these are the original discs found in the Aaronsen collection, Dr. Broadhurst," Consuela said. "We felt it was more appropriate to give you originals rather than duplicates."

"I'm sure the police will appreciate that, Consuela."

Annabel handed the printout to Consuela, and she gave it to Broadhurst, along with the envelope containing the discs. The Librarian pulled the discs from the envelope. Held them up like cards in a poker game, and said, "Perhaps you'd be good enough, Annabel, to give us the benefit of your knowledge of what's on these."

Annabel put her law training to good use, speaking slowly and deliberately and establishing eye contact with each person in the room. She spoke for ten minutes before getting to what she considered the most important material, the final portion of disc number five. She briefly mentioned her suspicion that Michele Paul might have been involved with John Bitteman's disappearance eight years ago. That comment raised eyebrows, and questions, but before Annabel could elaborate, Broadhurst was told he had an important call, and the meeting was temporarily put on hold.

Andre Lapin came to Annabel's side. "What makes you think Paul had something to do with the Bitteman case, Mrs. Reed-Smith?"

"Nothing you'd consider as evidence, Chief Lapin, nor would I if I was still practicing law. It's more a matter of the apparent animosity between them. Bitteman was going to—"

"Was this break planned?" a man she'd just met that evening asked, smiling. "Like a curtain falling on Act One? I can't wait for Act Two."

Lapin and the man started talking, allowing Annabel to slip away and go to where the Librarian had placed the printout on the edge of his desk. She picked it up and riffled the pages. She went to a page near the end, which she read carefully. She went on to the next page, and the next. Consuela looked across the office and saw the quizzical expression on Annabel's face. She came to her. "Something wrong?" she asked.

"Yes. These final pages don't reflect what was on the end of the fifth disc."

"Are you sure?"

"Let me look again."

After another fast perusal, Annabel said, "That material isn't here."

"Dolores must have forgotten in the rush to print that portion of it," Consuela offered.

"Probably," Annabel said, "or didn't include them with the other pages. I'll go back and see if she knows what happened."

"Sure you don't mind?"

"Not at all. In fact, if she didn't print those pages for some reason, I will from the duplicate discs we put in my locker."

Annabel was glad she'd worn flat, comfortable shoes as she almost ran through the tunnel leading to the Jefferson Building. She used her card to gain access to the stacks and stairway, went to her area next to what had been Michele Paul's space, squinted in the dim light provided by her desk lamp and a couple of low-wattage bulbs, opened the locker, removed her laptop, printer, and the envelope containing the duplicate set of the five discs, booted up the computer, slipped disc number five into the slot, opened the final file on it, and waited for it to appear on the screen.

What came up puzzled her. It wasn't the final file as she remembered it. Instead, what was on the screen was a long section preceding the final set of files. She sat back and bit her lip. The hard copy she and Consuela delivered to Broadhurst's office had obviously been printed from this duplicate set of discs. The missing pages should be on the original set back at Broadhurst's office, unless they'd been deleted from them, too.

She was certain of one thing: The disc on which she'd made selected copies of material from the floppy discs found in the Aaronsen collection contained those pages. She took it from her blazer pocket, substituted it for the other disc, and scrolled to the end. The missing fifteen pages started to come to life on the screen.

She connected her ink jet printer to the laptop and sent it into motion, each page slowly emerging like toothpaste squeezed from a broad tube. As the words were transformed from computer images to black-on-white, Annabel sat back and closed her eyes. This was no careless mistake, she silently, and unhappily, told herself. Those pages had deliberately been deleted.

The printing stopped. Annabel opened her eyes, picked up the printout, and scanned the pages once again. This time, her attention was directed at the initials sprinkled throughout the text—"LC," "BE," "WA," "DM." They were all there, as she remembered them to be. But what appeared on the pages she held was different from what had been on the screen when she ran the fifth disc from the envelope. It took her a moment to realize what the difference was.

A pervasive feeling of sadness gripped her as she again inserted the fifth of the five discs that had been copied from the original set and activated the Find and Replace function, instructing it to scan the disc for the initials "DM." It found none. Annabel ran the search again. The same result.

Until that moment, it had all been speculation, conjecture on Annabel's part. At first, the initials "DM" meant nothing to her, nor did many others contained on the discs. But then she began to wonder—when that moment occurred she couldn't remember—whether they referred to Dolores Marwede. It was plausible. Dolores had worked in the Hispanic Portuguese division during John Bitteman and Michele Paul's tenure there. She'd reacted strongly at the mention of Paul's name, and had made disparaging remarks about Bitteman.

"One more time," Annabel said, distinctly recalling that those initials had come up at least six times on that disc when she first examined it.

She swapped discs again, inserted the

single one on which she'd duplicated selected sections, and ran Find and Replace. The initials "DM" were highlighted.

"Damn," she muttered as she popped in other discs from the duplicate set and searched for "DM." Nothing. Those initials were gone, deleted, erased from the computer's memory.

Annabel sorted out what she'd just learned. The final fifteen pages on the fifth of five discs had been deleted when the duplicates were made, and the printout reflected that. Any mention of "DM" had been removed from the discs, which, by extension, meant it wasn't on the printed hard copy. The same thing undoubtedly was true of the original set of discs, which would easily be determined by returning to Broadhurst's office and using a computer there to view them.

Annabel put the disc of selected portions into her blazer pocket, returned the duplicate set of five to the envelope, and placed it on top of the fifteen pages she'd just printed.

She drew a deep breath in anticipation of leaving the area and returning to the meeting in the Librarian's office, started to get up, then settled back in her chair and thumbed through an internal phone directory until she found Cale Broadhurst's extension and dialed it. His secretary answered.

"This is Annabel Reed-Smith, Pamela. I need to speak with Chief Lapin."

"He's in a meeting with Dr. Broadhurst and—"

"I know that. I just left that meeting. This is an emergency."

"I'll get him for you."

Annabel's right foot tapped out her impatience as she waited for Lapin to come on the line. She was so intensely focused on what she would say to him, that the building should be sealed off and Dolores Marwede found and detained, that she failed to realize someone had come up behind her. When she did, it wasn't a sound that alerted her; it was more a sense that another person was there.

"Hang up!"

Annabel slowly swiveled in her chair and looked up at Dolores Marwede, whose expression was as frightening as the razor-sharp curved box cutter she held close to the back of Annabel's neck. Her face was distorted, a twisted mask of both fright and fear, pleading and threatening at once.

"Hang up!" Dolores repeated, grabbing the receiver from Annabel and slamming it down into its cradle just as Andre Lapin's voice could be heard through the instrument: "Mrs. Reed-Smith?"

"Give me that envelope," Dolores said. When Annabel didn't immediately comply, Dolores reached over her and swiped it from the desk.

Annabel attempted to collect herself, to will her breathing to slow down. "Dolores, I'm not your enemy," she said, knowing only too well that, at that moment, she was precisely that.

"You didn't have to do this," Dolores said. "Damn you!"

"I didn't do anything, Dolores, certainly nothing to hurt you. Put that knife down before you make another mistake. We can talk about this and—"

The ringing of the phone was deafening, causing both of them to jump.

"Don't answer it."

"The security chief knows I tried to reach him. I told Dr. Broadhurst's secretary it was an emergency. They'll be here, Dolores, any minute."

The phone continued to ring. Dolores took a few steps back, away from Annabel, the envelope pressed tightly to her bosom with one hand, the box cutter in the other.

"Dolores, listen to me," Annabel said, her voice not sounding familiar to her. "There's nothing to be gained by doing this, hurting me. I know it was you who deleted the material from those discs, those fifteen pages, your initials. But you can't delete the truth. Don't do something you'll regret. We can talk about it. Maybe I can help you."

The ringing stopped, the silence as jarring as the sound had been.

"You wouldn't understand," Dolores said.

"I can try."

Dolores looked uncertain of what to do next, whether to use the box cutter to attack Annabel and cut away the threat she posed, or to bolt, to run somewhere, anywhere in search of safe haven. Annabel extended a hand; instead of calming Dolores as intended, it caused her to stiffen and to thrust the box cutter at Annabel.

"Please, Dolores, put that down. It's over.

What's important now is for you to acknowledge the pain you're in and to help others understand."

Annabel's quiet, nonthreatening voice appeared to be having the desired effect. Dolores let out a sustained breath and seemed to sag before Annabel's eyes. Annabel had so many questions but asked only one: "Why, Dolores? Why did you kill Michele?"

Dolores spoke absently, matter-of-factly. "You didn't know him. You don't know how cruel he could be."

"I'm not surprised to hear that," Annabel said. "I knew his reputation."

"I wanted to be everything for him. He told me I was. He told me I was the only woman who deserved to be with him. He said I'd earned his love."

" 'Earned' his love? How did you 'earn' his love, Dolores?"

"When he killed John, I was there to help him."

"John Bitteman? Michele killed John Bitteman?"

"I hated John because Michele hated him. Michele was right. I wouldn't have killed John, and I didn't. I didn't know what Michele had done until he called me that night from John's apartment. He needed my help and I . . . I wanted so much to be there for him."

Annabel looked away for a moment, then back at her. "You wanted to help him to *earn* his love?" she asked, trying with only some success to keep the bathos from her tone.

"Yes."

"What did you do, Dolores, help him get rid of the body?"

They both turned their heads at the sound of people entering the Hispanic reading room below. The fright, the confusion was again etched in Dolores's face. Annabel slowly stood as someone opened the door at the foot of the narrow stairs. Dolores retreated as Annabel again offered her hand.

"Give me the box cutter, Dolores, and—"

Dolores's response was to wield the box cutter in a wide arc, missing Annabel's face by inches. With that, she ran from the area and disappeared into the stacks as Chief Lapin appeared at the top of the stairs. Consuela was behind him.

"Mrs. Smith, are you all right?" Lapin asked, coming to where Annabel stood, trembling.

"Annie, what happened?" Consuela asked.

"Dolores killed Michele Paul," Annabel said, suddenly feeling faint and having to sit.

"Dolores?" Consuela said.

"Yes."

"Where is she?" Lapin asked as two uniformed LC police joined them.

"Somewhere back there in the stacks. You'd better seal off the building."

Lapin spoke into his digital remote radio: "This is Lapin. Secure the building. No one leaves. We're looking for a library employee, Dolores Marwede. She's probably in the Hispanic stacks, but I can't be sure. Once the building's secured, send every available man to Hispanic." To Annabel: "Is she armed?"

"Yes, she has a box cutter, but don't hurt her, please. She's been hurt enough."

Lapin said to the uniformed officers, "Come on. Let's find her." The officers, guns drawn, entered the stacks.

Annabel stood. "I'm going with you."

"Ma'am, I think it's better if you don't," Lapin said.

"Help!"

They all turned to see Sue Gomara come

up the stairs two at a time, out of breath, frantic.

"What's the matter, Sue?" Consuela said as the intern stumbled into their midst and grabbed Consuela's arm.

"I know him," she said.

"You know who?" Consuela asked.

"The stalker. The guy who's been after me."

Lapin said to Consuela, "Why don't you take the young lady down to your office and calm her down. I'll be there after we find Ms. Marwede."

"Dolores?" Sue said. "Find her?"

Consuela put her arm around her intern. "Come on, Sue, let's do what he suggests. You can tell me about it in my office."

Annabel watched Consuela lead Sue Gomara to the stairs, then turned to see Lapin follow his officers. For a moment, she was tempted to join Consuela and Sue, but she shook off that decision and trailed after Lapin into the stacks, hundreds of floor-to-ceiling steel shelves housing the Hispanic division's vast collection of books. A series of low-wattage bulbs strung along the ceiling, dimmed each night by timers, provided barely enough light to see, everything in shadow, murky, lacking distinctive shape and form.

She saw that the two uniformed members of the library police had split up, coordinating their movements through their radios, light from their flashlights creating bizarre, erratic patterns on the ceiling. Lapin was a dozen yards ahead in one of the main aisles, off which hundreds of narrower aisles extended, each a cul-de-sac. He moved slowly, tentatively, radio in one hand, a revolver in the other, pausing as he reached each cross-aisle, weapon held vertically next to his right ear, a quick glance, then on to the next.

Annabel followed in Lapin's footsteps, her steps silent, holding her breathing in check. She stopped at an aisle veering off to her left that she'd been down more than once in search of books bearing upon Las Casas. She remembered that at its end was a short jog, no more than six feet long, running parallel to the main aisle and not visible from where she stood—or from the route taken by Lapin.

She turned into the aisle and moved with care, the faint light from the widely spaced bulbs above providing only gloomy illumination. Everything was bathed in gray; she ran the fingertips of her right hand along books as though that would help her see. Her eyes went to the floor and saw the box cutter where it had been discarded, half exposed, jutting out from beneath a bottom shelf. She picked it up, took the few remaining steps to where the aisles intersected, stopped, and raised her head, prompting her hearing into heightened acuity. The sound was a tight whine, animal in nature, wrenching.

"Dolores," Annabel said, pressing her back against the books and carefully peering around the corner. Dolores stood at the end of the short aisle, in a corner, barely discernible in the dismal lighting. Annabel fully exposed herself and took a few steps in the direction of the researcher-librarian.

"Please, don't," Dolores said. "Stay away."

Annabel extended her hands in a nonthreatening gesture. As she did, Dolores slowly sank to her knees, almost in slow motion, arms pressing the envelope containing the discs to her chest, that ethereal whine of a few moments earlier now reduced to a series of whimpers.

"I'm sorry, I'm so sorry," Dolores said. "I think I'm going to be sick," she said, turning from Annabel and vomiting.

When her body had stopped heaving,

Annabel closed the gap and reached down to touch her shoulder.

"Why don't we go see Consuela and others who'll want to hear what you have to say."

Annabel walked behind Dolores to the main aisle, where Lapin and some of his uniformed force were retracing their steps. Lapin instinctively pointed his weapon at Dolores.

"No, it's all right," Annabel said. "She's being cooperative. She's no danger to anyone—any longer." She handed Lapin the box cutter. "She never meant to use this."

Annabel went downstairs to where Consuela and Sue Gomara sat in Consuela's office. Consuela quickly stood. "Is it true, Annie? It was Dolores?"

"Afraid so," Annabel said. She sat, afraid that her trembling legs might fail her.

"My God!" Consuela said. "Why?"

"He hurt her too much, Consuela. Too much."

Annabel looked at Sue. The intern had obviously been crying, the dried tears creating makeup streaks on her cheeks.

"The stalker," Annabel said. "You found out who it was?"

"She says it's—"

Sue cut Consuela off. "It *is*! I know it. I'd know his voice anywhere."

"Who?" Annabel said.

"Dr. Vogler."

"Dr. Vogler?"

"That's what she says, Annie," Consuela said.

"I knew it five minutes into his lecture," Sue said, animated. "At first, I couldn't believe what I was hearing. Couldn't be, I told myself. But then I listened more closely, really concentrated on his voice and the way he talks, you know, almost like he might start stuttering any time. And he kept looking at me, not directly, but I knew he was. He was so nervous, like he couldn't remember what he was supposed to say, walking up and down in front of the room, always glancing at me. It's him! I know it's him."

"Did you say anything to him?" Annabel asked.

"Are you kidding? I got up and ran out of the room. I got here just when everything was happening with Dolores."

Consuela asked, "Sue, are you certain enough to bring charges against him?"

"Charges? I'd like to string him up, boil him in oil. Charges? You mean in court and all?"

"Yes."

"I don't know. I—"

Chief Lapin appeared in the doorway.

"Is she all right?" Annabel asked.

"Ms. Marwede? I wouldn't say so. Nothing physical, but she's a mental mess, that's for sure. You okay, Mrs. Smith?"

"Yes, I'm fine."

Lapin turned his attention to Sue. "Now, what's this about the person who's been stalking you? You say you know who it is?"

"Yes."

"Someone from the library?"

Lapin's radio came to life.

"Chief, it's Wozinzki. I'm down here in Manuscripts, Dr. Vogler's office."

"A problem?"

"Yeah, I'd say so. He's sitting at his desk. I'm out in his reception room. He bagged me out in the hall and started saying he did a terrible thing to someone, some intern named Sue."

All eyes went to Sue. She nodded.

"I'll be right there."

"Tell him to keep an eye on Vogler," Annabel said to Lapin. "He's liable to do something to hurt himself."

Lapin instructed his officer to stay with Vogler until he got there.

"Want to come with me, young lady?" Lapin asked Sue.

"No," she said, shaking her head for emphasis. "I don't want to see him ever again."

Lapin left the office. The three women sat in silence, each consumed with her own thoughts. Finally, Annabel pushed herself up out of the chair. "I have to call Mac," she said. "I want to go home."

39

Mac Smith moved quickly to his right, intercepted the baseline drive, and sent a two-handed rocket back across the net.

"That's game," Annabel announced happily.

Cale Broadhurst and his wife, Patricia, met the Smiths at the net and shook hands.

"You looked good out there," Cale said. "Like the old Mac Smith."

Mac laughed. "Nothing like a little surgery

to fix things up. I'm glad I didn't put it off. Made my knee as good as new."

He looked to Annabel, whose smile was pleasantly evil.

After showering, they drove to the Broadhurst home, where they celebrated Mac's return to tennis form with drinks and snacks. Talk soon turned to the library.

"I'm sorry," Annabel said after Cale had said something stern in passing about Dolores Marwede, "but I have a lot of compassion for her."

"Even though she took a swipe at you with a box cutter?" Mac said.

"Even with that," Annabel replied. "The woman was desperately in love with Michele Paul. He played off that, got her to help him dump John Bitteman's body off his boat, and kept stringing her along to protect his secret. I'm surprised she didn't whack him a lot sooner."

Mac laughed. " 'Whack him.' Spoken like a true mafia wife."

"Well, you made me an offer I couldn't refuse a few years ago, didn't you? I accepted your proposal."

"Isn't having compassion for someone like

Dolores carrying women's rights a little too far, Annie?" Patricia Broadhurst asked.

"I don't mean it as a matter of rights, Pat, but I believe her when she says she never meant to kill Michele. She was terminally in love with him."

"Terminal for him," Mac said.

"Yes, it was," Annabel said. "She'd reached the end of her patience and lashed out with whatever was close, in this case the lead weight on his desk. I spent an hour with Michele Paul, a disagreeable, anger-provoking hour. He was a horrible man."

"Hardly the sort of man women fall in love with," Cale said, "at least so deeply that they end up murdering him."

"For every man there's a woman," Annabel replied.

Pat said, "The discs she hid in the Aaronsen collection—those were John Bitteman's discs. How did *she* end up with them?"

"From what I've been told, Dolores knew Michele had taken them from Bitteman's place the night he murdered him, and knew where Michele kept them in his apartment. After she killed Michele, she ran to his apartment and grabbed the files and discs. There were things on those discs that referred to her, at least by her initials. As she said in her statement, she started to panic once the police investigation started but didn't know what to do with the discs. She dumped pictures and love letters from Michele in someone's trash can but couldn't quite bring herself to discard the discs the same way. She needed thinking time. She even considered trying to sell the discs to David Driscoll and use the money to get away. But she never had a chance to do that."

"She knew all about Michele Paul's deal with Driscoll, I assume," Pat said.

"Sure, she did," Annabel said, "and she played her own game of hardball with Michele, threatening to tell library management that he'd been working for Driscoll. I told Consuela after my interview with Paul that he reminded me of a bullfighter, waving his red cape and enticing people, particularly women, into his arena. He waved his cape at Dolores Marwede and kept sticking those knives, or whatever they call them, into her until she turned. It doesn't happen often, but in this case the bull killed the matador. Of course, even when a bull wins in the arena, its days are numbered. I'm afraid that's the case with Dolores, too."

"You're the criminal-law expert, Mac," Cale said. "What do you think she'll get?"

"Serious time, Cale. There's Michele Paul's murder and her role as an accessory in the Bitteman killing. Still, you never know how a trial will turn out. I know her defense attorney well. His only hope is to plead her as being mentally disturbed—mental impairment, insanity. The jury might demonstrate as much compassion for her as Annie."

"And what about David Driscoll?" Cale asked. "I'm furious at the scandal he caused the Library to suffer. Still, he didn't kill anyone—did he?"

"My prediction?" Mac said, sitting back and dabbing at his mouth with a napkin. "If the DA in Los Angeles can tangibly link Driscoll to the theft of that painting in Miami, his having hired the people to do it—and don't forget a security guard lost his life in that theft—they can charge him with conspiracy to murder. But that's a big *if*. Paying Michele Paul for his research broke your library rules, Cale, but it didn't break any laws, unless the IRS decides to take a look at the charitable deductions Driscoll was taking for his inflated donations to the library. Funny about rich men like Driscoll, they don't have to cheat the government. But it becomes a game of sorts, see how much they can get away with. Of course, if Michele Paul is named as an accomplice to Driscoll's tax fraud, that means the Library of Congress might have some explaining to do about the way it values contributions."

"Don't even say it, Mac," Broadhurst said.

"Unlikely, Cale. At any rate, if the DA can't make that connection between Driscoll and Miami beyond a reasonable doubt, I suspect the worst penalty he'll suffer is all the bad publicity, losing the esteem he enjoyed with the Library of Congress, and coming up empty with the Las Casas diaries and map. All this chaos and suffering for something that doesn't exist."

"Or *does* exist," Annabel said. "That Michele Paul and David Driscoll didn't come up with the diaries doesn't mean they aren't out there somewhere. As I said in my article, there's enough evidence in the literature— although maybe not beyond a reasonable doubt—that Las Casas did write his own diaries. If so, somebody has them. Hopefully, if they ever do surface, they'll end up at the Library of Congress."

"I'll drink to that," Cale said, raising his glass.

Later that night, Mac and Annabel sipped an after-dinner cognac on their terrace at the Watergate.

"I have to hand it to Cale," Mac said, "the way he handled the stalker situation."

"I don't agree."

"Oh?"

"I can understand Cale's concern about LC's reputation. On the other hand, John Vogler got off too easy. The terror he instilled in that young woman by his vile phone calls was dreadful. I wanted Cale to put some pressure on Sue Gomara to press charges. Instead, he called Vogler in, had him apologize to her, and sent him off on a leave of absence. He only did that, I think, because he managed to persuade Jim Hutson to come back to run Manuscripts. Vogler should have been punished."

"Cale's a pragmatist, Annie. Besides, where did my compassionate wife suddenly disappear to? Dolores Marwede 'whacks' somebody, as you so delicately put it, helps dump a body off a boat, and you feel for her. Vogler's a harmless, lonely eccentric."

"Tell that to the women receiving the calls."

"I know, and I think such people should be prosecuted. But Cale's major concern is the library and its reputation. I think in this case, the resolution makes sense. Life in a library is supposed to be quiet, reflective, helpful—not bloody or kinky."

"Like life in this household."

Before going to bed, they watched the news on NCN. Lucianne Huston reported from Iraq, where the administration had launched still more air strikes on Saddam Hussein's regime.

"He's still in power," Mac said, not happy.

"So is she. I sort of envy her, traveling the world like she does, reporting on monumentally important events."

"She did a nice wrap-up on the Paul and Bitteman murders."

"Yes, she did."

"You came off well in the interview she did with you."

"Thank you. How's your knee after the match?"

"Feels fine. Ready for bed?"

"I wasn't, but I am now."

"Somehow, I don't think my knee will be called into action tonight."

"Not with what I have in mind," she said, standing and pulling him up from the couch. "And leave any treasure maps at the door. You know where to find me."

ABOUT THE AUTHOR

MARGARET TRUMAN is the author of over a dozen bestselling novels of life and death amid Washington's monuments, institutions, and swirling social circles. She has also written two bestselling biographies—one of her father, the former president, and one of her mother—and a nonfiction exploration of first ladies. She lives in New York City with her husband, former *New York Times* editor Clifton Daniel.